COMMANDO

D1556394

Further Titles by Alan Savage from Severn House

THE COMMANDO SERIES

COMMANDO

THE SWORD SERIES

THE SWORD AND THE SCALPEL

THE SWORD AND THE JUNGLE

THE SWORD AND THE PRISON

STOP ROMMEL!

THE AFRIKA KORPS

COMMANDO

Alan Savage

This first world edition published in Great Britain 1999 by
SEVERN HOUSE PUBLISHERS LTD of
9–15 High Street, Sutton, Surrey SM1 1DF.
This first world edition published in the U.S.A. 2000 by
SEVERN HOUSE PUBLISHERS INC of
595 Madison Avenue, New York, N.Y. 10022.

British Library Cataloguing in Publication Data

Savage,   Alan
   Commando
   1.   World War, 1939-1945 - Fiction
   2.   War stories
   I.   Title
       823.9'14 [F]

     ISBN 0-7278-5492-5

Typeset by Palimpsest Book Production Ltd
Polmont, Stirlingshire, Scotland.
Printed and bound in Great Britain by
MPG Books Ltd, Bodmin, Cornwall.

Contents

PROLOGUE   1

PART ONE   THE SPEAR
Chapter One   The Tyro   11
Chapter Two   Training   29
Chapter Three   Bombs   50
Chapter Four   The First Mission   67

PART TWO   THE THROW
Chapter Five   The Woman   87
Chapter Six   The Plan   107
Chapter Seven   Preparations   126
Chapter Eight   The Raid   149

PART THREE   THE HIT
Chapter Nine   Belinda   171
Chapter Ten   The Big One   187
Chapter Eleven   Catastrophe   203
Chapter Twelve   Going Home   225

'Thou shalt not be afraid of any terror by night;
nor for the arrow that flieth by day.'

Psalms xci, 3

Prologue

The aircraft swooped low out of the sky, the black crosses on their wings clearly visible. This lot seemed to have run out of bombs, but their machine-guns carved swathes through the sand. Harry Curtis instinctively drew up his legs and huddled against the sand of his dune. Feathery grass tickled his cheek.

He thought this was no place and no position for a Guards officer to be in. Several of his men were doing the right thing, lying on their backs and firing their rifles at the *Messerschmitts*, an act of defiance even if they had no hope of hitting one.

"Christ, that was close," Lewis said. "You all right, young Curtis?"

"Yes, sir," Harry said.

They all worried about him, even Major Lewis, because he was so young: he had been passed out of Sandhurst less than a year ago, had received his commission the week before the War had started. He had been the happiest man alive, then. Every soldier wants, needs, to fight in a war. No soldier expected to have to come to this.

They needed to look after him because not only was he the youngest man in the battalion, but he looked it. His hair was fair, matching his blue eyes and fitting well with his quite handsome if totally innocent features: he only shaved once a week, and growing a moustache was out of the question. Equally he was slightly built, although no doubt given time he would fill out to match his height of six feet.

"Keep down," Sergeant-Major Tindall was calling. "Keep your bloody heads down. It'll be our turn soon enough."

1

Harry ignored the sergeant-major's admonition, to sit up, claw sand from his neck, and look out to sea. He did not suppose there had ever been a piece of sea this busy. He gazed at destroyers, freighters, small craft of every description from Thames barges to motor yachts, littering the surface of the calm water – thank God the sea was calm – waiting alongside the piers or approaching the Dunkirk beach just as close as they could without stranding, while the lines of men waded out to them.

He saw too the number of vessels burning or sinking, hit by the marauding aircraft who had managed to penetrate the RAF screen. As he watched, a plume of water rose skywards, close by one of the waterlogged columns. Several men fell out of line, to drift around helplessly. The rest continued their disciplined advance, towards hopeful safety.

"Makes you feel so bloody useless," Lewis said.

He was a heavy-set, swarthy, beetle-browed man who wore a moustache. He had been a regular all his life, had actually risen from the ranks to a commission, had fought in the Great War – would they still call it the Great War after this? Harry wondered.

He had always intended to be a regular. It was not a family tradition, but his parents were friends with a family who did have such a background. The Brands had been soldiers back to the foundation of the British Army: a Brand had fought under Marlborough at Blenheim. As a boy, Harry had listened to those tales of historical derring-do avidly. It had been all he had ever wanted to do.

More to the point, Brigadier George Brand had fought in the Great War. "It was pretty horrendous," he had said. "It won't ever happen again."

"You mean there won't be another war, sir?" Harry had been disappointed.

"Oh, there'll be another war," George Brand had promised him, "There will always be another war. No, I meant, we won't ever start digging trenches, and staying put. That was the horrendous part. No, no, the next war will be a war of

2

movement. You mark my words. The poor bloody infantry will hardly get a look in, apart from cleaning up operations."

Harry had believed him, but it seemed old habits died hard. In the six months he had been in France there had been precious little movement, and they had dug trenches.

"I thought we came here to fight," he had complained to Hardisty, his senior by a few months.

Hardisty had regarded him with contempt, as always. This was partly because Hardisty was an Etonian, while Harry's school was difficult to find on a map. But it was also the result of superior knowledge. "You have a lot to learn, young Curtis," Hardisty had said. "Modern warfare isn't a business of crash, bang, wallop. No, no. We wait for Jerry to come at us, then we stop him, then we hit him on the rebound."

Hardisty had been right, Harry reflected, up to a point. They had waited, for six whole months, for Jerry to come on at them, then they had rushed into Belgium to stop him and hit him on the rebound . . . but he hadn't stopped, and it was they who had rebounded, all the way on to this hellish beach.

The last time he had seen Hardisty it was as a headless body lying beside the road. Harry supposed it wasn't actually the first dead body he had ever seen, but the odd man keeling over during the rush up to the Dyle River hadn't possessed a positive identity. Hardisty had. He had vomited.

What was even more upsetting was that after six months at war, and a horrendous defeat, he had not yet seen a dead German!

"Here they come again," Lewis said. "Keep your heads down," he bawled.

The sergeant-major took up the call, while the planes thundered down and the sand spurted. Further along the beach a man started screaming, but there was nothing they could do about him; they had long run out of any medical supplies. Besides, he wasn't the only man screaming, or dying. Or dead. Harry had never supposed that an open beach could carry such a stench of rotting humanity.

"How did it happen?" he asked. "How did it *happen*?"

Lewis sighed. "Over-confidence, perhaps. Reliance on the power of defence. God knows. We invented the tank, for God's sake. Now we've been scuppered by them."

"Have we been scuppered, sir?"

"What do you think, Harry?"

"Well, sir, it'll be our turn soon enough. We'll get out of here. We've lost a lot of people, but . . ."

"People, Harry, are about the world's most replaceable commodity. I have no doubt some of us are going to get out. But we're going to have our rifles and sidearms, nothing more. A modern army needs tanks and guns to fight a war. And it takes a hell of a lot longer to make a tank or a gun than it does to take a civilian and make him into a soldier. You can take twenty, fifty, maybe a hundred men, and drill them and teach them discipline and how to shoot, in a matter of weeks, if pushed. You can't turn out a hundred tanks at that rate."

Tanks, Harry thought. He had never actually seen a German tank, either. The battalion had been pulled out, told to commence the retreat, when the strafing had become too heavy. The enemy armour had not yet come close enough to be seen.

"So what are we going to do, sir?" he asked. "Surrender?"

"Oh, I don't think we'll do that," Lewis said. "We still have the Navy. We must hope that Hitler will try to invade and come a cropper."

"But even if he does . . . that won't win the war?"

"No," Lewis agreed.

"And then the U-boats . . . we could lose anyway."

"You are a confoundedly pessimistic fellow, young Curtis."

"I'm sorry, sir. But there must be some way we can hit back at them."

"Patience, Harry. I'm sure the brass will think of something. Hello, looks like our number's come up."

An MP trudged across the sand towards them, the planes having been driven off again. "Major Lewis?"

Lewis stood up.

"We can take your people now, sir. If you'd proceed down

4

the beach. I'll show you where. Single file, sir. Presents less of a target."

"Fall in," Lewis bellowed. "Single file. I'll lead. Sergeant-Major, bring up the rear."

"Sir!"

"Where do you want me?" Harry asked.

"Next to me. You're our only remaining officer."

Harry gulped, and fell into line immediately behind the major. He hadn't truly realised the situation, although he remembered that he hadn't actually seen any other officer recently. Suddenly he understood that he was shell-shocked or traumatised or whatever was the current word in use, by the horrifying events of the past few days. He gritted his teeth, adjusted his steel helmet, and resolutely put one foot in front of the other.

Crossing the beach was more horrifying than lying on it. When they had come in, last night, there had only been sounds, and smells. They had gone to ground, as instructed, amidst the sand dunes to await their turn; the orders had been, first arrived, first out.

They had been so exhausted that it hadn't mattered then. All they had wanted to do after two days of marching and taking cover as they had been strafed, had been to lie down, drink the last of the water in their canteens, chew some iron rations, and sleep.

Today was different. If their bodies were still exhausted, their brains were alert. If they had not yet assimilated the magnitude of their defeat, they could understand that they were on the run. Now they were both hungry and very thirsty. But they could still smell. And now they could see as well. Harry could hear the murmur of unhappy sound behind him as they stamped on the beach, stepping over dead bodies, half-obscured by the sand, turning their heads as they heard cries of "Water!" from either side.

"Keep rank there!" Sergeant-Major Tindall called.

They obeyed him because they had been trained to do so. But they had no water anyway.

The gentle surf rippled at their feet. "Halt!" Lewis shouted.

Harry came to a stop, and heard the immense rustle close behind. In front of him the sea was like a millpond; here by the shore hardly a ripple disturbed the sand. Further out the wakes of the ships were churning the surface into a chop. Out there a destroyer waited, motionless apart from a slight roll, smoke drifting from her funnel. Closer in her launch was also waiting.

"You'll have to swim the last few feet," a Petty Officer called.

Between the launch and the beach, a dead body drifted by, face down, arms and legs outspread.

"All right, chaps," Lewis called. "Single file. No jostling. Sergeant Clifford, you lead. Stand beside me, Mr Curtis."

Harry stood beside the major, watched the men filing into the water, led by the sergeant. Several of them glanced at him, almost apologetically, as they went by. Now for the first time he realised how few there were, certainly not a hundred strong. It would be his turn in a matter of minutes.

"Easy does it." Sergeant-Major Tindall's voice was reassuring; he stood on the other side of the column, opposite the officers. "There's room for all."

"*Messerschmitts!*"

Someone had been looking up. Now they saw the six planes racing up the beach at hardly more than two hundred feet.

"Down!" Lewis bellowed.

"Down!" Tindall echoed.

Men dropped to their knees, and then to their faces, several half in the water.

"Those immersed keep going!" Lewis shouted.

Harry had also thrown himself down, half into the water. Now he looked up at the major, who continued to stand there, perhaps daring the planes to do their worst.

For God's sake get down, Harry wanted to shout. But it was too late. The roar of engines, the chatter of the machine-guns, was upon them. Lewis uttered not a sound, just fell backwards, the entire front of his battledress split open from neck to crotch, and replaced by splattering red.

Harry rolled on his face, watched the little surf also turning red, aware of a sudden sense of shock.

"Casualties!" Tindall was shouting. "If you can stand, stand!"

The guardsmen regained their feet.

"All right," Tindall said. "Move it. Slowly now. Single file."

Thank God for Tindall, Harry thought, as he sat up.

The sergeant-major stood beside him. "You all right, Mr Curtis?"

"I'm all right, Sergeant-Major."

Looking at his blood-stained uniform, Tindall was obviously doubtful. "The major is dead, sir."

"I'm afraid he is, Sergeant-Major."

"Yes, sir. You are in command, sir."

"Eh? Good lord!" He supposed he was.

"If you'd like to get up, sir."

"Oh, quite." Harry pushed down with his feet, and to his consternation his left leg gave way and he went down again, splashing into the water.

"Begging your pardon, sir, you is wounded," Tindall pointed out.

"By golly, Sergeant-Major, I believe you're right," Harry said. And fainted.

Part One

The Spear

I too have long'd for trenchant force,
And will like a dividing spear;
Have prais'd the keen, unscrupulous course,
Which knows no doubt, which feels no fear.
Matthew Arnold.

One

"I'll just take these away," Nurse Murton said, and gently plucked the crutches from under Harry's arms. "How does that feel?"

He swayed in the gentle breeze which flickered across the hospital grounds and ruffled his pyjamas. Nurse Murton, a large, jolly woman, had escorted him away from the rest of the patients, to the relative privacy of a little copse, so that he wouldn't be too embarrassed if he fell down.

"But you're not going to fall down, Lieutenant," she admonished.

Harry continued to sway for several seconds. His leg still hurt, but not seriously. It was his general weakness, his general uncertainty after the weeks in bed, the fortnight on crutches, that was difficult to handle.

Nurse Murton retreated several yards. "Now come to me," she said.

Harry drew a deep breath, and stepped forward. This was his good leg. When he started to bring up his wounded leg, it gave way, and he stumbled.

"No, no," Nurse Murton said. "You mustn't fall. Don't fall. Straighten up."

Taking another deep breath, Harry got himself straight. He was trembling.

"Good boy," Nurse Murton said. "Come to me."

Teeth clenched, Harry repeated the manoeuvre, and this time stayed straight. A moment later he was in her arms.

"Good boy," she said without embarrassment. "We'll be throwing away these crutches in another week."

11

"Excellent progress," said Dr Jackman later. "Nurse Murton says you're walking nearly as well as ever."

"Yes, sir," Harry agreed; the doctor held the rank of captain. "When can I leave?"

Jackman raised his eyebrows. "In that much of a hurry?"

"There's a war on, sir."

"You'd hardly know it down here," Jackman observed. "But I appreciate your anxiety to rejoin your regiment. However . . ." he put on his spectacles, read the report in front of him. "Physically, I would say in another week."

"Thank you, sir."

"There are other aspects of the situation, however," Jackman said. "You have an interview with Mr Roberts in one hour."

"Is that necessary, sir?"

"I'm afraid it is, Curtis. Oh, don't start worrying about being discharged. There is no possibility of that. But it is necessary for you to be assessed, and, well—"

"You mean Mr Roberts is going to decide whether or not I am still fit for combat duty?"

"Why, yes, I suppose that sums it up. I may say that all the men returning from Dunkirk had been similarly assessed. But of course there was no point in dealing with you, or any of the seriously wounded, until we knew you would again be *physically* capable of combat. So good luck with Mr Roberts, and before you can say Jack Robinson you'll be back in uniform."

Jack Robinson, Harry thought, as he sat before yet another desk. Mr Roberts wore a little moustache – possibly because of Hitler, Harry disliked men with little moustaches.

"Henry Arthur Curtis," the psychiatrist said, reading the file. "Now, Lieutenant Curtis, whatever I ask you, I wish you to answer with both truthfulness and candour. Providing it's what you really feel, I wish your answers to be the first things that come into your head. Do you understand?"

"Yes, sir."

12

"Very good. Born second of August 1921. Your father is a bank manager?" He looked up.

"That is correct, sir. Worcestershire."

"Good place to be, right now, Worcestershire. Brothers and sisters?"

"I have one brother, sir. He is in the Navy."

"Older than you, I imagine."

"Yes, sir."

"Now, women? Girls? Do you have a girlfriend?"

"No, sir."

Once again Roberts raised his head, "Why not?"

"There doesn't seem to have been time, sir."

"I see. But you would like to have a girlfriend, when there is time? I mean, it is one of your ambitions, in the course of time, to get married and have children?"

"In the course of time, sir."

"Very good. Sandhurst and the Guards. You had a good record."

"Thank you, sir."

"You were wounded in the leg. Where? I mean, where on the map?"

"On the beach at Dunkirk, sir. My men brought me out."

"That is good. Shows they liked their officer."

"I am very grateful to them, sir. That's why I would like to get back to them."

"Quite. Does your wound still trouble you?"

"When it rains, sir."

"Very good. Are you afraid of being wounded again?"

"Good lord, no, sir. Goes with the job."

"So, what were your feelings about Dunkirk, at the time?"

"That it was a bloody awful mess, sir."

"I see. You feel the Army is a mess, is that it?"

"No, sir. I do not feel the Army is a mess. The Army was, is, magnificent. The battle in France was lost by the politicians."

"I see. Tell me why."

"Well, sir, it was their business to foresee all the

possibilities, and even more the probabilities. They had the example of Poland before them. When Hitler struck Poland, he struck hard. There was no shilly-shallying, no hesitation, no chivalry. It should have been obvious to everyone that when he struck in the West it would be equally ruthless."

"So how should our people have handled it?"

"Back in September, sir, they should have told the Belgian Government, either you let us come in now and take up strong defensive positions, or we will not come in at all."

"The Belgian point of view was that such a step would have provoked a German attack."

"In September, sir, the Germans were fully committed to Poland. Having given the Belgians the choice, if they refused, we should then have concentrated either on invading Germany right away, or on creating a very strong defensive position, an extension of the Maginot Line, if you like, all along the French border, not only with Germany but with Belgium as well."

"If we had not gone to Belgium's rescue, Curtis, it would not have gone down well with public opinion."

"With respect, Mr Roberts, wars are not won by worrying about public opinion. As it was, worrying about public opinion, about international protocol, earned us a beating. We went rushing into Belgium, took up unfortified and unprepared positions, and expected to stop the German Army. That was ludicrous."

"I see. Do you think we can beat the Germans?"

"In fair fight, yes."

"So what would you like to do, now?"

"Fight them, sir. But this time with no holds barred, no diplomatic niceties. Just fight them. That's the only way we are going to beat them."

"I see. Well, I think that covers everything."

"Sir?"

"Is there something else?"

"I don't know, sir. I had supposed it would be, well . . ."

14

"Finding the right square for various holes? I'm not here to assess your intelligence quotient, Curtis. My business is to assess your capability as a fighting officer."

"And what is your assessment, sir?"

"I'm afraid I can't tell you that. Nor is it my business to determine whether or not you are again fit for active service. I will make out my report, and that, together with your medical report, will be forwarded to the War Office. I'm sure you'll be hearing from them soon enough."

"Can you at least tell me whether I'm sane?"

Roberts gave a quick smile. "I don't think there is a sane person in this world at the moment, Curtis. You're not too different to some others I know. Just remember that second lieutenants are required to do what they're told, not try to decide what they should be told. Leave that until you're slightly higher in rank."

"Yes, sir."

Roberts stood up, collected his papers and put them in his briefcase. "Oh, and one more thing. Get yourself a girl-friend."

"Sir?"

"Shouldn't be difficult. You're young, good-looking, com-missioned, come from a good family, and are serving in a top regiment. And you're a wounded hero. Have a go. Who knows, you might enjoy it."

"So, have you been promoted, or got the chop?" Armistead asked.

Armistead was as near to being a friend as Harry had made in the hospital. It wasn't that he was basically unsociable, but he felt that most of the other patients were just happy to be out of the firing line, for as long as possible, while he was only anxious to get back into it, as rapidly as possible. The thought that the Germans might start their invasion – which everyone assumed was imminent – while he was still wearing hospital pyjamas was intolerable.

Armistead was a captain on the staff who had been knocked

down by a truck during the retreat and had his leg broken. Thus they had shared the same physiotherapy classes. Armistead would not be returning to a fighting unit, but he did want to get out of hospital, if only to find out what was really going on.

"Haven't a clue," Harry said. "I've an idea he thought I was mad. Because I want to kill Germans."

"I shouldn't think that will prove a handicap at the moment," Armistead said.

"He also . . . well . . ." Harry could feel the heat in his cheeks. "Said something about women."

"What about women?"

"Well . . . he said I should have one."

"And why not, indeed." Armitstead shot him a glance. He was a short, somewhat tubby man, with a round face. "Don't you have one?"

"He seemed to find that odd, too."

"Are you trying to tell me that you're a virgin, young Curtis?"

"Well, sir . . . there hasn't really been time . . ."

"How much time do you need?"

"Well, sir, school, and Sandhurst, and then the regiment . . ."

"You had holidays."

"Then there was cricket, and tennis, and rugger . . ."

"Sublimation gone to hell. How old are you?"

"I was nineteen last month."

"And you've never even been with a tart?"

"Well, no, sir. I had sort of hoped . . ."

"That one fine day you would run into a beautiful, well-bred girl who would willingly invite you to her bed. That's woolly thinking, Curtis. Not what we expect from a Guards officer. If your prospective soulmate is well-bred, she will not invite you into her bed. And even if she did, you would then have the problem that she probably knows less about sex than you do. So we have frustration all round. The only possible solution would be marriage. But you can't marry. As you say, you're just nineteen. The Army frowns on marriages under the age

16

of thirty, except in very exceptional circumstances, such as a vast private income. Do you have a vast private income?"

"I'm afraid not, sir."

"So that's definitely out. Not that I would recommend marrying during a war, even if you did have a private income."

"I'm sure you're right, sir. But why is it important, anyway? It seems to me the Army has been doing a bit of woolly thinking as well. Their tame psychiatrist recommends I get myself a woman, but he must know as well as anyone that I couldn't possibly marry her, so therefore . . ."

"You keep mixing up sex with marriage," Armistead said severely. "The Army accepts that men will be men. It may not want them to marry, but it does want them to be men. They want to be sure you're not queer. Don't get me wrong. I have nothing against queers, and the slightest study of military history, certainly of the Greeks or the Middle East, should convince anyone that being homosexual does not decrease one's value as a soldier. In fact, if you think of people like Epaminondas it may actually increase it. But those were different times, different mores. Today it is perceived wisdom that a queer cannot command men into battle. Are you a queer?"

"Good lord, no, sir. Well, I've never thought about it."

"Quite. But you do think about sex."

"Well, sir . . ."

"I don't imagine you find Nurse Murton sexy, although she might well surprise you. But what about that pretty little red-headed nurse in Ward C?"

"We've never actually spoken," Harry confessed.

"Hm. I see you're moving quite freely."

"Oh, yes, sir, thank you."

"Well, do you know what I am going to do, Harry? I am going to get us a weekend pass and take you up to London."

"Can we do that, sir?"

"Of course. Roberts is still here. I'll have a chat with him and have him recommend it. Then they'll have to let us go."

Armistead actually had a car, an Austin Seven. Even more remarkably, he had petrol for it, and a stack of coupons.

"One can get anything one wants, even in wartime, if one knows where to look." He grinned. "Perhaps I should say, *especially* in wartime."

He wasn't proposing to drive up to London, of course, only to the nearest railway station, but that was several miles away from the recuperation home, deep in the Somerset countryside.

"How does your leg get on with the clutch?" Harry asked.

He had been taking driving lessons just before the War had started, and hadn't actually got his licence yet, but he was interested in anything mechanical.

"Hurts like hell, if you must know. But the quack says it's good therapy."

Two wounded officers had no difficulty in obtaining tickets, and seats, and they were in London that evening. In Somerset, as Captain Jackman had suggested, there had been little evidence that the War was still on; even the odd airplane had clearly been on a training flight. But as they approached the capital, the evidence of recent air raids became more obvious.

"Actually, most of the damage is in the south-east," Armistead said. "I believe the airfields down there have been bombed to hell. Pity again that we have to sit and take it, and not be able to hit back."

London was an undamaged paradise, at least so far as could be seen. The train arrived in Paddington Station just on dusk, and as the black-out was in full force, it was difficult to see anything clearly. But there was an atmosphere of high excitement, the capital had been bombed for the first time that afternoon.

"The docks, it were," someone told them. "I suppose it had to happen. It's a bloody mess down there."

The Underground was brightly lit, and the trains were running on time. The two officers homed on Piccadilly Station, and emerged into the warm evening air, to find themselves in the midst of crowds of people, eerie in the darkness.

Harry had only been to London on two previous occasions in his life, but Armistead apparently knew the West End very well. He first of all checked them in to a small hotel off Trafalgar Square, where he had reserved two rooms, then took Harry to a restaurant off Shaftesbury Avenue where he was apparently well known, and where the food and wine were excellent.

After the meal they walked back toward Piccadilly, and turned up Rupert Street. "Now," Armistead said, "I have a treat for you."

He led Harry up a flight of steps at the end of the street; the building was quite large, and was surmounted by a huge windmill, discernible even in the darkness. The door was closed, but opened to his knock, and they were admitted through the black-out curtain into a brightly lit lobby, filled with photographs of attractive girls, quite a few of them naked even if decorously posed.

"The Windmill Theatre," Armistead announced. "The mecca of any self-respecting serviceman."

"You'd think they'd shut down," Harry suggested. "If the Germans are bombing the city."

"They didn't bomb the city," Armistead pointed out. "They have no reason to. They bombed the docks. That's fair enough, I suppose. As for the Windmill, their motto is, *We Never Close.*"

He joined the queue at the ticket office, bought two seats, and ushered Harry through another curtain into what might have been a cinema save for the fact that the seats at the rear were empty, while those at the front were fully occupied. The show was live, the various tableaux being enacted to the beat of a drum and piano.

An usherette was waiting to check their tickets. "Anywhere you like," she said.

"Shouldn't we at least try to find our numbers?" Harry whispered.

"Waste of time," Armistead said. "We're not going to stay in them."

He led a mystified Harry to the first vacant seats nearest the stage, which were about six rows back. Here they sat, to watch the girls perform. Harry, unused to seeing the naked female form, was at once amazed and, as he had to admit to himself, aroused. As with the photographs, the girls either wore just enough or moved sufficiently quickly to conceal their pubes, but at each end of the stage there was one of the artistes, posed facing the audience, quite nude and standing absolutely still – their pubic hair had been shaved, and Harry presumed that went for all the other girls as well.

"They can appear naked as long as they don't move," Armistead whispered.

Harry stared at them, and was distracted by the end of the number, which appeared to have been the finale. The curtain came down, the lights went up, and most of the men in the front row got up and left. They were indeed mainly servicemen, Harry observed. But if the show was over . . . ? "That was bad timing," he said.

"Don't you believe it. Best time to arrive," Armistead said. "The show is continuous. Let's move."

Because the men in front of them were climbing over the seats to reach as far forward as they could. Armistead followed their example, and Harry followed his, advancing two rows, to within four of the stage. While they were doing this, the curtain went up again, and a comic appeared. He didn't attract much attention, and several of the men took newspapers from their coat pockets and began to read.

"That's a bit rough," Harry commented.

"Goes with the trade," Armistead said. "These chaps are learning. They say if a comic can hold the attention of a Windmill audience he's got it made."

Obviously this man did not have it made, although some of his jokes were quite good. But after a few minutes he departed, and the newspapers were put away. Then the show began again, with the same format, dances and songs from the girls and the few male partners, while two new girls stood motionlessly naked at each end of the stage. But a few items later there was the highlight of the evening, apparently, the fan dance performed by one of the girls alone, in which she strutted the stage, as naked as the girls in the tableaux, but with a large fan in each hand with which she allowed only the briefest glimpses of her groin and buttocks between feathery swirls.

The audience, and by now the seats behind Armistead and Harry had again filled up, certainly liked this number, and stamped and clapped, Harry as vigorously as anyone.

Then the performance ended, the men in front left, and Armistead and Harry reached the front row.

"How long does this go on?" Harry panted.

"Well, now we're here, we can stop until the very end," Armistead said. "Enjoying the show?"

Harry felt it would be churlish not to say, "Yes, indeed, very much." And it was certainly titillating. But the numbers in each performance were exactly the same, and even looking at variated parts of the female body began to grow boring after a while. Harry had no very pronounced ideas about sex – as he had told Mr Roberts, he simply had never had the time – but what he did have were intensely private. When he finally got together with a girl he wanted it to be just the two of them, far away from anyone else. He felt he would have enjoyed the show much more had he been watching it alone; the stamping, clapping men lowered the tone.

He was heartily relieved when at last they emerged into the night air. "Now what?" he asked. "Is it possible to date one of those girls?"

Armistead looked at him in amazement. "You have got to be joking. I mean, it *is* possible, but only after a proper introduction. Those girls are artistes, you know, not whores."

"Oh," Harry said humbly. "So it's home to bed."

"We didn't come to London to go to bed, young Curtis. At least, not by ourselves. What we are going to do now is get ourselves a drink."

"The pubs will be closed."

"Correct. But I know a tidy little club, where we'll be

welcome, and where we might do ourselves a bit of good. How much money do you have on you?"

"Ah . . . about ten pounds, I think."

"That should do it. Come along."

Harry dutifully followed him down a succession of dark streets, still surprisingly busy despite the hour – but then it was Saturday night – until they arrived at another of those doors which opened to a knock.

"We're friends of Niki's," Armistead explained.

They were admitted by a very large man who had clearly been an unsuccessful boxer in his day, judging by his battered features. In the dimly lit hallway he looked them up and down, ascertained that they were wearing officers' uniforms, and gestured at the stairs. They went up, and were accosted by another man at the top. This one wore a dinner jacket but was hardly more prepossessing.

"Friends of Niki's," Armistead said.

Once again they were looked up and down, then the man nodded, and opened the door. "She's at the bar."

This was difficult to locate, because of the haze of cigarette smoke as well as the crowd of people in the not very large room. There were men of every description, most of them in uniform, although as at the Windmill there was a smattering of civilians, most very flashily dressed, and even more girls than at the theatre, although the majority of these had to be more properly described as women; their ages varied from eighteen to forty plus, Harry estimated. They also were dressed, in varying degrees, and were nearly all smoking. Harry found himself coughing.

"You'll get used to it," Armistead said, and pushed his way through the throng, Harry at his elbow, until they reached the bar.

"Hello, there," said the barman, and immediately placed two wine glasses in front of them.

Armistead handed over some silver. "Niki about?"

The barman jerked his head,

"Ah," Armistead said.

22

Harry was sipping his drink. "What is it?" he asked.

"Champagne. We only serve champagne," the barman said. "Saves mixing drinks, see?"

It didn't taste like any champagne Harry had ever drunk in the past. But he would be the first to admit that he didn't know all that much about wine.

"Well, hello," said a deep contralto, and he found himself gazing at a tall, slim woman, with a mass of yellow hair clouding her bare shoulders. She wore a strapless evening gown that was maintained in position by extremely large breasts, and presumably some stiff wire. Her features were bold, but quite attractive, save for the hardness of her blue eyes and her flat mouth. But this was presently smiling. The smile did not reach the eyes. "You're new here," she remarked.

"Captain John Armistead," Armistead said. "RASC. I came once before. With Captain Linton."

The woman looked him up and down. "Of course, I remember," she lied. "And this is . . . ?"

She turned her smile on Harry, and this time it was almost genuine.

"Lieutenant Harry Curtis, Brigade of Guards."

He decided not to name his regiment – she could probably tell he was a Guards officer from the insignia on his uniform.

"How nice," she said. "I'm Niki."

She extended her hand, and Harry gave it a gentle squeeze. He was trying to estimate how old she was, decided it was probably at least twice his own age.

"So what part of the War are you involved in?" she asked. "Or is that top secret?"

"Not in our case," Armistead said. "We're just out of hospital."

"How nice," she said. "You must show me your wounds, when we have a moment. Excuse me."

Some more newcomers had just come in.

"Does she own the place?" Harry asked.

"Good lord, no. She manages it for some vice lord."

"Vice lord? Should we be here?"

"It is a fact, young Curtis, that there is no pleasure without vice. And where would a man be without pleasure? Hello, she's coming back. I think she fancies you, Harry."

At that moment a three-piece combo struck up a slow number, and Harry discovered that there was a small dance floor at the far end of the bar. With a dozen people on it there was hardly room to move.

"Would you like to dance?" Niki asked Harry.

"I'd love to," he said, honestly. Having spent the entire evening staring at beautiful women he was in the mood to hold one in his arms.

They crowded the dance floor even more, which meant that they crowded each other to the limit. Bodies glued together, they hardly moved, just swayed together in time to the music. Niki's head rested on Harry's shoulder, her hair tickled his nostrils. It smelt delightful.

"Were you very badly wounded?" she asked.

"Yes, and no," he said.

Her head moved as she looked up at him.

"It wasn't life threatening," he explained. "Apart from loss of blood, and they soon sorted that out. But my leg was broken in three places, so it took a long time to heal. They only took out the last steel pin a fortnight ago."

"Oh, you poor boy," she said. "And are you now going to be invalided out?"

"Not if I can help it."

"You mean you *want* to go back to fighting and being wounded again? Next time you might be killed."

"I have a score to settle," he said.

"Very romantic, I'm sure. Where are you staying?"

"An hotel Armistead knows."

"I'm sure it's a crummy joint. You could spend the night here."

"Here?"

"I've a double bed."

He gulped. "You've only just met me."

24

"So? My business is sizing men up. And I'd say you measure up."

To his consternation, she slid her hand down his tunic, in between their closely pressed bodies, and gave the front of his pants a quick squeeze.

"Oh . . . ah . . . I have to tell you that I only have ten pounds."

"Oh, really, sir," she said. "When I invite a man to my bed, there is no charge."

"I do apologise."

"You can make up for it, later. Excuse me." More new arrivals.

Harry wondered if he had put up a monumental black, and wandered back to the bar to consult with his mentor; he was feeling sufficiently randy to find Niki most attractive, but he was totally out of his depth, both as to what he would be required to do, and how to go about it. While she, with her obvious vast experience of men, would probably laugh at him. That thought was quite terrifying.

Armistead was still at the bar, but deep in conversation with a dark-haired woman on a stool, their heads close together, while he stroked her thigh. It was clearly not a tête-à-tête to be interrupted.

He leaned on the bar, and a fresh glass of champagne was placed in front of him.

"Ah." He reached into his tunic for his wallet, and the barman shook his head,

"On the house, mate. The boss gave me the wink." He grinned. "You got it made. But stay sober."

To Harry's great relief, the club began to empty just after midnight. It was less anxiety to get to bed with Niki, than an uncertainty that he would be able to stay awake, much less sober, for very much longer.

From time to time he danced either with Niki or with some other woman introduced by Niki. They were all very sexy, and good dancers, and as the music remained slow and languorous, he couldn't help feeling that way too.

At some time during the evening, Armistead had disappeared, without so much as a see-you-later. With him had gone the dark-haired woman, so presumably she also had a double bed awaiting occupation. Which left him very much on his own, save that he wasn't going anywhere.

"You look tired." Niki was standing beside him.

"I suppose I am. This is the longest I've been on my feet since the march to Dunkirk."

"You were there? You must tell me about it. But the first thing we need to do is get you off your feet. Joe, you'll lock up, will you?"

"No problem," Joe said, giving Harry another grin.

But by now he was too tired to care about other people's opinions. What had he said to Mr Roberts? That wars are not won by bothering about public opinion? Neither are women, he thought, and realised that he was, definitely, drunk.

Niki escorted him through a door at the rear of the club, which gave access to a little flat, lounge and kitchenette, bedroom, bathroom.

"Neat," he said.

"Convenient," she corrected. "It goes with the job." She went into the bedroom, took the bottle of champagne from the ice bucket on the table beside the bed. "This is the real thing."

"I'm not sure I should have another," he said.

"I agree with you. Not right now, anyway. What you need is a shower. I know I do."

She released her dress, which slid down past her thighs to the floor, and stepped out of her shoes. She was wearing no underclothes. Now she did a little twirl. "You like, I hope."

Harry licked his lips. "Very much."

He stepped towards her, and she held up her hand. "Shower, first. You *are* going to take your clothes off?"

"Oh. Yes." Hastily he took off his uniform, turning his back on her to remove his underwear.

"Don't tell me you're a virgin," she remarked.

"Well, you see . . ."

"Let's be having a look at you."

He turned round, slowly.

"All of that going to waste, all of these years. Don't tell me, you were brought up to the cold bath and averted eyes routine."

"Well . . ."

"It's always been a puzzle to me how the English middle class manage to keep their breed going. This shower will be hot." Then she bent to look at him more closely. "Great God in the morning!"

"It's healed, really. But I'm told I'll have the scar for the rest of my life."

"And how. Do you realise that a couple of inches to the right and you wouldn't be any use to woman or beast, or even yourself?"

"I was born lucky."

"So let's make you luckier yet." She led him into the bathroom, scooped her hair on to the top of her head and secured it with a ribbon, and turned on the taps. A few seconds had the flow adjusted to her satisfaction, and she beckoned him. "Come along. I'll do you, and you'll do me."

Harry stepped against her in the small stall. He put his arms round her to hold her closer yet, and she turned up her face so that he could kiss her mouth. He kept her there for some seconds, until she pulled her head back. "I suppose some things just come naturally."

She reached past him for the soap, began rubbing his back. "Always save the best until last, I say."

He continued to hold her tightly against him, his erection trapped between their groins, while he cautiously slid his hands down to her buttocks. He desperately wanted to hold her breasts, but as she had said, always save the best till last. Were a woman's breasts the best part of her? He had never thought beyond that stage, being ignorant of everything else.

Then – "What's that noise?" he asked, listening to the weird wail cutting across the night.

"Eh? Oh, that's an air raid siren."

27

"A what? You mean there's another raid? On London?"

"Lord, no. It's a false alarm. They have them quite regularly. Anyway, they were here this afternoon. Over the docks, anyway. They'd hardly come back again tonight."

"Oh." His hands closed on her buttocks. Then he released her again as the first bombs fell.

Two

"Jesus Christ!" Niki shouted, leaping out of the shower stall and grabbing a towel. "They *are* back again. The bastards!"

She tossed another towel at Harry.

There were more explosions, gradually coming closer.

"What do we do?" he asked.

She had run into the bedroom, was dragging on her clothes. "Get the fuck out of here," she said.

"They're not likely to bomb the West End," he protested. "There's no military target here."

"When those bastards decide to bomb, they just bomb. Think of Rotterdam. Will you hurry up?"

Harry dragged on his clothes, with some difficulty.

"I know," she said sympathetically. "We'll get him up again when the raid is over."

She opened the door, led the way into the hall. The lights were still on, but as they closed the flat door, they went out.

"Damn and blast and shit," Niki complained. "Don't move."

Harry stood still, and heard her fumbling behind the bar. A moment later a torchlight beam cut across the darkness.

She opened the door, led him down the stairs.

"Is there anyone else in the building?" he asked.

"Not at this hour. Underneath are just offices."

Now the explosions were really close, and as they reached the ground floor the entire building shook.

"Shit," Niki commented. "It's just along here." She opened another door.

"Wait a moment," Harry said. "I want to look out."

"You'll get your fucking head blown off," she remarked, and kept on going down the stairs.

Harry went to the street door, parted the blackout curtain, and opened the door. He looked out at a night sky criss-crossed with searchlight plumes, and when he stepped away from the doorway he could see an immense fire towards the river, where some kind of refinery or fuel dump had been hit. Anti-aircraft guns were blasting away, but at some distance, and there was no indication that any German planes had been shot down.

He went back inside, closed the door, and felt his way through the blackness to the cellar entrance. The torch beam came up to help him down the steps.

"So?" Niki asked. "What did you see?"

"Not a lot."

"I have more to show you," she promised him.

Next morning there was little evidence of the raid, at least in the West End. But there were still clouds of smoke rising from the south and east. There were crowds on the street, staring and commenting, but movement, at least on foot, was fairly easy. Harry returned to the hotel in the middle of the morning, to find an agitated Armistead.

"Where the hell have you been?" the captain demanded.

"Doing what we came to London to do," Harry replied, urbanely. He was still on a high. It was not merely the woman, although Niki was unlike any woman he had ever met, and not merely because of her liberal use of four-letter words. It was also the sensation of having sex, on the floor, in the middle of an air raid. Talk about *Gotterdämerung*, he thought.

"With Niki?" Armistead asked incredulously. "Shit! Didn't you know there was an air raid on?"

"We heard the sirens, and sheltered in the cellar. Fortunately, we were the only people there. Where did you go?"

"Into an Underground Station," Armistead said. "Seems they

are designated shelter areas."

"Good thinking. And did you have your little friend with you?"

"No," Armistead said morosely. "She ran off. But you, young Curtis, you seem to be learning fast.

"It's the only way," Harry said, happily. "What's the plan for today?"

"To get the hell out of here before Jerry comes back."

"Do we have to?"

"Yes – and you are coming with me," Armistead said. "I'm responsible for you." The railway stations had been bombed, if not very accurately, but there were considerable delays. Harry, having promised Niki to return to the club that night, tried telephoning her but couldn't get through. Then it took them two days to get back to the hospital, having spent a lot of their time waiting on draughty platforms for trains which either had been delayed or didn't run at all.

But for the disappointment of having to abandon Niki, Harry was content, and he knew Niki would understand. He had had an *experience*, of which he was heartily proud. And which he intended to renew when next he could get to London, when he would be the one with the know-how and the experience, and the cachet into Niki's midnight world.

He felt a thorough man.

But he was also exhausted; three months in hospital was no training for a jaunt like that.

He slept very heavily the first night back, and was awakened by one of the male orderlies with the information that Captain Jackman wished to see him.

Before breakfast? Hastily he dressed and reported, gulping as he saw that seated beside the doctor was Brigadier Brand.

"Sir!" He stood to attention and saluted.

"At ease, Curtis. You know the Brigadier, I believe?"

"Yes, sir."

"He wishes to have a word with you. I'll leave you to it, sir."

"Thank you." George Brand was a tall, spare man, with a thin face and a small moustache. In his case there was not the slightest resemblance to Hitler, and besides, he was an old friend of the family. "Sit down, Harry."

Harry sat down in the chair before the desk, cautiously. Was he going to be hauled over the coals about the London trip? But how could Brand possibly know about it, already?

The brigadier had moved to Jackman's seat behind the desk, and now he opened a file. "You've had a busy war."

"It's been rather static, sir. Eight months sitting on my tod in France, a week's frantic activity, and then three months lying on my tod here."

"I spent a lot of that time in Norway," the brigadier said, sadly. He tapped the file. "It says here that you don't really approve of the way things have been handled."

"I'm sorry, sir. Mr Roberts said to let it all hang out."

"Oh, indeed. It's good to do that, from time to time. And now I gather you've been seeing the sights of London. Did you enjoy them?"

"My activities were interrupted by the Luftwaffe, sir. Are we going to let them get away with that?"

"The word is that they were acting in response to the RAF bombing Berlin a few nights ago. Anyway, that is not our province. It says here that you are anxious to rejoin your unit, and resume the fight."

"Yes, sir, I am."

"Are you one hundred per cent fit?"

"No, sir."

Brand raised his eyebrows.

"I will need to do some training. The facilities here are somewhat limited."

"I see. But I was speaking of your health. Your leg."

"Only a twinge now and then, sir. It stood up to the London trip very well."

"Excellent. You do realise that merely rejoining your

32

regiment will not guarantee you a crack at the Nazis?"

"You mean Hitler is not going to invade, sir?"

"It would be suicide for him to attempt to do so, while the Navy is in being. And before he can eliminate the Navy, he needs to eliminate the Royal Air Force. And he's not succeeding in doing that, as yet. In fact, considered opinion is that the raid on London a couple of nights ago, and there has been another one since, incidentally, is an admission that he is not winning that particular battle and may be switching to terror bombing, as he did so successfully in Poland and Holland. Hopefully, he'll find our people are made of sterner stuff. And of course we're now into September. Having regard to the normal Channel weather pattern, if he can't get his people across by the end of this month, he's going to have to call it a day until next spring, at the very earliest. So you'll see that the possibility of actually being able to confront the Germans on Dover beach or wherever is a remote one."

"Than what is going to happen, sir?"

"It is likely that there is going to be a fairly lengthy period of stalemate, certainly until next year. He has to devise a way of getting his people across the Channel, if he is going to knock us out. One presumes he will continue this bombing campaign, but this is costing him more than us, not so much in aircraft – for all the wild claims being made in the newspapers the ratio is only about five to four in our favour – but in trained pilots. We recover all of ours who are not killed outright, he loses *all* of his who are shot down, whether killed or not. This is a big problem for him. I have the highest regard for our fighter pilots, but I am bound to say that the Germans are, or were, at least as capable. But you don't train a first-class fighter or bomber pilot in a matter of days or even weeks."

"So what is he going to do, sir?"

"As I said, it's a problem. He possesses probably, at this moment, the best trained and best equipped army in the world, and certainly an army with the highest possible morale. But what's he going to do with it? He also possesses three-quarters of Europe outside Russia. But the people he rules, in the conquered territories, certainly, aren't very happy with the situation. So, is he going to use his army as a vast garrison? That's a sure way to have soldiers lose their cutting edge. His best bet would be to try to do an Alexander or Napoleon, and push his way through to India. I'm sure you know there are quite a few elements in the sub-continent who would welcome him. But that would be an immense undertaking. I assume that by diverting a large force to North Africa in support of the Italians he could push us out of Egypt, simply because we have to maintain most of our forces here to repel the invasion, if and when it comes. But after that . . . Palestine, the Arabian desert, Iraq and Iran, the Hindu Kush . . . that's quite an undertaking. No, no, Mr Hitler has his problems."

"And we can do nothing, but wait and see where he goes next," Harry said, bitterly.

"Well, of course, you are absolutely right, in the short term. We have the nucleus of a very fine army of our own, once it can be re-equipped, and that is going ahead as fast as possible. But it is going to take time, and as I have just said, even when it is completely re-equipped, we are going to have to keep our main force here until we have finally seen off the invasion threat, and that could be the end of next year. What we need to be doing in that time is to encourage revolt in the conquered countries against the Nazis or Nazi-supported regimes. This is a bloody and unpleasant business, even if it has to be done. However, Churchill has come up with the idea of creating a military force which can attack and confound the enemy, a small body of determined men, who could be put ashore on enemy-held territory, shoot up his people on the spot, destroy vital facilities, and generally make him realise that we are still in and fighting. Winston has in mind a sort of British equivalent of the German storm-troopers."

"What a brilliant idea," Harry said.

"The idea, yes. The name, not so good. The phrase storm-trooper has all manner of unpleasant connotations to the average English man and woman. So we've persuaded him to change the name to Leopards. That has a good historical ring: the Plantagenets fought under the standard of two or three leopards. So tell me, are you interested?"

"Me, sir?"

"Why do you suppose I have been telling you all this?" the brigadier asked. "I didn't come down here just to give you a summary of the present situation, Harry."

"I'm sorry, sir. I was so absorbed by what you were saying . . . you would like me to join this force?"

"I am asking you to volunteer for a special operations group."

"Yes, sir. Would it mean leaving the Guards?"

"In the first instance, you would be seconded to a Leopard unit, retaining your Guards appointment. But, if the idea takes off, as we all hope it will, yes, the Leopards will become a regiment of their own, and you will be transferred."

"I see," Harry said thoughtfully.

"Of course I respect your loyalty to your regiment, Harry," Brand said. "I'd be disappointed if it were otherwise. However, again, if this thing takes off, the Leopards should, very quickly, become the elite regiment in the British Army, and it is certainly the only one with any prospect of actually getting to grips with the enemy, barring that very unlikely invasion scenario. I may say that with your Dunkirk experience, should you succeed in qualifying as a Leopard, you will almost certainly get an extra pip."

"Thank you, sir. Did you say, qualify?"

"I'm afraid the Leopards are going to have to attain a higher level of physical fitness, and even more important, mental commitment, even than in the Guards, Harry. That's why, when I was given the task of recruiting suitable officers, I immediately thought of you. My initial inclination was confirmed when I read Roberts' report: he describes you as being quite fanatical in your wish to get back at the Nazis. Now, we aren't looking for fanaticism. As I said, we're looking for commitment. But I believe you have that. I am also told that you are now fully recovered from your wound. I appreciate your feeling that you are not yet one hundred per cent. We can make you that. You are also a fighting soldier, with experience in the field."

"I have to confess, sir, that I have never actually fired at a visible German."

"But you have been fired at, Harry, and stood up well. So?"

"Oh, yes, sir. I will volunteer."

"Excellent. You understand that this is top secret?"

"I thought it might be, sir."

"Very good. Your assembly orders will be along in a day or two. Until then, this conversation did not take place." He stood up.

Harry also stood. "Will you be commanding the Leopards, sir?"

"I would like to. But they tell me I'm too old. Like most things in life, war nowadays is becoming a young man's game. Good luck."

"My name is Lightman," the major said, looking over the faces in front of him.

They were an ill-assorted bunch, Harry thought, and he felt rather like a new boy on the first day of school. But they were all new boys, even, presumably, the major. They had arrived from various units all over the country, each from a separate regiment. Harry wondered if this was deliberate, and decided that it probably was. The Army obviously intended that this outfit should create its own *esprit de corps* from the very outset.

They were also, he estimated, having not yet actually been introduced to any of them, a widely disparate group of men, their only common factor being that they were officers, and that he estimated they were all under twenty-five – he did not think even the major was thirty. And judging by their accents, he reckoned there were Scots, Irish and Welsh, as well as English, in the group, and certainly not all had been to public schools. He wondered how many had seen action.

"Welcome to the Leopards," Lightman said. He was a

craggy-faced man, of somewhat short, chunky build. More interesting was the woman seated beside him. She could also be described as short and chunky, if in a far more attractive fashion. Her black hair was cut short, and surrounded an attractively purposeful face. Even in uniform her figure suggested solid comfort. Or was that reflection prompted by his sudden close acquaintance with the female species? "If your surroundings are a bit bleak," the major was saying, "that is because, firstly, our very existence must remain top secret, and secondly, we are not here to enjoy ourselves."

Harry could believe that. The camp was situated on the Welsh coast, in as desolate a stretch of country as one could wish, and consisted of nothing more than a half-dozen wooden huts, of which this was the largest. From the proximity of the kitchen he gathered this was to be their mess as well as their assembly hall. It was certainly not intended as a place in which to relax, as the furniture consisted of nothing more than the wooden benches on which he and his companions were seated, and various trestle tables, behind one of which at the head of the room Major Lightman was presently standing.

There was, however, a rifle and pistol range, and the whole area was surrounded by an electrified fence, powered by the generator which grumbled ceaselessly from its own hut to the rear of the rest. They meant business.

"You are the first Leopards," the major was saying, "or, hopefully, you *will* be the first Leopards, when we have assessed your capabilities. The course is designed to take six weeks. For that period no one will be allowed to leave the camp, so there is no point in applying. Nor will you be allowed to write to your families. Incoming mail will be distributed, as and when it is received by your recent units. Now let me point out straightaway that this is not to be a unit composed only of officers. But the officers *in* this unit are going to be expected to lead, far and away beyond any normal concept of command. That is to say, you will not be overseeing your men into an assault course, you will be leading them through it. You will also be required to be fitter than your men at all times. As you, and your men, will be operating in conditions of extreme danger, the men you lead must have, at all times and under all circumstances, complete confidence in you as their leader. This must be demonstrated on every occasion. In other words, you will order no man to do anything or go anywhere, unless you have first of all done it yourself. Understood?"

He looked over their faces, and waited for a response. There was none. Not, Harry supposed, that anyone would have dared dissent.

"Now, I must tell you," Lightman went on, "that the Leopard idea was no sooner put forward than it was acted upon. Prematurely. We sent a small group of volunteers to carry out an attack and demolition raid on Boulogne. Then we sent another small group of volunteers to carry out a landing on the Channel Island of Guernsey. The two raids of course had vastly different objectives. As I have said, Boulogne was a destroy and disrupt operation. Guernsey was to ascertain the condition and morale of the people there after being taken over by the Germans. I have to tell you that both raids were failures. The forces were too small to be adequate, and they were insufficiently trained. In Guernsey there were problems with the big tides and high seas often encountered in the Bay of St Malo, with the result that some of our people were cut off on shore for a considerable period. Most of them were recovered, but they accomplished nothing of value, and several of the islanders, who attempted to help them, had their lives put at risk. These two failures have caused the entire concept of the Leopards to be reconsidered. Hence the call for additional volunteers. Now our aim is to create units of not fifty men, but five hundred, which, properly trained and led, and equipped with everything conducive to making them a top-class fighting force, will be able to operate, in enemy held territory for, if necessary, days on end without support. It goes without saying that these will be high-risk operations, and that we can expect heavy casualties, from time to time. If you understand what I have been saying, you will realise that the heaviest casualties may be expected amongst the officers in each unit. I don't want anyone to be in any rosy glow about this, however romantic the notion may sound. I also wish it understood that your business will be killing the enemy, and destroying his infrastructure, by any means, fair or foul, that can be devised. There will be no chivalrous warnings, no chivalrous hands out to a wounded foe. Your business, gentlemen, is death and destruction, murder and mayhem. Do I make myself clear?"

Once again he looked over their faces, dwelling for a moment longer on Harry's face than on the others. He knew all about all of them, Harry realised, was not only aware that Harry was the youngest present, but suspected that a Guards officer might be more inclined to wish to fight an old-fashioned, chivalrous war than any of the others.

"Your training starts tomorrow morning. If, before then, any man here has any doubts as to his ability to qualify as a Leopards officer, I would like him to come and see me, privately. The decision to withdraw from the training programme will not in any way detract from his record as an officer, nor will it be known outside this group, and you are all bound to secrecy. If," he added, again looking from face to face, "any of you has problems of a more domestic nature, my adjutant, Captain Forester," he indicated the woman, "will be happy to hear of it and will do her best to alleviate it. Now go to your quarters as assigned. Dinner will be in one hour."

Their names and hut numbers were on the notice board.

"Hut C," Harry said.

"Here," remarked a tall, lanky man. He wore a moustache, but he also did not remind Harry of Hitler.

"Harry Curtis."

"Kevin Tate."

They shook hands.

"Count me in. Jonathan Ebury."

Ebury was shorter than the other two, and stockily built. Harry decided he had been wrong in his original estimate, and put Ebury down as very probably over thirty. He had a red face and did not really look in the best of condition.

They trooped across to C hut, which predictably was even more spartan than the mess hall, with bunk beds, a single table and chair and hanging lockers.

"One upper and two lower," Harry remarked. "Shall we toss?"

He did not intend to surrender any prerogatives on account of being obviously younger than the other two.

"I'll take the upper," Tate volunteered.

"Right-ho."

They dumped their gear.

"What do you reckon?" Tate asked.

"No batmen, it appears," Ebury remarked.

"Strictly do it yourself," Harry agreed.

"Guards, is it?" Tate asked. "Or was it?"

"Still is," Harry said. "Buffs?"

Tate nodded, and looked at Ebury. "RE?"

Ebury grinned. "They say I'm an expert with explosives. All I have to do is get into shape."

"I've an idea that goes for all of us. What price her ladyship?"

"I suspect it's strictly look but don't touch," Harry recommended. "She belongs to the boss."

Dinner was at least served, by two stony-faced orderlies, but it was very plain fare, with nothing more than water or tea to drink. Lightman presided, Captain Forester at his elbow, and after the meal was over, he addressed them again.

"There will be a film in half-an-hour," he said. "It will be brief. Then I suggest you all have an early night. Reveille will be at zero five zero zero, and we will commence with a five-mile run. This is what you might call an introductory offer." He gave one of his quick, wintry smiles. "Within a fortnight the morning run will be twenty miles."

Ebury gulped, audibly.

"That will be followed," Lightman went on, "by arms drill, assault training, lectures, and after lunch, PT."

"When do we get our men, sir?" someone asked.

"When you are accepted as Leopard officers," Lightman said.

Next morning it was raining.

"Par for the course," Tate commented.

In addition to the wet, they had also accumulated two drill sergeants, who accompanied them on their run, as did Lightman. Captain Forester was not to be seen. The only casualty was Ebury, who collapsed from exhaustion towards the end.

"We'll get you into shape," Lightman said, encouragingly.

Harry hoped he was right; he felt sorry for the little man, who obviously had talents far beyond those of an ordinary line soldier.

Worrying about Ebury apart, the course was most interesting, if exhausting for all of them. Harry had, of course, done assault training with the Guards, but nothing as intense as this, as in addition to the usual burrowing through tunnels and barrels and across swampy ground with full kit, the kit itself was unlike anything he had previously encountered, and weighed some fifty pounds – including such items as spare clothing, spare magazines for their tommy-guns, water-purifying tablets and a first-aid kit as well as iron rations for three days – with which he was expected to run a hundred yards in not more than twenty seconds.

In addition they were required, in full kit, to scale a vertical cliff close to the camp, using ropes and crampons to go up some hundred feet as if they were mountaineers. Here there were several failures, but Lightman remained encouraging.

They were also taught specialist combat techniques, using both fingers and hands and even elbows to strike at possible enemies in the most lethal manner. A doctor came down to show them pressure points and fatal areas, from the Adam's Apple or the simple clapping of the hands, hard, over an enemy's ears, to the paralysing chop at the base of the neck. The drill sergeants taught them throwing techniques as in ju-jitsu, but as Lightman said, "That isn't really of too much value to us. The essence is to be able to eliminate the enemy without him being able to make any noise. Once there is noise, use your firepower."

And they were taught the use of the most lethal piece of equipment they possessed; a length of steel wire which could be looped over a man's head and drawn tight round his neck in hardly more than a second.

"Makes me glad I'm one of us and not one of them," Tate commented.

"Don't you imagine 'them' are similarly equipped and trained?"

"Ah, I'm sure their storm troops are. But we're hardly likely to run into any of them, are we?"

Harry hoped he was right.

Their weapons themselves consisted of tommy-guns, although each man was also issued with a revolver and a long, straight knife, with both a point and a razor sharp blade. There were also sundry accessories such as knuckledusters.

"I may say," Lightman told them, "that every man in your command will be similarly equipped and trained."

"Will there be any heavy stuff, sir?" Harry asked.

"In the first instance, no. For two reasons. Every tank, every gun, every heavy machine-gun being made at the moment has to go to the regulars while the invasion remains a possibility. The second reason is that our business is to raid, get in, do as much damage as possible, and get out again with as few casualties as possible. It will therefore not be practical to deploy any heavy equipment at this stage. When, as one would like to think will happen, we are developed to divisional strength, that will be a different matter."

They had all had a rigorous medical examination before being accepted, even for training. After six weeks, the doctors were back again, poking and thumping. Then they were all summoned into the mess hall, to face Lightman.

"Passing out parade," he said with one of of his smiles. He looked down at the list in his hand, then up again. "You will each be given a sealed envelope, which you will carry with you. You are being given four days leave, to visit your families, or, ah, friends. The sealed envelope is to be opened twenty-four hours after you leave here. Inside you will find instructions as to where you are to report at the end of your furlough, together with travel documents to get you there, and sufficient money for your expenses. In the case of those of you who have not made the grade, the instructions and documents will be towards rejoining your original units. Now, let me repeat what I said when you first came here: this is a top secret exercise. You are to tell no one, not even your parents or your nearest and dearest, what you have been doing, or what, in the case of those of you selected, what you are hoping to do. To divulge any of this information will not only be a criminal offence, which could lead to a court martial, but it could also endanger the lives of your comrades here and many others besides. Any questions?"

"Just what are we to tell the folks at home, sir?" Tate asked. "They all know we have been incommunicado for the past six weeks. Doing something."

"You will tell them that you have been selected for training in the handling of a new weapon. The weapon is top secret, so you are unable to say anything about it, or even where you have been. I may say, gentlemen, that this is not actually a lie, except in so far as you have not been training with a new weapon, you have been creating it. I will now wish you good luck, and goodbye, at least for the time being. A truck will be along to pick up you and your kit for conveyance to the railway station tomorrow morning. Until then, why, I think you deserve a night out."

He shook hands with each man in turn, and Captain Forester handed over the large, heavy brown manila envelopes, murmuring "Good luck," as she did so.

Harry found her intensely attractive. This he knew was in part the hubris created by his training, the knowledge that he could kill with a blow, added to his experience with Niki, which made him feel that any, and every woman would surely fall for his charms the moment he turned them on, as well as the plain fact that she was the only woman with whom he had come into contact for six weeks. He also knew that every other man in the camp probably felt the same way – except perhaps for Lightman, who presumably had already had her. Yet he couldn't help murmuring, as he took his envelope, "Are you going home too, Captain Forester?"

"Yes, I shall," she said.

"Not anywhere near Worcester, is it?"

"I live in Kent," she explained. "With my husband."

Yet that night, when they were for the first time released from duty, she accompanied them to the village pub, which was not all that far away. Predictably they all got very drunk, and wandered around the yard afterwards, waiting for their transport.

"Let's *do* something," someone said.

"Let's have Forester's knickers off for a start," Tate said.

"You dare," she said. But she was laughing; she had had as much to drink as anyone.

They surrounded her. "You, Ma'am, because it's you," Tate said. "May name the chap with the honour."

"Bastards," she said, continuing to laugh. "All right . . ." she looked around their faces. "You!" She pointed at Harry.

"Me?" He had deliberately been hanging back, embarrassed. He reckoned he was the most sober person there.

"You, is what the lady said," someone shouted, and he was pushed forward, to gaze at Belinda Forester, lying on her back on the ground, her legs in the air.

Then he was as enthusiastic as any of them, reached for her, pushed his hands under her skirt, found the silk, enveloped in warm and pleasant smells and feels, dug his hands into the elastic and pulled down, cursed the darkness which prevented him seeing properly, and was then jerked backwards, the knickers in his hands. "What are you going to do now, big boy?" she asked.

The yard filled with light as the transport van rolled in, and they all released her to run towards it, laughing. Belinda Forester snatched the knickers from Harry's hands as she joined them.

"Does he really think we're going to wait for twenty-four hours to learn our fate?" Tate asked, when they returned to their hut.

"It might be a good idea," Harry suggested.

Had it really happened? She was a most delightful woman, additionally because she had taken the ragging in such good part. And she had chosen him! But she was also his superior officer. All of their superior officer. Suppose she preferred charges? But somehow he knew she wasn't going to do that. So . . . but surely they would never meet again?

"I think I know mine," Ebury said. "Back to the Engineers, I imagine. Well, it's been fun knowing you fellows."

"What are you going to do with your leave?" Harry asked.

"Oh, I'll spend it with the wife."

"Wife? You mean you're married, too?"

"Why, are you?" Tate asked, somewhat sceptically.

"No, no, I mean . . ."

"I have a kid," Ebury said.

Harry looked at Tate.

"I didn't think they'd use married men on a high risk op like this," Tate commented.

"I volunteered. Special skills. All gone to waste because I can't climb a bloody cliff."

His fingers moved up and down the envelope.

"Please don't open it here," Harry begged. "Lightman is sure to know if you have."

Ebury hesitated, then pushed the envelope into his bag.

"So," Tate said. "I reckon, if we're selected, we're certain to meet up again. Until then, the best of luck, Harry."

"And to you, Kevin." Harry shook hands, and then with Ebury. They had become good friends. Six weeks, and hardly a cross word. Of course, they had all been so exhausted when off duty, and so concentrated when on, that there had been no time for rancour or petty disagreements. And now, home. Harry hadn't been home since July of 1939. As it was now the beginning of December 1940, that was damn near eighteen months. His mother and father had, of course, been allowed to visit him in hospital, twice. But in the ward those had been relatively public occasions, matters of mutual reassurances. He wondered what he'd find, at home?

Jupiter, certainly. The huge black dog, a cross between a Newfoundland and a Red Setter, rose from his habitual midday position under the cherry tree, and barked at the intruder, then galloped forward, wagging his tail, as he recognised his master.

"Jupe, you old devil." Harry closed the gate on to the quiet suburban street, dropped his kitbag, and stooped to hug the dog, being pushed over so that he found himself sitting on the gravel path.

"Jupiter? Who is it?"

Alison Curtis looked out of an upstairs window. She was short-sighted, but being an intensely pretty woman as she approached fifty, was too vain to wear spectacles.

"Me!" Harry called.

"Oh, Harry!" The face disappeared, and they both reached the front door at the same time, Jupiter getting mixed up with their feet. Alison hugged and kissed her younger son. "It's so good to have you back. But . . . no warning?"

"You know that's the way the Army works, Mother."

She stepped back to look at him. "You're looking well."

"I'm in the pink. And you?"

"Aches and pains. Is there any news?"

"I imagine I've been more cut off than you these past few weeks. At least we may be pretty sure they aren't coming this year, now we're virtually into winter."

"George Brand said something about a new weapon."

Harry nodded, ushering his mother and the dog into the house and closing the door. "All very hush-hush."

"Will it stop Hitler?"

Harry grinned. "All new weapons are intended to do that. Whether it will or not is another matter. Dad well?"

"Oh, yes. I must ring the office and tell him you're home. Then he'll be back early."

James Curtis was a bank manager in nearby Worcester.

46

"And then we must have some of your old friends in."

"Do I have any old friends? I mean," he added hastily, "still about here."

"Oh, well, most of them are doing something. But there are a few. There's Yvonne Clearsted. You must remember Yvonne Clearsted."

"Ah, yes," Harry conceded.

"I think she had ideas about you," Alison said. "She'll be so glad to see you again."

"Ah, yes," Harry said again.

The only thing he really remembered about Yvonne Clearsted, when last they had met nearly two years before, was that she had pimples. They had been to kindergarten together, and he had pulled her pigtails. As to whether she had been fond of him, he didn't believe that, they had only met at the odd tennis party or church fete during the school holidays.

In any event he was at the moment feeling decidedly ambiguous regarding women, even his own mother. When last *they* had met, he had been a total innocent, lying in a hospital bed. Harry post-Niki was a totally different person to Harry pre-Niki. The post-Niki Harry felt he knew a great deal about women, the pre had known nothing. The experience, coupled with the lethal training he had just received, the supreme physical fitness he was now enjoying, added to the dangers he had been told lay ahead, taken all together with the last night at the camp, when a woman who in her own way was every bit as sophisticated as Niki had picked him out of the crowd for an act of sublime if unfulfilled intimacy, were inducing a continual euphoria, a hubris which he knew his parents would never be able to understand.

Not that he was at all sure how he wanted the sexual side of his life to progress. At the moment, his only dream was to get back to London, and Niki's club. And Niki. He was still meaning to do that at the end of this furlough, if only for one night. He told himself he had no illusions about her. In addition to being old enough to be his mother, if she was working for a vice lord she no doubt serviced *him* fairly regularly, just as she no doubt slept with any of her clientele who tickled her fancy. That she did not charge those she liked more than the average did not alter the fact that she was basically a prostitute. What his parents would say . . .

But having been terrified of the whole idea in the beginning, he now felt comfortable with her and about her. No doubt she had found him a boring tyro, although she had seemed to enjoy it. He had certainly enjoyed it. The idea of trying to replace that matter-of-fact straightforward approach, here we are, a man and a woman, each possessing something the other wants, so let's get on with it and have fun – an attitude he felt might be shared with Belinda Forester, were she not both married and bespoke and a senior officer – with the hypocrisy of will she, won't she, shall I, shan't I, dare I, dare we, which would be necessary should he go after a girl of his own age, and even more, his own class . . . Armistead's words of warning of what might lie in that direction were burned in his brain.

Anyway, *good* girls, as they might be described – and into which category he supposed he should even put Belinda, who had merely been drunk – would be thinking of marriage or at least an engagement. That was quite out of the question, with a war on, with him probably engaged in a high-risk operation, quite apart from his age.

"I'll invite Yvonne and her parents to come over," Alison said, sitting at her desk and pulling out a pad of paper and a pencil. "And the Brownings. You remember the Brownings. They have a boy in the Army, too. One of the Highland regiments. And Gillian Parks. You remember Gillian?"

Crikey, he thought. Not Gillian Parks? "Mother," he said earnestly. "I am only home for two days."

"Two days? You mean you won't be here for Christmas?"

"I'm afraid not. Two days. There is a war on, you know."

"But you just said there'd be no invasion this year."

"I believe that. But . . ." hastily he bit off what he had been carelessly going to say, that the Army was planning to hit back. "We still need to be ready."

Hit back, he thought. He carried his kitbag up to his room, looked around himself with some nostalgic satisfaction. His cricket bat leaned in a corner – had he really once made a century with that bat? – his gloves and pads and box beside it. Funny, he thought, in view of the training he had just received, in which going for a man's genitals with either knife or hands was highly regarded, they had not been issued with boxes.

He opened his wardrobe, looked at his civilian clothes, his dinner jacket, his bow ties, he wondered, when he left here in two days time, if he would ever see any of this gear again, much less use that bat.

He sat on the bed, pulled the envelope from his bag. He had only left the training camp six hours ago. Lightman had said to wait for twenty-four hours before learning his fate. But as Tate had said, did the major really suppose any of his protégés was going to wait that long?

Harry slit the envelope.

Three

Bombs

H is travel voucher was made out, firstly to London, and then to Fort William in Scotland, from where he would be directed to his unit. He was there!

No less important was the information that he was now Lieutenant Curtis.

This will not be gazetted for several months, the typed letter said, *for obvious reasons, as the name of your new regiment has not yet been finalised. Nor is it necessary to rush out and get yourself a new pip, as you will wear no insignia in your new appointment. You will be fitted for your uniform when you join your unit.*

At least there was nothing about not telling his parents about his promotion.

His instructions were precise. He was allowed three days at home. On the fourth day he would report to a London headquarters, where he would be given additional orders, with a view to reporting to his unit by the evening of the fifth day. That fitted his plans perfectly. That he only intended to spend *two* days at home was his business.

"Lieutenant Curtis. That sounds very good," John Curtis said, shaking hands. He had indeed come home early.

"I'm afraid I won't be gazetted until I return to the Guards

50

after this assignment," Harry explained, not knowing if he was ever going to return to the Guards.

"But we can still call you lieutenant," his father smiled. "I gather your mother has organised a party for tomorrow. They'll all be tickled pink."

"Yes," Harry said grimly.

They walked on the lawn behind the house, Jupiter frisking about them, noisily.

"So how's the leg?" John Curtis asked.

"Oh, right as rain. I've been doing some pretty hard training the past six weeks, and hardly a twinge."

"With this new secret weapon."

"Yes, Dad. Please don't ask me about it."

"I wouldn't dream of it."

"Tell me about Paul."

"Oh, he's watch-keeping on a destroyer. Convoys, mainly. We never actually know where he is, unless, like you, he suddenly turns up on the doorstep. Puts a strain on the old ticker."

"At least he's fighting the enemy," Harry suggested.

"Not so's you'd notice. He tells us it's a dead bore. He's never seen a U-boat. Now you tell me, Harry. What's the true situation?"

"I wish I knew, Dad. Like I told Mum, it's pretty well accepted that there cannot be an invasion now before next spring at the earliest. But the pundits seem to think Hitler can't wait that long to use his army, somewhere, somehow."

"The Middle East?"

"That's the most likely bet. You should ask George Brand. He walks the corridors of power."

"I *have* asked George. But he's not very forthcoming. And they're still bombing the hell out of London. Aren't you glad you're not being posted there?"

"I was there," Harry said absently. "The night of the first raid. 7th September."

"Eh?" his father asked. "What were you doing in London?"

"I got some leave from the hospital. Went up with a pal.

We'd planned to spend a weekend, but on the Saturday night down came the bombs, so we got out the next day."

"Good lord! What was it like?"

"Ah . . . you'd have to say it was hairy. But not as bad as the beach at Dunkirk."

"You were able to shelter?"

"Oh, yes, in a basement. I was in no danger, Dad, really."

His father grinned. "It's amazing, isn't it. You were in France, you were at Dunkirk, and here I am worrying about a few bombs. So you didn't have much of an opportunity to enjoy yourself?"

"Ah . . . no," Harry said. "Not as much as I would have liked."

It felt extremely odd to wake up the next morning, without the sound of a bugle call, and without having to leap out of bed and set off on a twenty-mile jog. Just lie in bed and think, savour the fact that he was now a full lieutenant, and that he had been accepted as a Leopard. High risk. But incredibly romantic.

And then do nothing all day but read the newspapers and play with Jupiter. And brace himself for Mother's party . . . and be considerably surprised.

Yvonne Clearsted had shed her pimples, and indeed had developed a very good complexion. She was taller than he remembered, and thinner too – perhaps she had been dieting by cutting out chocolates and boiled sweets, which were in any event about to be rationed, if the papers were to be believed. She had long, straight yellow hair which appropriately framed her long straight face and features. Hair apart, Harry did not suppose she would ever be a woman to have heads turning when she entered a room, but she was a considerable improvement on his memory of her. And she certainly seemed pleased to see him.

"Harry," she said, her voice low and soft. "What a war you have been having, I'm told."

"And you?"

"Oh." She shrugged. "I'm at the library. People read a lot, in wartime. I suppose it's the blackout."

"Now, now, Yvonne, you mustn't monopolise our hero," Gillian Parks said.

Again Harry was pleasantly surprised. Gillian Parks had been one of the kindergarten mistresses at the school attended by both Yvonne and himself. When he had been eight, she had been about twenty. So now she had to be in her early thirties, he supposed, a stocky, somewhat plump and therefore decidedly voluptuous woman, with dark hair and horn-rimmed spectacles. She too was no beauty, but her somewhat blunt features were enhanced by her smile. Spectacles apart, she reminded him, vaguely, of Belinda Forester. Now to his consternation she took him into her arms for a huge hug and a kiss on the mouth.

"I remember *spanking* you," she whispered. "Do you?"

Suddenly he did. She had made him bend over and given him six of the best with a strap. For . . . he couldn't really remember what.

"Bit difficult to do now, eh, Gillian?" Yvonne asked, coldly.

"I bet it'd be fun." Gillian released him, reluctantly. "Your Ma tells me you've been wounded. Where?" Her eyes drooped as if expecting it to be somewhere vital, at least to her as a woman.

"In the leg. A couple of bullets broke my thigh bone in three places."

"Oh, good lord!" Yvonne exclaimed.

"I'm all right now," he said. "Right as rain. Just scarred a bit."

"You poor boy," Gillian said. "But now you're home. For Christmas?"

"No. I return to duty tomorrow night."

No need for them to know it was not actually for two days' time.

"Tomorrow?" Both women spoke together.

"I'm sorry. I wish I could stay, believe me."

"Well, at least you can come round to the school and have a

cup of coffee tomorrow morning," Gillian said. "We can talk about old times."

She screwed up her nose as she looked at him.

Yvonne glared at him.

"Oh, I thought I might stop by the library as well," Harry said.

He stood with his parents to wave their guests goodbye; it was a thoroughly nasty December night, chilly and with a steady drizzle.

"Good friends," John Curtis said. "That girl fancies you, Harry."

"Ah . . ." which one, he wondered. But they both did. Even Gillian. But obviously Gillian, remembering how she had spanked him. The thought suddenly made him feel quite randy. For Gillian Parks, simply because she reminded him of Belinda? Gillian had to be the most confirmed spinster in the world, he would have supposed. Who still remembered the pleasure of spanking little boys. What a hoot. A session with Gillian would set him up nicely for his projected meeting with Niki – and might even enable him to stop thinking about Belinda.

Hubris again. Would that mean he was a cad? Not if she wanted it. Needed it, after the way life had got away from her. Besides, suddenly, after Niki and the intensive training he had just undergone, which included Belinda, he wanted to *know* every woman in the world.

Harry went, as he had promised, to the library first. He enjoyed libraries, because of the quiet. Yvonne was seated behind the main desk, with another woman, much older, and actually blushed as he appeared.

"Ah," said the other woman. "Our local hero. I have been hearing all about you, Lieutenant Curtis."

"I only wish there was something to tell, ma'am," Harry said. He looked meaningfully at Yvonne, then went off to stand behind a tall bookshelf, out of sight of the desk.

A moment later she joined him. "I didn't really expect you."

"Why not?"

"I thought you'd have too much to do, on your last day."

"Nothing I'd rather do than this," He lied.

"Oh. Well . . ." she was flushing again. "It seems odd, to meet again, for so short a time."

"I'll be back."

"Will you, Harry?"

"Of course. This is where I live."

"And me," she said. "So . . . I'll be here."

"Good." He took her in his arms.

She made a strangled sound, which grew as he held her tightly against him and kissed her mouth. But she wasn't exactly fighting to get free, and she tasted good, and felt even better: there was more to her than he had suspected.

He let his hands slide up and down her back, but not below her waist, he didn't know what might be her reaction to that. Then he took his mouth away.

"I can't tell you when," he said.

"I know. I'll be here." She looked right and left, but the aisle remained empty.

He kissed her again before leaving.

Harry didn't know if he'd made some kind of commitment. As there had been no witnesses, he could easily avoid it, if he was a cad. But the fact was, she was the most likely prospect at the moment. It was a marriage that would delight both his parents and hers, he thought. Not to mention Yvonne herself.

And him? He doubted it. But he was suddenly in the mood to create stability, have something more than his home and even his parents and Jupiter to come home to. As for what happened after that . . . there would always be Niki.

He *was* a cad.

And setting up to be an even worse cad, he thought, as he arrived at the school on the stroke of ten-thirty, just as the children were flooding out of the building into the yard to play.

I was one of those once, he thought, and wondered if they too would grow up to fight in a war? It could even be the same war, he thought, unless something dramatic occurred.

He pushed open the gate and went in. The children stopped their shouting and aimless running around to stare at him. A woman appeared in the classroom doorway.

"Hello," Harry said. "I'm Harry Curtis. I used to be a pupil here, a few years ago."

"Oh, Mr Curtis," she said. "Gillian said you might stop by. Come in, do. Oh, please shut the gate."

Harry obeyed, walking between the gaping children.

"This is Lieutenant Curtis, children," the woman said. "He used to be a pupil here, just like you."

"He's a soldier," said one of the little boys, authoritatively. "He's wearing uniform."

"Have you killed lots of Jerries?" asked another.

"Lots and lots," Harry said.

"But you don't have a medal," said a little girl. "You should have a medal."

"Lots and lots of medals," suggested another.

"They haven't got around to me, yet," Harry explained, and looked at the mistress, hopefully.

"Now, children, leave Mr Curtis be," she admonished. "Get on with your games. Do come in, Mr Curtis." She stood back to allow him past her. "Mr Curtis is here, Gillian."

Gillian appeared at an inner doorway. "Why, Harry. I didn't really expect you."

"You're the second person to say that to me this morning."

She raised her eyebrows. "Ah, you've been to the library."

"As promised."

"Come in. You'll excuse us, Marjory."

The other teacher simpered, and Harry went into the staff room.

"The old place hasn't changed much," he remarked.

"Not at all," she agreed. "Save for the lack of a couple of coats of paint, and we've been told there'll be no more of that for the duration."

He heard the soft thud of the door being closed behind him.

"Tea?" she asked.

"Thank you." He sat down, watched her. She had the sort of body that cried out to be held, hugged, caressed . . . and then what? Both of these women were mantraps. Unlike Niki.

She placed the cup of tea in front of him and sat opposite with her own.

"When are you away?"

"My train is at four."

"To where? Or shouldn't I ask that?"

"You shouldn't. But actually, in the first instance I'm going to London. I'll make another connection there."

"How I envy you. I wish I were coming with you."

"To London? It's being bombed all the time."

"That makes it even more exciting. But it always was exciting. London is my favourite city. And do you know, I haven't been there for two years."

"Good Lord! I was there in September. The night the bombing started."

"That must have been terrific."

"Well . . . it was a terrific night, yes."

"You had a girl," she suggested.

"Well . . ."

"I lost my virginity in London," she remarked.

"Eh?"

"I'm sorry. It just slipped out."

But he knew it hadn't, it had been carefully timed. And why not? He knew she was pretty desperate.

"So did I," he said. "On that night in September."

They gazed at each other.

"Then we have more in common than my having once caned you," she said.

"I suppose we do."

"Do you hate me for that?"

"Good lord, no. I'd forgotten all about it till you reminded me."

Her tongue came out and circled her lips. "Does it shock you, that I should be a fallen woman?"

"You, a fallen woman. For a—"

"It was an affair," she said positively. "I met him at a teacher's training school, and well . . . one thing led to another." She sighed. "I actually thought he was going to marry me." Her cheeks were pink. "I don't know why I'm telling you this."

"Because we share a bond," he suggested.

"What bond?"

"You once spanked me."

"Oh." She gave a shy smile. "You were a terrible little boy. You were sitting next to me during lessons, and you put your hand up my skirt."

"Did I really? Good heavens. I do apologise. Do you think I've changed?"

She gazed at him, and again her tongue came out and circled her lips. "Would you like to do it again? And . . . maybe get your own back for the spanking?"

"That might be fun." He looked left and right.

"We couldn't possibly do it here," she said. "Marjory might come in at any moment. Anyway, break will be over in a few seconds. What time did you say your train was?"

"Four o'clock."

"Well . . ." another quick circle of her lips. "Today is half-day at school. I'll be home by two. We could, well . . . you could call. If you can spare the time. Before your train."

"I can spare the time, Gillian. But are you sure you want to?"

She kissed his cheek. "Oh, I want to, Harry. How I want to."

"Well," John Curtis said. He had broken his usual routine by coming home from the office to be with his son for a last luncheon. "All ready for the off?"

"I think so, Dad."

"Such a brief visit," Alison grumbled. "When will you be back again, Harry? When?"

"Now you know I can't answer that, Mother. Even if

58

I knew, which I don't. Some time next year, if all goes well."

"Next year," she muttered.

Her husband reached across the table to squeeze her hand, looking apologetically at his son. "What time is your train?"

"Two-thirty. I really should be going."

He went upstairs to collect his gear. Both parents were in the hall when he came back down.

"You *are* going to come back, Harry?" Alison asked.

"Of course I am, Mother. Don't I always?"

He kissed her, shook hands with his father, and walked down the path to the street. War, he thought, which involves lying even to one's parents. Save that the War had nothing to do with this lie. Or did it? He would never have been in this position at all but for the War, and Dunkirk, and the hospital, and Armistead, and Belinda's knickers . . . and Niki.

Did he know what he was doing? He wasn't sure he did, but he certainly intended to do it. Niki had opened a Pandora's Box of knowledge and desire in his mind, compounded by the knowledge that he might, at any moment, be called upon to live his last few seconds on earth. Before then he wanted to sample as much of life as possible, and life, on a sudden, meant women.

Perhaps the desire for women had always been there, thoroughly repressed and suppressed by the regime of cold baths and cricket bats to which he had been exposed throughout his youth. Now he wondered what Gillian would be like, how far she would be prepared to go. He rather felt it might be all the way. Unlike Niki, she wasn't actually old enough to be his mother, but she was old enough once to have spanked him.

"I hope your neighbours won't comment," he remarked, as she closed the door behind him and shot the bolt.

"Fuck the neighbours," she said.

She was breathless, still wore the white shirt and navy blue skirt of a schoolmistress, although she had taken off her tie and loosed her hair. She had also taken off her glasses.

Harry laid down his kitbag.

59

"I don't suppose there's much time," she said.

"Unfortunately, no."

"So . . ." her tongue made one of those quick and anxious appearances. "What would you like to do?"

"Kiss you."

She was in his arms, her tongue reaching for his, while her nails scoured up and down the back of his tunic. When she took her mouth away, they were both breathless. "Harry Curtis," she said. "The moment I saw you again, yesterday, I thought to myself *there is a man.*"

"That's very kind of you. The moment I saw you, I thought, there's a pair of knickers I'd like to get into."

He checked, amazed by his boldness, while she smiled. "And you shall. What about Yvonne?"

His head jerked. The question had come out of the blue.

"Well . . . my parents think she's the ideal girl for me to marry. So do her parents, apparently. And so does she, I think."

"Have you had her?"

"Well, of course not. I mean, I only saw her again, last night."

"You only saw me again, last night."

"Yes, but . . ."

"A gentleman does not immediately climb on board a young lady," Gillian remarked. "But a middle-aged frump, now . . ."

"You're not middle-aged," he protested.

"Getting there." She gave another sigh. "So, marry that girl, and be happy, Harry. I'm not jealous, really. Just lonely."

He took her in his arms for another long, intimate kiss. Then she led him to the stairs and went up in front of him. He watched her legs moving. They were surprisingly good legs. Even more surprising, he realised she was not wearing stockings. And above the legs, her buttocks also moved, entrancingly, against her skirt.

As they reached the top, he surrendered to impulse, and leaned forward, to grasp her knees and then quickly slide his hands up her thighs, to hold her buttocks, and discover she was not wearing knickers, either.

She gave a little shriek, and fell to her hands and knees.

"You said I could spank you," he said.

"Would you like to?"

"I'd rather feel you. May I feel you?"

"You may. All over."

The train hummed over the tracks on its way south. Harry sat in his first-class compartment and gazed out of his window at the faint images rushing by. It was already dark, and with the black-out it could have been the pit of hell out there. The lights on the train had been out from the start, controlled from the guard's van, so that no one could carelessly switch one on and reveal their presence to any marauder in the sky. There were a couple of other people in the compartment, but Harry had no idea who or what they were.

Nor did he wish to communicate with them in any way. He felt utterly content, and not a bit guilty. He was embarking on a great adventure. That his life might be endangered only added to the spice of it. He did not believe he would be killed. He had never believed that. But then, no soldier ever believed that. Not even Hardisty.

And in the meantime . . . he had, looked at in the terms of his school and upbringing, and the mores of 1938, behaved in a most reprehensible manner. But Christmas 1940 was a million light years away from the Christmas of even 1939, much less 1938.

And what had he actually done? His conscience was attempting to condemn him because he had been brought up to believe that one did not make advances to a woman, and certainly one did not take her to bed, without honourable intent. That was entirely correct, in the abstract world which had now disappeared, perhaps forever, certainly for the duration of this war. One lived, knowing that death might be just around the corner, and one died, when the moment came, hopefully with the knowledge that one *had* lived.

Whatever he had done, it had been what Gillian wanted. She too had been affected by the War, in a way that so far had not reached people like Yvonne. She had wanted an hour of life, to sustain her for the coming months.

Had it really been only an hour?

She had asked for nothing in return, no commitment, no promise. Only a "look me up when next you're home." No man could ask for anything more than that.

No, his real guilt was caused by the fact that all the time he had been with Gillian he had been fantasising that she was really Belinda Forester. Even worse, his mind had been roaming ahead, to this evening, and Niki. He did not even know her last name. But even in a cold, damp, and extremely hard-floored cellar, she had given him the experience of his life. No doubt the bombs dropping all around them had helped their mutual urgency. That and the fact that it had been his first sexual experience. Now, for all that had happened since – or because of it – he desperately wanted to renew his worship of so much acquiescent beauty. He had dreamed of nothing else for six weeks.

The train was slowing, and a few minutes later the guard appeared in the doorway, a shadowy figure.

"There's a raid on," he said. "We can't get into Euston. We're stopping here."

"Where is here?" someone asked.

"It's not far," the guard said. "Just follow the track."

The train stopped. Harry reached up to the rack, pulled down his kitbag, and strapped it on. Then he climbed down and joined the considerable number of other passengers on the footpath beside the track. Looking ahead he could see the bright lights of burning fires, and now he could hear too, the crashing of bombs, the wailing of sirens, the drone of airplane engines, the searchlight beams criss-crossing the sky, bringing into focus the massive shapes of the barrage balloons hovering above the city.

"Strewth," someone commented.

Harry was inclined to agree with him.

They walked, muttering to each other. Harry did not engage in conversation. He was thinking that Niki would be down in her cellar, but as it was still quite early in the evening, she'd probably have all her clientele with her. Damn!

On the other hand, the raid would have to end some time. And in fact, long before they even reached Euston, the all-clear was sounding. Now the wailing of sirens was louder, but so were various bangs and crashes as buildings fell down and gas mains exploded.

They reached the station, which had been hit and was surrounded by fire-engines and police cordons. The Underground Station was also closed, as a station, although there were quite a few people down there, apparently prepared to spend the night on the platforms. Harry continued on his way above ground, walking through areas of scattered, smouldering rubble, and equally, and without warning, areas which were relatively undamaged. He passed groups of people pulling at piles of wreckage, apparently feeling there might be living people underneath, and skirted bodies of firemen directing their hoses at burning buildings.

War comes to Britain, he thought. Old George Brand had supposed attacking London was a mistake. But this city was having its guts torn out.

It was eleven o'clock before he reached Piccadilly Circus, tired but still full of energy, thanks to his six weeks of Leopard training. By now the pandemonium caused by the raid had died down somewhat. He was still surrounded by noise: bangs and crashes, sirens and shouts and occasional screams, but the intensity had diminished.

He reached the corner he was looking for, and was checked by a policeman. "Mind how you go."

"Eh?" Harry had a quite painful sensation.

"There's a couple of craters down there," the policeman said. "You don't want to fall into one. Where are you going, anyway?"

"Ah . . ." he had no idea if the club was legal or not. "I have a friend who lives down there."

The policeman gave a grim smile. "She don't live there now." He ran his torch, quickly, up and down Harry's uniform, and added, "Sir."

"What do you mean?" Harry ran round the corner, and checked. The entire row of buildings on the left hand side of the street was a mass of rubble. "Oh, my God! But where are the emergency services?"

"This happened last night, sir," the policeman said.

"Last night?" While Mother was throwing her party, and he was chatting up Yvonne and Gillian.

"That's right," the policeman said. "Nothing to be done here now."

"But the people . . . the Foxy Club . . ."

"Ah, so that's where you were going, sir. I thought that might be so. Well, I'm sorry, sir, but the Foxy Club took a direct hit. God knows what they were aiming at."

"But the people . . . they were in the cellar?"

"Not all of them, sir. You know how it is. After the first dozen raids or so it became the thing for the night birds to say bugger them, if you'll pardon the expression, and sit it out. Or dance it out. Especially if they were tanked up. Terrible mess it was. Bodies scattered everywhere. Were you looking for anyone in particular?"

"Well . . . I knew the manageress. Niki."

"Oh, yes, Niki. Everybody knew Niki. They identified her by a ring on one of her fingers. She was fond of that ring."

Everybody knew Niki, Harry thought. He should punch the fellow on the nose. But no one knew Niki any more, nor ever would.

He felt sick.

"You all right, sir?" the policeman asked.

"Yes, I'm all right," Harry said.

"Well, you want to take care. Here they come again. My advice to you, sir, would be to go down the Tube. They'll look after you there."

Harry spent the night in the tube station, with several hundred other people. They were all amazingly cheerful,

64

chatted, organised little sing-songs, and tried to keep their children in order. They were also very well looked after by volunteer workers with mobile canteens, who kept bringing round cups of tea and trays of biscuits.

Several people spoke to Harry, but he replied merely to be polite. He felt absolutely shattered, without quite understanding why. Niki had undoubtedly been a beautiful, flamboyant woman, on their one night together she had been good-hearted to him. But she had also been a middle-aged – relative to himself – tart. They would never have met but for the war. They could never have had a relationship, save during the war. And now that was history, because of the war. He knew the main component of his feelings was guilt. He had had nothing to do with her death. He could not have saved her life even had he been there, he could only have died with her. But he had been shagging Gillian, glorying in the feeling of mental and sexual freedom to which Niki had introduced him, while she had been lying in the midst of a heap of rubble, so blown to bits, if the policeman were to be believed, that she could be identified only by her ring.

He was obsessed with the feeling of the obscenity of it all. But he was also overwhelmed with the anxiety, the determination, to get into that obscenity as rapidly as possible, to kill or be killed, to avenge. As soon as it was daylight he left the station and returned to Rupert Street – the Windmill still stood – and beyond, to gaze at the rubble, the crater where the Foxy Club had once been. Then he reported to the address he had been given.

It was not very imposing. A door, and then a room, empty save for a table and two chairs. Behind the table there sat a sergeant, with a pile of papers in front of him.

"Lieutenant Curtis," he repeated. "Half a mo, sir." He riffled through the papers, extracted one. "Here we are. Yes, sir. Your unit is in Eastleigh. I'll just fill out a travel voucher."

"Eastleigh?" Harry queried. "I already have a travel voucher, for Scotland."

"Ah, yes, sir. It was to be Scotland. But that show is over."

"I'm not with you," Harry said. "What show is over?"

"The Leopards, sir. They've been wound up and disbanded."

Four

"Would you mind saying that again?" Harry asked.
Coming on top of the events of last night he felt totally disoriented.

"I don't know the details of the matter, sir," the sergeant said. "All I know is that the idea has been terminated, and I am instructed to return all officers to their previous units."

"What a foul-up," Harry commented.

"However, sir, if you would like some more information, Major Lightman did say that any officer who wished could join him for a farewell drink at lunch time at the Ritz Hotel. I'll make your voucher out for this afternoon, shall I?"

"We've fallen foul of the Establishment," Lightman said, while glasses of sherry were handed round. Only four officers had so far turned up, and neither Tate nor Ebury were amongst them.

"In what way, sir?" someone asked. "We haven't done anything, yet."

"I am speaking of the Army Establishment," Lightman said. "What we are planning got leaked, as these things usually do." He looked around their faces, as if wondering if one of them might have been responsible. "With the result that a whole covey of generals, past and present, and colonels, ditto, got up in arms. An elite regiment? they screamed. What's wrong with *my* regiment? It's the best in the British Army. Create this regiment, and you'll at the same time create an inferiority complex in every other regiment."

"With respect, sir," Harry said.

"Oh, quite, Harry. The Brigade of Guards is an elite force. But you see, it is elite at least partly because it was there first. The Guards regiment were the first regulars. No one can argue with that, or that they have maintained their position. But what we were trying to do was create a brand new elite force. I understand Winston is hopping mad. But there we are; I don't imagine even Winston can take on the whole Army." Once again he looked over their faces. "I would like to think, however, that your six weeks training has not been wasted, that you are now better soldiers, and that you will be able to convey something of what you have learned to your men. I would also like you to know that I have enjoyed meeting you and working with you. Good luck."

Once again Harry felt utterly shattered. Being a Leopard had given a purpose to his war. Perhaps it had also driven him a little way over the top, imbued even his personal relationships with a do or die, here today gone tomorrow, attitude. Now it was back to the grind of being virtually a garrison soldier, again with not an enemy in sight, no matter how they might know he was *there*, just across the Channel, glaring at them as hard as they were glaring at him.

With nothing to think about save the imagined image of Niki's splendid body, blown into a thousand pieces.

Lieutenant-Colonel Brewster was charm itself. "Harry Curtis," he said, shaking hands. "I've heard a lot about you."

They hadn't previously met, as Brewster had not commanded Harry's battalion in France.

"All good, I hope, sir."

"All very hush-hush. I gather you've been training with a new secret weapon."

"Yes, sir," Harry said cautiously.

"Oh, I'm not going to ask you about it. Although we could do with a few secret weapons around here, I can tell you. I'm assigning you to C Company. I'm afraid they're nearly

Commando

all recruits, but Bannon is doing a good job of licking them into shape. He'll be glad to have you along."

"Thank you, sir."

Harry had actually met Peter Bannon, although again they had not served together. The captain was a very tall man, with a hooked nose and a somewhat languorous manner. But he was a good soldier and a stern disciplinarian.

"Welcome," he said. "There's an old friend waiting for you."

"Sergeant-Major!" Harry shook Tindall's hand. "It's good to see you."

"And to see you, sir, looking so fit again." Tindall's craggy face broke into a smile.

"I see you've picked up the MM."

"God knows what for, sir."

"Saving my life on the beach, I should think. Have we any of that lot with us here?"

"Half-a-dozen, sir. The rest are fresh lads. Conscripts," the sergeant-major said, disdainfully. "But we'll make soldiers of them."

The other lieutenant in the company was John Bright. He was older than Harry, but also a recent draftee into the regiment, and regarded Harry with a good deal of awe.

"I wish I'd been at Dunkirk," he confided.

"It wasn't a lot of fun," Harry remarked.

"And then secret training . . ."

"Now, that *was* fun," Harry said. "Although I don't know how much use it's going to be."

Yet, as Lightman had said it should, it could not help but rub off. The battalion had nothing to do but train, while mounting patrols along the sea front and gazing at the cold grey winter waves. Harry trained his platoon harder than any other. His methods caused grumbles, but he met them all with a smile and a word of encouragement, and his men could not help but respond when they realised he would ask them to do nothing he did not do himself. After a month they were fitter than any others in the battalion, and senior officers came to look. Even a

69

general turned up one day to watch him putting his men through their paces.

For what? he wondered. If Christmas and New Year were bleak, January got bleaker. There was actually fighting going on in Egypt and Libya, where the Eighth Army was socking it to the Italians, but it wasn't happening anywhere else, except at sea and in the skies. There was no prospect of any German attempting to cross the Channel before May, and it was apparent to almost every British soldier that it wasn't going to happen then, either.

Equally, there was no way any British soldier was going to cross the Channel to invade occupied France. It was the most complete stalemate there had ever been in war, by Harry's reckoning. Even in the long years against Napoleon, before the British had got a toehold in Portugal and Spain, they had continued to pump invasions into Holland, all unsuccessful and very costly in terms of men and material, but at least they had been in contact with the enemy. This stagnation was soul destroying.

Nor could he fully fit into the social life of the Officers' Mess or the town of Eastleigh, or indeed that of Southampton, only a few miles away. Being virtually in the front line, should there be an invasion, those residents who had not been evacuated certainly indulged in a here today gone tomorrow philosophy, however false this may have become. Southampton, as a major dock area, had suffered severe bombardment in the early days of the Blitz, before the Luftwaffe had shifted its targets, first of all to the RAF airfields of the south-east, and then, on that fateful September day, to London. Raids against seaports, however, remained on the occasional agenda: Southampton had been heavily bombed three times in November, and the area welcomed the low cloud and heavy weather of the winter months.

Beneath the rain and the blackout the inhabitants of the city kept as much of a social life going as possible, built around the pub and the cinema, with a special welcome always kept for the officers of the local detachments. Opportunities for more than just a chat and a drink were always available, but Harry had no inclination to take advantage of them. He felt as if his sexual instincts, so alive and eager only a few weeks before, had been anaesthetised by Niki's death.

Even Brewster was moved to comment that all work and no play makes Jack a dull boy. Mr Roberts' psychiatric report was of course on file, and Brewster had obviously studied this. But there was nothing about Niki in the report, and Harry's anxiety actually to engage the enemy did not fully explain his dedication to training and nothing else. He discovered that the colonel had actually contacted his parents in an endeavour to find out what had happened in his past, apart from Dunkirk, that could explain his extreme motivation.

This became apparent when Harry received a letter from his mother, but as she also knew nothing of his private life since joining the Army all she could do was ask him in turn if all was well. He replied non-commitally. With her letter, which had been addressed to the General Army Post Office, there was one from Yvonne. This he binned, unread. Female relationships could have no more part in this war.

Harry was totally surprised when, at the end of the month, he received a summons to Brewster's office.

"Here's a rum do," the colonel said. "You have been seconded."

"Sir?"

"That's what it says here. You are to report to Fort William, in Scotland, immediately. To join a special unit." He peered at his junior officer. "Do you know about this?"

Harry opened his mouth and then shut it again. "I didn't expect it to happen, sir."

Could it really be happening?

"Would this be the unit you spent six weeks training with after leaving hospital?" He glanced at Harry's file. "You were with a special unit then too."

"Yes, sir."

"Secret weapons, eh?"

"Ah . . . yes, sir."

"And now they want you back again. They must think highly of you. Well, you will have to go. And not a replacement in sight. Good luck, Harry. Maybe we'll see you back again, one of these fine days."

"What are you?" Bright asked later. "Some kind of special warrior?"

"I have no idea," Harry confessed.

"How'd you get this job, anyway?"

"Well, when I was just about to leave hospital, I was invited to volunteer for special training."

"With a secret weapon?"

"In a manner of speaking."

"Nobody ever asked me to volunteer for anything," Bright grumbled. But he wished Harry luck.

Harry could hardly believe it was happening. Lightman had been the picture of dejection when they had met in London before Christmas. Now . . . could the show possibly be on the road again? He had said Churchill was hopping mad at the abandonment of the Leopard idea . . . perhaps the old man *was* capable of taking on the Army establishment!

He was given very little time to think about it, except when sitting in a train. He left for London at the crack of dawn the next morning, was met at Victoria by an MP who escorted him across London and saw him on to a train at Paddington for the journey north. It was next morning before he finally arrived in Glasgow, by which time he was tired and stiff and badly needed a shave. But here he was met by another MP, who saw him on to another train heading north. This was hardly an express, and the track threaded its way through the valleys of the southern Highlands. It was lunchtime before he arrived at Fort William.

But also joining the train in Glasgow, to his great delight, was Jonathan Ebury.

"Jonathan, you old son of a gun!"

They shook hands.

"Harry! Lightman told me I just missed you, in London, back in December."

"That was a bit of a sad occasion. But this . . . you reckon it's on again?"

"Can't be anything else."

"And you're . . . well . . ." Harry surveyed his friend. Ebury had certainly lost a little weight, but not that much; nor did he suppose the little man was any fitter than he had been at the end of their training programme.

Ebury grinned. "I'm included. Seems they'll take the odd expert, no matter what his physical shape."

"Well, it's jolly good to see you. Here's hoping we get posted to the same unit."

Fort William gave the impression of being a sleepy little seaport. Situated at the west end of Loch Ness, it serviced both the loch and the Western Isles. But there was a large number of soldiers to be seen.

Not that they were allowed much time in the town. They had a hasty lunch in the local NAAFI, and were then placed in a truck and driven north, in a country which was both wild and, at this time of the year, extremely cold; to either side of the road the snow lay quite heavily on the hills.

It took them nearly an hour to reach their destination, which was first signalled by a barbed wire fence and a large gate, beyond which was a guard hut. The sign read: *MINISTRY OF DEFENCE: KEEP OUT.*

Inside was a huge encampment, with several long barracks in the course of being constructed. Despite the weather, it appeared that most of the men were presently housed in tents.

Not that they were being allowed to get cold. Large squads were drilling and training. From the sound of rifle fire others were on the range. At the far end of the camp, as in Wales, there was the sea.

"Home from home," Ebury muttered.

Identification passes were inspected, and the MPs on the gate allowed them through. They were driven to the command post, where the Union Jack drooped in the light breeze, and a few minutes later found themselves standing before Lightman who, they discovered, had been promoted colonel.

"Welcome back," he said, shaking hands.

Captain Forester was, as usual, seated beside him, her face expressionless.

"Glad to be here, sir," Harry said. "Ma'am." *What* an attractive woman – but that was possibly a mixture of memory and his utterly chaste winter. "But . . . confused."

"It's a confusing business," Lightman agreed. "Sit down."

They sat before his desk.

"Very simply," he said, "one should never underestimate the Prime Minister. He banged a few heads together, and here we are again. There have been one or two changes, however. We have a new name. We are no longer Leopards. We are Commandos." He looked from face to face. "Does that mean anything to either of you?"

"Commandos was the name given to bands of Boer sharp-shooters, who raided our lines of communication towards the end of the South African War," Harry said.

"Well done, Harry. They were quite formidable for a while."

"But we beat them in the end, sir."

"Only in a manner of speaking. There were still several Commando groups in the field when the Boers finally surrendered. And to be frank, we beat them by rather reprehensible methods, burning their farms and locking up their women and children in concentration camps. Well, the Nazis may be destroying our homes as fast as they can, but God willing there is no way they are ever going to get their hands on our women and children. So the original concept is very much back in effect. And Winston wants action, just as quickly as we can do it. You've got just one month to lick your people into shape, and then we get to work."

"Where, sir?" Harry asked, eagerly. "Back to France?"

"I'm not going to tell you that, Harry. Where we are going, and what we are going to do, is known to only a handful of people, and will stay that way until we are on our way. Just bear in mind that wherever we go, it will be by sea. Train your men accordingly. It will also, as it will be the beginning of March, be very cold. Bear that in mind too. So, get started."

It was quite the most intense month's work Harry had ever experienced, making their six weeks on the Welsh coast seem like a holiday camp. The Commando regiment had been expanded to its full complement of five hundred men, split into five companies. Ten out of the twelve original officers from the Welsh training camp were present, including Kevin Tate, and there were three newcomers. The men themselves were, like their officers, all volunteers and were drawn from every regiment in the Army. There were even several guardsmen, although none from C Company of Harry's battalion.

"I've heard about your training methods, Harry," Lightman said. "We'll have some of your own people through soon enough. When we're allowed to expand. But," he told his assembled officers, "we need to bear in mind that right now we are on probation. Winston has gone to bat for us in the biggest possible way. But if we are going to be allowed to exist, much less expand, as he dreams, into a complete division, ten thousand men with our own airborne section and communications and artillery sections, this raid has got to be one hundred per cent successful. That means the maximum damage and casualties inflicted on the enemy, the minimum on us."

Now, in addition to the hard grind of drill and physical training to raise their men to the highest possible level of fitness and immediate obedience to orders, and teaching them all the arts of killing, silently and quickly, at close quarters, they concentrated on field tactics, the ability to approach an enemy position unseen and unheard. These tactics included such relatively obvious instructions as, in daylight, always keeping the sun behind, thus enabling one to control the direction of one's shadow and where possible merge it with others, to basic farmyard drill which was completely strange to many of the men, and the officers too, where they had been born and bred in cities.

The sergeant-major instructor knew a great deal about the

business. "You'll often have to approach an enemy position through wooded country," he told them, "but what I have to say applies to cultivated land as well, which may well contain orchards. These contain birds, and birds are a dead giveaway to any sentry, if they are disturbed. Now, certainly at night, birds are not disturbed by a steady rustle, such as you would make walking through grass. What really gets them going is the clink of metal. Remember this. Cattle are another potential hazard. If it is some time since they have been milked, they will approach any human entering their field. They may want to lick your face. They will certainly moo, and that could be disastrous. If you get approached by an amorous or distended cow, the only safe thing to do is milk it.

"When you are in position vis-à-vis an enemy, as may well happen over considerable periods of time, remember that repetition is your most deadly enemy. An enemy sentry, or worse, sniper, may be overlooking your position. If he notes movement, he will keep watching that spot. If the same movement is repeated, and again, he will draw a bead on you and be ready for the next time, when he will kill you. When you have to move, do it in a different direction every time. When you have to crap or pee, do not go to the same place more than once.

"When you are about to engage an enemy, especially at night, you will need to blacken your faces. This can be done in a variety of ways, by using burnt cork, or graphite, or soot, or even lamp black, whatever is most readily available. But under no circumstances use the most readily available substance of all: earth. This is liable to come away and expose you at the worst possible moment.

"Remember always, silence is not only essential, it means survival. The slightest noise can alert an enemy. Learn to keep your bodily functions under control Going into action is a nerve-wracking business: it creates wind. If you must fart, release it slowly, no rapid-fire machine-gun stuff. If you have to sneeze, don't. You can cut the necessity by pressing the upper lip against the base of the nose . . ."

"Makes me want to fart just thinking about it." Harry's captain was Tom Lockyer, who had been at the Welsh training camp. Harry had not seen a great deal of him then, but they both knew each other's worth. Lockyer was an urbane, good-humoured man, who took life very much as it came. But he was concerned about the other lieutenant, Harbord, who was one of the new volunteers, and who exuded a great deal of nervous energy, which occasionally led to sharpness with the men.

"He has good credentials," Lockyer said. "And I am sure will meld in. But I think you should have word with him."

Harry nodded. He also reckoned he should have a word with Company Sergeant-Major Johnson. The sergeant-major was a little man, a bustler who was very popular with the men.

"Raring to go, they are, sir," he told Harry. "Just show them an enemy."

"And no complaints?"

"Well, sir, when were there ever soldiers who didn't have complaints?"

"Food?"

"Oh, no, sir, the food is good."

"Women?"

Not even the officers were allowed off the camp for any light relief. Harry supposed there was not a man who was not drooling over Captain Forester, the only woman to be seen. That he might drool more than most was his business. But she was as unobtainable as the moon. At least, Harry remembered, until their training was complete.

"Well, sir, this is a monk's existence, that's for sure. But they knew that when they came here. And it's not as if it was for very long, is it, sir?"

"So they say. Thank you, Sergeant-Major."

"Sir!" Johnson slammed his heels together and saluted.

"Oh, there's just one thing more," Harry said casually. "How do you think Mr Harbord is settling in?"

"That is not for me to say, sir."

"Yes, it is, Sergeant-Major. I asked you."

"Well, sir, I am sure he will settle in very well. Keen as mustard, sir."

"The men like him, do they?"

"Well, sir, like I said, he's keen as mustard."

"And they're not? You just said they were."

"Well, sir, if I may put it this way, it's easier to be keen on the little things as an officer than as an enlisted man. Don't get me wrong, sir. Our men will follow their officers anywhere. I think they're just anxious to get on with it. I would say Lieutenant Harbord feels so too, sir. But underneath I'd say they're all a bit agitated. None of these men have your experience, sir, of France and Dunkirk. They don't know what to expect."

Harry smiled. "There is a butter rationing in force, Sergeant-Major, in case you hadn't heard. Thank you."

"God, to be out there, *doing* something."

Clive Harbord was a curly-headed blond with a baby face but a good pair of shoulders. He stood on the beach outside the camp and stared at the restless waves. Just visible in the gathering gloom was the shape of the nearest island, Eigg.

"Well, there's not a lot to be done immediately, out there," Harry suggested. "Unless you happen to be in the Navy."

He wondered how Paul was getting on. He, and everyone else, had been completely cut off from their families for the entire month they had been here.

"Ah, but that's where we'll be going first, isn't it?" Harbord asked.

"I imagine so. Looking forward to it?"

"Oh, yes. Can't wait."

"Well, everything comes to he who waits, so they say. In our case I would say there's no doubt of it. So we should just relax. And wait."

"Easy for you to say, old man. You've done it all, already."

"Would you believe that I have never killed a man?"

Harbord turned his head, sharply. "You were in France. You were at Dunkirk."

Harry nodded. "The trouble was, while they were shooting at us, we didn't have too many of them to aim at."

"But you've been under fire. You know what it's like."

"Yes," Harry said, and seized his opportunity. "It's not as bad as it seems in the abstract. Because you're part of a unit. If it's a good unit, every man will trust the man beside him not to let the side down, and they should all trust their officers to do the right thing, lead from the front, make the right decisions." He grinned. "Even when it's a bloody awful decision."

"That's what we're trying to do here," Harbord said. "Create a good unit."

"Absolutely. But it's not just a matter of drill and PT. Your men have got to *believe* in you. They also have to feel that you believe in them. You know, a smile, a slap on the shoulder can bring a man up to scratch where he hasn't been."

Harbord shot him a glance. "You don't think they believe in me? I always lead from the front."

"Of course you do. We all do. But sometimes it seems to me that you're a bit over critical of those bringing up the rear."

"I want them to be quicker, faster, better than anyone else."

"I think you mean they must be *as* quick, as fast, as good as anyone else. You can't ask more than that."

"Are you criticising my methods, old boy?"

"I just wonder if they might not be counter-productive, when the chips are down."

"Ha! Didn't someone once say that the only way to lead men into battle was to make them more afraid of you than of the enemy?"

"I think you'll find that was said a very long time ago," Harry suggested. "Nowadays, and especially in an elite force like this, you need their respect, certainly, and hopefully their admiration. I don't think fear should be allowed to come in it, whether of you or of the enemy."

"What do you think?" Lockyer asked.

"I think we must wait and see, sir," Harry said. "He's a good officer. And he's certainly enthusiastic."

"Yes, well, I'm afraid we're not going to be able to wait

and see. We have our orders. Embarkation tomorrow afternoon."

"And still no idea where we're going?"

"Not a clue. I imagine the old man will enlighten us once
we're at sea."

Next afternoon, just on dusk, five destroyers entered the bay.
The Commandos had already been assembled, in full combat
kit, and now they splashed through the shallows to gain the
launches which would carry them out to the waiting ships, and
would also be used to land them at their destination.

"Aren't you coming with us?" Harry asked Belinda, who was
standing on the beach ticking off each company as it embarked.

"Not bloody likely," she said. "I get seasick."

"But you'll be here when we get back," he suggested.
"Something to look forward to."

"I'll be here, Lieutenant Curtis," she assured him. "Just be
sure you do come back."

He presumed she didn't mean it personally.

There was only a light breeze, and the sea was calm; it was
now that Harry did indeed have a sense of *déjà-vu*, save for the
time of day and the fact that it was near freezing, whereas at
Dunkirk it had been a warm June day.

The sailors welcomed them on board, and the three officers
were shown to the sleeping quarters they would share with the
ship's officers.

"David Bingham," said the lieutenant to whom Harry had
been assigned.

Harry shook hands.

"I'm sorry it's a bit cramped," Bingham said. "I've cleared
a space in that locker for your gear."

"Thank you. Have you any idea how long we're going to be
bosom buddies?"

"I was told approximately thirty-six hours out, and thirty-six
hours back, if all goes according to plan."

"Thirty-six hours being . . ."

"Say a thousand miles, give or take a couple. We'll be
cruising at twenty-five knots."

"A thousand miles," Harry said thoughtfully, mentally envisaging a map of the Western European seaboard, "That seems to rule out northern France or the Low Countries."

"Could be Biscay," Bingham suggested. "It's just about a thousand miles from here to Bordeaux."

"Biscay," Harry mused. But Lightman had said it would be freezing cold. That hardly applied to Bordeaux, even in March. "I don't suppose you have an atlas?" he asked. "As opposed to charts, I mean."

"There's one in the wardroom library," Bingham said.

Bingham took Harry and Harbord on a tour of the ship, as soon as they were at sea and he was free of his immediate duties as Executive Officer. Lockyer was on the bridge with the lieutenant-commander who was captaining the vessel. He was very proud of *Ambitious*, as she was named, although she was not very large, just over three hundred feet long and displacing less than two thousand tons. Nor was she very new, having been launched in 1926. But she could, he claimed, make thirty-seven knots if pushed. She had two funnels, as well as a high bridge, beneath which, looking forward, were two of her four-point-seven-inch guns, mounted singly; the other two were aft. She also had six twenty-one-inch torpedo tubes as well as a couple of pompoms for aerial protection.

"What's your crew?" Harry asked.

"A hundred and thirty-eight. So you'll see that with your lot on board, we're just about doubled up."

They were not required to dress for dinner, but it was still a very formal occasion, even if the destroyer was now hurtling through the night, plunging slightly and rolling to the wake from the vessel in front. The loyal toasts were drunk, and the conversation became general, with great care not to involve the current operation. But after the meal Bingham unlocked the glass-fronted bookcase to take out the atlas, and the two men opened it on a side table.

"Now, what are you at?" asked Lockyer at their shoulders.

"Just checking, sir."

Lockyer grinned. "You have the same information I do.

A thousand miles, bearing north. Or at least north-east. The Norwegian coast."

Bingham produced a pair of dividers and marked off the distance. "Not a lot there. These islands . . . Lofoten. Ever heard of them?"

"Can't say I have," Lockyer mused. "Harry? He reads a lot," he explained to the naval officer.

"I think they have some fish processing plants," Harry said.

"Doesn't sound very worthwhile. Still, we must presume the big boys know what they're doing. Anyone for a hand of bridge?"

By dawn they were out of sight of land, racing through a still calm sea. But after breakfast the destroyers slowed and then stopped, and each put down a launch to convey the company commanders to the flotilla leader.

"Here's where we learn the truth," Harry said, as he watched Lockyer being motored up the line of ships.

"This is also probably the most dangerous part of the whole business," Bingham remarked, leaning on the rail beside the two lieutenants. "If a U-boat were to come along now . . ."

"Shit!" Harbord said. They were on the bridge wing, and could look forward to where the deck was crowded with Commandos. "Should we be having some kind of drill?"

"We don't have the time," Bingham pointed out. "And it wouldn't do a lot of good. Our hulls may be steel, but they're paper thin. If a torpedo were to strike us, we'd be down in seconds."

"God, you're a cheerful bastard," Harbord commented.

It was certainly nerve-wracking, as the destroyers rolled gently in the low swell. Every man on every ship was watching the calm surface of the sea, for the first sight of a periscope. Harry found his throat was quite dry. Was he afraid? Odd, he thought, this was the first time he had ever considered that. On the beach at Dunkirk he had been dazed by the enormity of what had happened and was still happening, but although he had been surrounded by dead and dying men it had never occurred to him that he might be one of them at any moment. He had not actually felt the bullets smashing into his leg, he had been on board the destroyer before the pain had overwhelmed him.

Now suddenly he felt vulnerable. Because he was a soldier, and this was a sailor's world. But there was more to it than that. The personal cocoon of invulnerability that every soldier has to have had been ripped away by Niki's death. She, like Gillian, or even Yvonne, and certainly like Mum and Dad and Jupiter, had been included in that cocoon, because he wanted them to be. But that hadn't done her much good. Nor would it do the others much good were a stray bomb ever to land in the Worcester suburbs.

The amusing, and even more frightening, aspect of the situation was that everyone thought he was a nerveless fighting man. Because he had been at Dunkirk! When he tried to tell them that he had not actually ever done any fighting, they thought he was being unduly modest. So when they went into action, tomorrow, he would be leading from the front. All the officers would be, but he was the man who would be expected to perform. Apart from people like Lightman himself.

"They're coming back," Bingham said.

They watched the launches cutting through the water. The slings were waiting, and no sooner had the boat come alongside than it was being raised, while the propellors were already turning. The lieutenant-commander on the bridge had been as anxious as anyone.

Harry and Harbord were immediately summoned to the wardroom, where Lockyer was waiting for them.

"Here's what you were waiting to hear," he told them. "We go into action at dawn tomorrow."

"May we ask where, sir?"

Lockyer grinned. "Your guess was right, Harry. Lofoten. The codeword is Claymore."

Part Two

The Throw

Be bloody, bold, and resolute; laugh to scorn
The power of man.

William Shakespeare,

Five

"There are things we need to remember," Lockyer said. "First and most important, these islands are inhabited by Norwegians. These people are our allies, and are therefore not to be harmed in any way, unless they are obviously helping the Germans. Impress this on your men. We are informed by our agents that there is a sizeable part of the population who wish to get out, and we will take these people with us when we leave."

"Bit of a tall order, sir," Harbord commented. "These ships are crowded enough as it is."

"I understand, after we leave the islands, we shall be making a rendezvous with a larger vessel, which will take off our passengers. However, this is the second point. We are going in at first light, and the intention is that we should be out again by noon. Six hours. We have to assume that the Germans, before they are overrun, will be able to make radio contact with the mainland, and that aircraft will be present, certainly by noon, with no doubt naval units and ground troops to follow. It is therefore very necessary that we stick to our timetable. Now, as to what we are about . . ." he spread a map on the table. "Our target is called Svolvaer."

"Doesn't look very big," Harbord remarked.

"It isn't very big. Now, here is the town. Here to the left are the fish factories. These are the main targets. But they are not our targets, Colonel Lightman will take care of those himself. Our business is the capture or destruction of the headquarters of the German garrison. This building here." He prodded a large square outside the town to the north-east. "It is also the barracks for the garrison itself. Therefore we must anticipate resistance."

"What is the size of the garrison, sir?" Harry asked.

"We are told approximately a hundred men. Mainly sailors, as these islands are regarded by the Germans as a naval station."

"Piece of cake," Harbord suggested.

"They will be outnumbered, certainly if we need to bring additional forces to bear. But speed is essential, this headquarters is certainly also their communications centre, and this must be knocked out the moment we get ashore. You should also bear in mind that these are tough, experienced fighting men, that they have a very high morale, and most important of all, that they are battle-hardened, which our people are not as yet, on the whole. Keep your men well in hand. Now, the Navy will put this company ashore in two launches, fifty men to each. When we land, we stay in the same formation. Harbord, you'll be with me in Group A, Curtis, you'll command Group B. You'll have the sergeant-major with you. We land here." He prodded the beach at the base of the pier. "Then it's into the town, and through it on the double, unless we run into organised resistance. I consider this unlikely. When we reach the headquarters, we regroup for our assault. I do not propose to summon the garrison to surrender, there is not sufficient time. All of their radios must be knocked out as rapidly as possible. Understood?"

"Yes, sir," the two lieutenants said together.

"Very good. Now here are some more of these maps. See that your men understand both the topography and what we have to do."

It remained a very long and anxious day, as the flotilla raced north. All eyes were now on the sky rather than the sea, as a submarine could hardly hope to keep up with much less hit a destroyer travelling at thirty knots. Were they to be found by a German patrol plane they could be bombed out of existence well before they could reach their target.

But the sky remained as empty as the sea.

"I believe we're going to make it," Lockyer said. It was his business to be optimistic.

The officers spent the day with the NCOs and men, going over the maps, explaining just what they were required to do. Enthusiasm ran high, as did confidence. With reason, Harry supposed, given the odds in their favour, of both surprise and overwhelming superiority in men. Only the sea and the sky were truly dangerous, and these remained empty.

In the latitudes into which they were entering, in March dusk was early, and the darkness was intense. The Commandos had an early supper, and retired to their borrowed bunks and hammocks. Harry wondered how many of them would actually get to sleep. He was sure he wouldn't, as he lay in his narrow berth, moving to the surge of the ship, both forward and from side to side, listening to the constant slapping of the waves against the hull – paper thin, Bingham had called it – wondering what would happen if they struck a mine. Again, going on Bingham's description of what would happen if they were torpedoed, he didn't suppose he'd reach the deck in time. One more statistic. One of several hundred statistics.

He found himself thinking, and then dreaming, of Belinda Forester. Even in his dream he wondered why, but it was intensely erotic. He awoke with a start as Bingham's hand closed on his shoulder. "Four o'clock," the lieutenant said.

Harry swung his legs off the bunk, splashed water on his face. He had slept fully dressed and it was simply a matter of pulling on his boots, strapping on his revolver and other equipment, and finding his helmet and valise. This he slung on his shoulder by its strap.

"What's it like up there?" he asked.

"Pretty clear. Dawn in half-an-hour."

Harry pulled on his gloves, made his way up the ladders,

discovered it was remarkably warm, even in the open air, and took his gloves off again.

The company was assembling, the men clearly excited but remaining quiet. Harbord was marching up and down, checking their equipment.

Lockyer stood beside Harry. "Okay?"

"Okay, sir."

"Here's the dawn."

Light was coming over the mountains to the east. The mountains! They were fairly close inshore, still racing along. If there were islands ahead of them they were lost in the general bulk of the land.

Then they saw twinkling artificial light.

"They don't know we're coming," Lockyer said, with satisfaction.

The destroyer began to lose way and Bingham joined them. "Fifty men to each launch," he said. "Sorry about the squeeze, but it's the best we can do. Good luck. We'll be waiting for you."

The ship slowed to a stop, rolling in its own wake. The launches were put down, one to each side, and the men clambered down the netting as they had practised so often in Scotland. The three officers were last on board: as arranged Harry had the starboard boat, Lockyer and Harbord the port.

At sea level the darkness remained intense, even if more and more light was showing to the east. The men were packed so close that chins were resting on the backs of those in front. Harry was in the bow, where he was joined by Sergeant-Major Johnson. "All present and correct, sir."

Harry heard a man vomiting – probably nerves, he thought, although they had hardly had the time to gain any sea legs.

The engine growled, and the launch moved away from the side of the ship. All around them launches were leaving other ships, each one packed with men. All the destroyers had stopped, save one, she was moving slowly ahead, to lead them, gradually increasing speed as she saw all of the ten launches were functioning properly. She was clearly visible, as the light improved, and now, behind them, the rest of the flotilla was moving forward.

In front of them there now opened a little harbour, in which were moored several fishing boats as well as a motor-torpedo-boat. But the Navy had seen these and opened fire; even the four-point-seven-inch shells wreaked havoc on the wooden hulls and within seconds all were burning and sinking. The little warship did not have time to fire a shot in reply before she too was overwhelmed.

This was obviously the first intimation the German garrison had that they were under attack. Alarm bells rang and someone blew a bugle. The ten launches surged to their appointed landing places, several into the harbour itself, some of these brought up alongside the jetty, expertly handled by the sailors. The others crunched into the sand of the beach. Harry leapt over the bow into ankle deep water, and led his men up the gentle slope, gun levelled, towards a delightful-looking little town, bathed now in the warm glow of the rising sun. Windows were opening and dogs were barking, as they ran up the main street. Harry waved at the heads looking out, shouting at them to stay inside; although as he spoke no Norwegian he didn't suppose he was making much impression.

Then a shot was fired from the end of the street.

"Go down," Harry shouted. "Return fire." He himself moved into the shelter of a doorway, and then, as the hostile fire ceased, waved the Commandos forward. They ran up the street behind him, and came across a German sailor, lying on his back, dead. Obviously he had been a lone patrol. It was impossible to determine which of the Commandos had actually drawn first blood for he had been hit several times.

"The barracks," Harry said, moving on.

Now there was noise all around them, explosions mingling with the gunshots. They rounded the corner, and encountered more fire. But it was very wild, and no one was hit. Nor could they ascertain precisely where it was coming from.

The other half of the company emerged from the next street. "Where is that shooting?" Lockyer asked.

Harry pointed at the large building across the square. "I reckon that's it."

Even as he spoke, there was another flurry of firing from the windows, again wild.

"They haven't got their nerves back, yet," Lockyer said. "Harbord, take thirty men to the left. Be quick but be careful. Curtis, thirty to the right. I'll take the centre. Blow your whistles when you are in position."

"Orders, sir?" Harry asked.

"As before. Take the building. Destroy all radio equipment. Kill everyone in the building who doesn't surrender. But bring out what papers you can find. Harry, you take the upper floors. Harbord, you'll assist in cleaning up the ground floor defence."

"Supposing there are Norwegians in there?"

"There won't be at six thirty in the morning. Move."

Harry led his men, bending double, to the right of the building. The firing had now become sporadic, as the Germans were waiting to see just how their attackers were deploying, and equally trying to ascertain their numbers and fire power. He reached a position to the right of the building, waved his men to take cover, and blew his whistle. A few seconds later there was an answer from the other side, where Harbord had also reached his position.

Harry checked his revolver, was pleased to see that his hand was perfectly steady. He had in fact not felt afraid at any time during the attack. But then it had all been so easy, thus far.

Another blast on a whistle, this one louder and more prolonged, and at the same time Lockyer's section opened a heavy and sustained fire on the front of the building. Harry waved his men forward, and they charged across the small yard. There was a door, and Harry went to this. It was locked, but he blasted the lock with revolver fire and it opened, to admit him into a dark corridor. He paused inside to reload, three men at his back, and a German seaman looked round the corner. Harry fired at him and he disappeared.

The rest of his men were crowding into the corridor.

92

"Up," Harry said, moving along the corridor. At the end he paused, listening, but it was difficult to tell what was happening because of the enormous firepower being used at the front of the house.

He stepped into a wide hall. To his left were the front rooms and the front doors. These were being hotly defended, but there had been casualties. The man who had looked round the corner was lying a few feet away, gasping and bleeding and clearly dying. Harry gulped – the man had not been armed.

But there was no time for reflection. Or for following his instincts to attack the defenders in the rear. That was Harbord's job, he had his orders. He pointed to the right. Here was a flight of stairs. "Sergeant-Major, check the back." Harry himself took the stairs up to the first floor, throwing open doors to left and right. The first room was the communications centre, and contained two sailors. One man was trying to use the telephone, the other was tapping on a Morse key. Harry opened up with his tommy-gun, supported by his men, and the two Germans crashed to the floor in a welter of blood, while sparks flew from their sets.

"Make sure those are fully destroyed," Harry said, and returned to the corridor. The rest of the rooms, apparently offices, were empty. At the end of the corridor there was another staircase. "Check the next floor," he told his sergeant, and started on the offices.

He ripped open drawers and hunted through their contents. He did not read enough German to understand most of it, but he crammed them into his valise for examination by the experts.

In the third room there was a safe, embedded in the wall.

"That's what we want," he said. "But it'll have to be blown. Corporal, report to Captain Lockyer and ask him for a demolitions expert."

"Yes, sir." The corporal ran down the stairs.

One of the privates sniffed. "Something's burning, sir."

"The whole damn building, I shouldn't wonder," Harry agreed.

He heard a woman scream.

The men looked at each other in amazement. "Stay here," Harry told them, and ran into the corridor and to the stairs leading up. At the top there waited a very agitated looking soldier.

"There's a woman . . ."

"I gathered that." Harry went past him into the corridor. Here several doors stood open, revealing various bedrooms. At the end of the corridor two more of his men, and the sergeant, stood hesitantly, looking into the room. "Stand aside."

The sergeant retreated. "There's a woman in there, sir."

"So I understand. Is she armed?"

"Well, no, sir. But . . ."

Harry stood in the doorway and looked at the bed. In it there was certainly a woman, half-wrapped in the sheets and blanket, but revealing enough to indicate that she was naked. Staring at her, he was aware of some very uneasy vibrations. She had a mass of yellow hair, which he thought might normally be straight but which was currently tangled from the night, a face of quite classically beautiful features, and, he reckoned from the various glimpses of white flesh emerging from the covers, a body to match.

The whole was incredibly as if Niki had come back to life, only younger, and even more lovely. And German?

More realistically, he could understand his men's reluctance to proceed, without at least laying themselves open to a charge of indecent assault.

"Ah . . . *Wer geht es Ihnen?*" He didn't suppose it was the least good, but it was the best he could think of on the spur of the moment.

"I speak English," she said in a low voice.

"Thank God for that."

"My name is Veronica Sturmer," she answered his question.

"Ah . . . you're German."

Her mouth twisted. "Partly."

"Well, Fraulein, are you aware that there is a battle going on, and that you are in the middle of it?"

"I know there is a battle," she said, somewhat irritably. "Conrad said to stay here."

"Conrad being . . . ?"

She shrugged, delightfully. "I suppose you could say that he owns me. At the moment."

"Well, that's about to change," Harry said.

"You will protect me?"

"Ah . . . yes, if I have to."

"Begging your pardon, sir," the sergeant said. "But I think this building is on fire."

The sound of the shooting had stopped, although there was still a great deal of noise. But the scorching smell was growing stronger by the moment.

"Do you have any clothes?" he asked Veronica Sturmer.

"Yes, I have clothes."

"Then would you mind putting them on?"

"Certainly." She threw back the covers, and Harry retreated hastily. Perhaps Niki had looked just like this once, but it had been a very long time ago.

"Outside," he told his men, who withdrew, reluctantly. He went with them. "Please hurry," he called through the door.

"I reckon someone should keep an eye on her, sir," the sergeant said. "She could be arming herself, or getting some grenades together . . . or anything," he finished lamely as his officer looked at him.

"I think we'll let her get on with it, Sergeant," Harry said. "Go down and see if there's any sign of the demolitions expert. If he's not here soon, he needn't come."

"We could try blowing it open with grenades, sir."

"I'm not sure they'd work. And anyway, it's the contents we're after, not the destruction of the safe."

"Yes, sir." The sergeant went down the stairs.

A whistle was blowing, from quite close at hand, and a moment later Sergeant-Major Johnson came up, panting. "We have to get out, sir," he said. "The whole lower floor is alight."

"Damn," Harry said. That meant the safe was lost. "All right,

Sergeant-Major, evacuate your men. You go with him," he told the waiting privates.

"Aren't you coming, sir?" Johnson asked, looking curiously at the half-closed bedroom door.

"In a moment," Harry said.

Johnson glared at the privates, who were trying not to laugh. "Come on," he said. "You heard the order."

They clumped down the stairs.

"Fraulein," Harry said through the door. "We simply have to hurry."

"I am ready." She was wearing a green dress with a matching cardigan, stockings and high-heeled shoes, her chic appearance spoiled only by the woolly hat pulled down over her ears. Incongruously, she carried a handbag.

Now they could hear the roaring of flames and the crackle of burning wood, while when they reached the stairhead they looked down on a swirl of dark smoke.

"We will not get through that," Veronica Sturmer said.

"Damn," Harry commented. "Is there another way?"

He could hear his men shouting from beyond the smoke, but they couldn't help him now.

"There is a window at the back," Veronica said, and ran along the corridor. Harry went behind her, threw up the window, and looked down. Amazingly, the back yard, which had been turned into a vegetable garden, was empty. But it was three floors away.

"Can you climb down?" he asked.

"No," she said.

Harry hesitated, then ran into the nearest bedroom and pulled the sheets off the bed. These he knotted together, tying one end to the bed itself.

Smoke was now billowing up into the corridor, making him cough, and he could hear the crackle of the flames. He reckoned they had about a minute left.

He dropped the sheets out of the window. They did not reach the ground, but he estimated the end was within twelve feet.

"I cannot climb down that," Veronica said.

"Right," he agreed. "Put your arms round my neck, and hang on."

"You are very brave," she commented, hanging her handbag round her neck before obeying, nestling against his back.

So are you, he thought, many a woman would be having screaming hysterics by now.

"Remember," he said, "don't let go. Getting out of the window is going to be tricky."

He backed to the window, gazing at the steadily increasing smoke in front of him. "Put your legs out."

She released him to take off her shoes, and dropped them out, then put her arms round his neck again, holding her left wrist with her right hand, and backed into the window. He heard her scrabbling about, and giving a little grunt as her back scraped the sash. Then the weight suddenly increased.

"Please hurry," she begged.

He backed into the window himself, while smoke swirled down the corridor, and now the entire staircase gave way, crashing to the floor below with a cloud of sparks. He held the sheet in both hands, swung one leg over the sill, listened to shouts from below as his men finally found their way into the garden, and swung his other leg through, suddenly very aware of the weight of the woman on his neck and shoulders. Then he went down with a rush, hands slipping on the sheet before it began to tear.

But they were past the first floor. "Let go!" he shouted.

Her weight disappeared, and she gave a little shriek. He held on for a couple of seconds more, so as not to fall on top of her, then dropped himself. The ground was surprisingly close, and he landed easily, breaking his fall with his hand and rolling over and over. Immediately he was surrounded by men, picking him up and dusting him off.

Others were doing the same for Veronica, while she straightened her skirt and looked for her shoes.

"You saved my life," she said.

"Goes with the job." Harry looked up at the blazing building;

it had been a very close run thing. "What's the situation up front, Sergeant?"

"Everything under control, sir. Apart from the building."

"Casualties?"

"Some of the Germans, sir. We have one wounded. Lieutenant Harbord."

"Good lord! You'd better come with me, Fraulein."

Veronica hurried behind him. "Will you take me to England with you?"

He checked, looked at her. "You are a German combatant. You are a prisoner-of-war."

"I am half-Norwegian," she said. "In blood. I am a Norwegian citizen."

"Would you like to explain that?"

"My father was German. My mother was Norwegian. My father . . . died, some years ago. Before the war. So my mother returned here to live. This is her home. She arranged for me to become a naturalised Norwegian."

"I see. So how come you got together with friend Conrad?"

She shrugged. "They are the masters, here. Conrad is the master of them all. Please . . ." she held his arm. "If you leave me here . . . the people think I am a collaborator. They will lynch me. At the very least they will shave my head and beat me up."

That was unthinkable, even if Harry supposed she *was* a collaborator. "We'll talk with my captain," he said.

The surviving Germans, and there were a considerable number, were assembled in front of the burning building, looking both shocked and disconsolate. With Lockyer was Ebury.

"You've something for me to blow," Ebury said.

"It's in there."

"Shit," remarked the little man. "Then I'd say it's lost."

He wandered off.

"Still, a complete victory," Lockyer said.

"I'm told Harbord bought one," Harry said. "That was bad luck."

"Bad luck hell," Lockyer said scathingly. "Silly clot shot himself in the foot drawing his own revolver. I've sent him back to the ship. Now it's time for us to get organised. We're taking these prisoners with us."

"Where are we going to put them, sir?"

"That's the Navy's business. You!" He beckoned the naval commander. "You speak English?"

"Some," the German said.

"Fall in your men and march them down to the dock for embarkation. Your walking wounded will go with you. Stretcher cases may be carried."

"And our dead, Herr Captain?"

"We'll have to leave them. I'm sure the Norwegians will give them a decent burial. There are only seven, right?"

"Seven good men," the commander said.

"No doubt. Now . . ."

"There's this woman, sir," Harry said.

"What woman?" Lockyer seemed to notice Veronica for the first time. "Good God! Where'd she spring from?"

"The building, sir. I brought her out."

"Veronica," the commander said, and spoke rapidly in German. To which Veronica replied with some vehemence.

"Do they know each other?" Lockyer asked Harry.

"I would say yes. She was in bed when we found her. I think it was his bed."

"Good God! Talk about the spoils of war. Well, tell her that she is free to return to her people."

"That's just it, sir. She doesn't have any people. She would like to be taken to England."

"As what? A prisoner-of-war or a Norwegian patriot?"

"It would actually be a bit of both, sir. And I don't think she cares in what capacity she is taken, just so long as we get her out of here. Apparently, once the German presence is withdrawn, the locals may take it out on her."

"Well, we can't have that," Lockyer agreed. "I'm not sure what the colonel is going to say. Bring her along, anyway, and we'll sort it out at the dock."

The commander was speaking again, urgently, in German. But Veronica was clearly refusing.

"What're they on at now?" Lockyer asked.

"Conrad wishes me to go with him," Veronica said. "Stay with him. I do not wish this. I wish to go by myself."

"Madam," Lockyer said, "I am regarding you as a prisoner-of-war, for the time being. Which means you will go how, and when, and with whom, I choose. Fall in."

The morning was by now well advanced, and the shooting had stopped. Apart from the headquarters building, which continued to blaze merrily, there was smoke rising from the fish factories on the far side of town. These apart, there was little evidence of the recent skirmish, and the people of Svolvaer were out in force, a considerable number carrying suitcases or wearing knapsacks, obviously prepared for evacuation.

There was also a crowd of excited children and even more excited dogs, who gathered round the Commandos marching their prisoners down to the harbour, jeering and shouting in Norwegian at the Germans. Veronica had dropped to the rear of the column, so as not to be with Conrad, and she was quickly identified, whereupon the shouting grew in intensity.

Harry had also fallen back, both to look after the rear of the British force and to keep an eye on her, for he regarded her as strictly his prisoner. "What are they saying?" he asked.

"I told you," she said, maintaining her remarkable composure, although there were pink spots in her cheeks. "They are shouting obscenities, and saying what they intend to do with me. You will not let this happen, please."

"Certainly not," Harry said.

"What will happen to me?" she asked. "In England."

"That depends on how the authorities decide to treat you. If they regard you as German, you will go to an internment camp."

"For how long?"

"The duration of the war."

"I do not think I could stand that."

"It's not a very pleasant prospect."

Commando

"And if they decide to treat me as a Norwegian patriot?"
"Then you'll go to a Norwegian centre, I would say, until they find somewhere for you to live, and work for you to do."
"That would be worse. Being confined with other Norwegians, I mean."
"Well . . ."
"Listen, I can be of great use to you."
"I'm sure you could, Fraulein, But it's not on."
"I do not mean *you*. I mean Great Britain."
"How?"
She glanced left and right, at the men around her. "I will tell you on board the ship."
"Right-ho. Although you'd do better to tell the colonel."
Still surrounded by the crowd of children, who had now been joined by many of their mothers, equally vociferous, they reached the waterfront, where Lightman was issuing instructions.
"You will send your prisoners out in batches of ten," he told his company commanders. "They'll be divided up amongst the ships. That goes for you too, Lockyer."
Lockyer's company had by far the largest number.
"The ladies will be taken on board the command ship," Lightman went on.
"There, you see, there are other women embarking," Harry said. "They'll take care of you, Fraulein."
"They are Norwegian," Veronica said. "I cannot be shut up with them. They will . . ."
"All right, all right," he said. "I'll see what I can do." He approached the colonel. "With respect, sir."
"Is it true you nearly got yourself burned to death, Curtis?"
"Nearly, sir. But we have a problem. The young lady."
Lightman looked at Veronica, and like Lockyer a few minutes earlier, did a double-take. "Good Lord! Where did she come from?"
"I brought her out of the headquarters building, sir."
"You mean you rescued her."
"Well, sir . . ." Harry said modestly.

101

"I assume you forgot my orders, that no aid or comfort was to be given to any enemy who did not immediately surrender?"

"She did immediately surrender, sir. I couldn't leave her to burn."

Once again Lightman peered at the patiently waiting Veronica. "You haven't been improper with her, I hope."

"No, sir. All she wishes is to be taken to England."

"Hm. Has she anything to offer? I mean . . ." he grinned. "Apart from what we can see."

"She says she does, sir. But in any event, she is afraid that if she is left here, she will be lynched as a collaborator."

"I suppose that's possible. Very well. Put her with the other women."

"That's the problem, sir. She's afraid they will lynch her too.

"Mr Curtis, they will be on board a British warship. That simply cannot happen."

"Even when several women are locked in a cabin by themselves, sir? It could be pretty unpleasant."

Lightman gazed at him for several seconds. "You're sure you have nothing going with this tart?"

"Only that I saved her life, sir. And I do not feel that she is a tart. She claims to be in possession of some information that may be of great use to us."

"And you believe her?"

"I think it may be worth following up, sir."

"Very good, Curtis. She's your prisoner. She can travel in your destroyer. You will have to make what arrangements you can for her. Just bear in mind that she is to sleep alone, and that if she makes the slightest claim that she was assaulted or in any way interfered with, by you or anyone else, you are going to be for the high jump. Understood?"

"Yes, sir."

"And immediately upon our return to England, she will be handed over to the proper authorities for interrogation and investigation."

"Yes, sir."

"I must first go to my home," Veronica said.

"Eh? We have a schedule to keep."

"You expect me to leave Norway in the clothes I am wearing and nothing else? Besides, there are papers I must get. They will be to your advantage."

Harry hesitated, then signalled two of the men to accompany them. As they walked away from the dock the crowd gathered round them, shouting and screaming in Norwegian. Presumably more obscenities, Harry thought. He was more concerned when someone threw a stone.

He faced them, and they withdrew a few yards, still shouting.

"It is here," Veronica said, stopping before a quite well-to-do, two-storeyed house.

Harry tried the door. "Locked."

"But of course. Or these people would have looted it." She took the key from her bag and opened the door.

"Stay here," Harry told the two Commandos. "And keep those people away."

He followed Veronica into a well-furnished lounge.

"Upstairs," she said, and climbed the stairs in front of him. He watched her legs. He had never had the time, in the gloom and the haste, to study Niki's legs. But they could never have been as perfect as these.

She opened a bedroom door, went in. He remained in the doorway, watching her. From the top of the wardrobe she took a suitcase, and laid it on the bed. Then she opened the wardrobe and took out some dresses. These she folded carefully into the suitcase. From the bureau she took a selection of underwear, packed them in turn, then added various toiletries from the dressing table.

"What about all the other stuff?" Harry asked. "The furniture. Is it yours?"

"Let's say it *was* mine. Down to this morning."

"And now you have to abandon it?"

"I can't take it with me." She opened a desk drawer and took out an obviously well-filled and heavy manila envelope. This also she placed in the suitcase, closed it and locked it. Then she straightened. "Now I am all yours, sir."

They gazed at each other.

"Some other time," Harry suggested.

She pouted. "I think you do not like me."

"I think I might like you very much," he told her. "But right now I'm on duty."

Bingham was not amused. "As Hardy might say to Laurel," he remarked. "Here's another fine mess you've got us into, old man. Mind you, it's easy to understand how it happened."

He gazed at Veronica, who was standing by herself at the rail, watching the last of the Commandos embarking. Above the islands the smoke continued to pall.

"I'd be careful what you say," Harry suggested. "She speaks perfect English."

"A Norwegian fisher lady?"

"I suspect there's a hell of a lot more to her than that," Harry said.

"Which I am sure you intend to investigate. The question is, where the hell is she going to sleep? We can't very well leave her on deck with this lot."

The decks of the destroyer were littered with German prisoners-of-war and Norwegian refugees, not to mention the Commandos themselves.

"She'll have to use our cabin. I mean, your cabin."

"Oh, yes? And what do we use?"

"We'll stay on deck, with this lot. Or we can nap in the wardroom. It's only for one night."

"God save me from romantic army officers," Bingham grumbled.

"I hope you're not getting into deeper than you want to, Harry," Lockyer said, as they stood together on the bridge wing watching the islands, and the mainland of Norway receding into the distance. The skies remained clear, the wireless equipment at the German headquarters had been destroyed, and it was possible that an insufficient message had been got off. Or maybe they were just being lucky. Certainly, with their crowded decks and accommodation below, an air strike could be catastrophe.

"Good lord, sir," Harry said. "I don't imagine I shall ever see her again, once we get to England."

"That would probably be a very good thing."

"There is just the matter of what we do with her, sir. She does not wish to be treated as a German prisoner-of-war, and she is afraid of being dumped in with a lot of Norwegian refugees who might know, or learn, something about her."

"She should have thought of all that before she climbed into bed with that commander."

"She would claim he didn't give her much choice. She doesn't strike me as the sort of woman who would prefer death to dishonour." Niki certainly would not, he reflected. "The point is, she claims to have information which could be of great value."

"Well, she would, if she thought it would help her case."

"Absolutely. But it might be worth investigating."

"All right, have a go. Just remember not to get too close."

Choosing his time was difficult. The destroyer was almost literally packed to the gunwales. This not only reduced her speed but as most of the extra weight had to be carried on deck it made her slightly top-heavy so that she tended to roll, even in the still calm sea. Privacy, whether on deck or below, was at a premium.

Feeding the many passengers was another problem; the ship's galley got to work almost immediately, passing round soup and sandwiches and tea in a steady routine. Quite apart from the prisoners and refugees, very few of the Commandos had felt up to eating anything before beginning the attack, and they were now starving.

"I reckon, by the time we've finished serving lunch it'll be time to start serving dinner," Bingham remarked. As the ship's executive officer he was in charge of these domestic arrangements. "How's your glamorous friend?"

"I have no idea," Harry said, and seized his opportunity. "Would it be in order for me to go and find out?"

Bingham grinned. "I think we can allow you that privilege." He looked at his watch. "I'll expect you back up here in half-an-hour."

Harry grinned in return. "I can do a lot in half-an-hour."

"I'm sure you can. Just don't push your luck."

Six

Harry had escorted Veronica down to Bingham's cabin when they had come on board, and left her there. He had considered asking Bingham for a sentry to be placed on her door, or indeed using one of his own men, but had decided against it, merely telling her to stay out of sight. Now he was glad of that decision, as he knocked.

She opened the door. "I hoped it would be you."

She was wearing a dressing gown, rather to his dismay.

"Are you all right?"

"Should I not be all right? Come in."

She held the door wide, and he entered the cabin.

"I have been fed," she said. "Your sailors think of everything."

"It's their job."

She closed the door. "Is this the other time you spoke of?"

"Sadly, no. I need to talk to you. About what happens when we get to England."

"I do not wish to go to a camp," she said.

"I'm going to see what I can do. You spoke of possessing information which could be of value to us."

"I do." She sat on the bunk.

"Tell me."

"Will you not sit beside me?"

"I'll stand, for the time being." He leaned on the bulkhead to counter the roll of the ship.

"You do not like me," she said again.

"Tell me," he said again, not wishing to be sucked back

into personalities.

She sighed. "My father is General Hans Sturmer."

"Is? You said he was dead."

"I thought he was dead at one time. But he is alive."

"You are saying that your father is a German general? But you were living in a remote Norwegian fishing village? I'm afraid that doesn't altogether make sense, Fraulein."

Yet he had felt all along that she was far more than she seemed.

"It does, if you will listen to me. My mother was actually born on Lofoten, yes. My grandfather was manager of the fishing factory. My mother was very beautiful, and very talented as a singer. Well, that is obvious, is it not?"

Looking at her, Harry couldn't argue with her reasoning, even if he hadn't yet heard her sing.

"So my grandfather sent her to Vienna to study music. This was just before the start of the Great War, you understand. It was in Vienna that she met my father, who was a German military attaché to the Austrian Government. They fell in love and married, and when the war started, the Great War, my father sent her to his home in Germany for safety. I was born in Germany. I grew up there. I was seventeen when Hitler came to power."

"And you became a Nazi."

She shrugged. "I did what all my friends did. It was a very romantic time. I had no real interest in politics. I did not know what my father was doing, or why. And then, suddenly, you could say the roof fell in. My father had opposed Hitler's plans for war, and he had been arrested. My mother was told he had been condemned and shot. This was still before the actual outbreak of hostilities, you understand. Fortunately, my mother had friends in high places. She was personally known to the Fuehrer himself. So she, and I, were saved from involvement in my father's disgrace. But we were told to leave Germany, to return to my mother's original home in Lofoten, to say nothing of what had happened, and to keep out of harm's way. My mother did this. It was a bitter homecoming, I can tell you. My grandfather had died, and my grandmother had never approved of the Nazis or of my mother's marriage to one. Thus she had never approved of me, as having been born of them. There was very little money, after the life in Berlin, and very little social life either. I was given a job, as a bookkeeper in the factory. It was dreadful. Then the war started, and the Germans invaded Norway. Up till then we had not believed the war would affect us. But before we properly understood what was happening, they had landed in Lofoten and taken us over. The shock was too great for my mother. She had a heart attack and died. My grandmother had already died, so I was left an orphan."

"You're saying this was last year," Harry said. "How old were you?"

"I was twenty-four years old, last year."

"I see. And then?"

"I lost my job at the factory. I had very little money. I was reduced to selling various pieces of jewellery left me by my mother. I did not know what to do. Some of the men in the town made advances. None of them offered marriage. Or any means of escaping Lofoten. Besides, to prostitute myself in such a small community . . ." she fluttered her eyebrows.

"So you went to friend Conrad," Harry suggested.

"He was different. He had money. He drank champagne. And he said, when he had completed his tour, he would take me with him, back to Germany."

"And you believed him?"

"What was the alternative? Commit suicide?"

"Yours is a very tragic case, Fraulein," Harry said. "But probably not such an uncommon one, in places occupied by the Nazis. As you said, in your instance, he was the master, and you obeyed, or suffered. Unfortunately, there is nothing you have told me that can possibly be of the least use to my government, or the Allied cause."

"Except that my father is alive."

Harry frowned. "So you said. Is that important? I mean, I am sure it is important to you. But to us?"

"Listen. I told you, he was arrested for opposing Hitler. There was no plot, so he was not executed. There was simply a fearful quarrel."

"Your father was that important? How come I have never heard of him?"

"Because that was his, and Hitler's, choice. My father was, is, the greatest living exponent of ciphers and code-breaking. The Nazi Government, ever since it came to power, has been tapping into the British radio and telephone systems. All that was happening in government circles in Britain between 1933 and 1939 was copied and transmitted to Germany. Most of this, all that was important, was in code or cipher. It was my father's task to decipher all of this material and inform the Fuehrer. Unfortunately, not all of what he learned was what the Fuehrer wanted to hear. He learned, for example, of the development of radar before such a concept was accepted in Germany. The Fuehrer dismissed its possibilities as nonsense. Then my father learned of the development of the Spitfire engine. When he told the Fuehrer that the British were about to produce an aircraft that might just be superior to the Messerschmitt, Hitler lost his temper entirely, accused my father of deliberately trying to undermine the morale of the Luftwaffe, and as I said, had him arrested. That he was not shot, or sent to a cencentration camp, was because there were generals and air force officers who felt that my father might just have a point."

Harry whistled. "And to quote the Bible, it all came to pass. So the Fuehrer relented, and your daddy was freed. Now your tale becomes rather romantic, Fraulein. But I still fail to see where it can be of any interest to us. Save that we need to be more careful in our use of ciphers in the future. I assume you can prove all this?"

"I have my birth certificate, and my mother's marriage

certificate, and a recent letter from my father. They are in the envelope in my suitcase."

"Well, I will report what you have told me to my captain, but I am not sure it is going to help you keep out of stir. Rather the reverse, as it seems to establish beyond doubt that you are German and not Norwegian, even if your mother had you naturalised. Thus you are, technically, an enemy alien. I must get back on deck."

She caught his hand as he stepped towards the door. "You still do not understand. My father has been returned to his old duties, with his rank and superiority intact. That is why he felt able to send for me."

"Your father sent for you? When did he do this?"

"He arranged for me to visit him, last autumn."

"In Berlin?"

"No, at his headquarters."

"And after that he returned you to Lofoten?"

"Questions were being asked because of the nature of his work, and my Norwegian nationality. He feared for my safety, and told me to return to Lofoten until he could arrange for me to leave permanently."

"I assume he funded you for the interim period. But you still went to bed with friend Conrad."

"Father said no one should suspect what we were hoping to accomplish. He still has enemies. He was hoping to obtain an order, in a few days time, authorising my permanent removal to France. Until then, no one was to know of it."

"Maybe we turned up at the wrong time."

"Listen," she said urgently. "I have told you, my father has been entirely reinstated, because so much of what he predicted has come true. But do you not see? He is not only engaged in deciphering and decoding your material, he also has at his fingertips and in his brain all the codes being used by the Germans."

Harry stroked his chin.

"And he is stationed at a place called Ardres, just outside

Calais. It is a top secret establishment, as far forward as is regarded as practical, to give him better access to your signals. If your people were to launch a raid on Calais, just like the one you have just carried out on Lofoten, you could get him, and bring him out."

"And then?"

"He would co-operate with you. I know this. Basically he is against Hitler and the Nazis, and he is sure this war will turn out badly for Germany."

"But he has never tried to leave before."

"It is not a very easy thing, to escape Nazi Germany, certainly when you are well known."

"And once we got him out, you would expect to be reunited with him."

"Is that unreasonable?"

"Not in the least."

"Then will you help me?"

"I'm afraid this is too big for me to handle. I'll have to report to my superiors."

"If it was found out . . ."

"It won't be. Just sit there and keep your fingers crossed."

Lockyer felt it was a bit too big for him to handle as well when, early the next morning the destroyers made their rendezvous with the cruiser which was to take off the prisoners and refugees, he and Harry were ferried across to the flotilla leader to see Lightman, Harry having given instructions that Veronica was not to be transhipped with the other prisoners.

"You said she'd only be with us for one night," Bingham groused. "I'll get rheumatism. I hope you know what you're doing, young Curtis."

"I think the brass will go for it," Harry said.

Lightman listened to what he had to say. "Quite a saga," he commented at the end. "Do you believe it?"

"She has documentary proof of her identity, sir. Our intelligence people should be able to confirm whether or not there is a General Sturmer, and what position he holds in the German Army."

"True. But I think there are certain aspects of the situation you do not seem to have considered."

"Sir?"

"Firstly, this whole thing could just be a ploy on the young lady's part to get out of Norway, without having to go to either a rehabilitation centre or an internment camp. If she was indeed hoping her father would be able to have her join him permanently, why didn't she just wait for us to leave and the necessary papers to arrive?"

"Because, sir, as I explained, as it was well known to the people of Svolvaer that she had been sleeping with the German naval commander, she estimated, probably correctly, that with us withdrawn and the German garrison liquidated, if only on a temporary basis, she would be lynched or at least badly beaten by the islanders."

"That doesn't affect my point. She was determined to get off of Lofoten, by hook or by crook, and equally determined to obtain her freedom, no matter what sort of cock and bull story she might have to concoct to do so." He held up a finger as Harry would have spoken. "It's just a point to be considered. Here's another: if everything she told you is true, it might just be another ploy, to get her father out of Germany."

"I had thought of that, sir. But if he could be of such value to us."

"We do not know that he will, Harry."

"Well, of course, it would have to depend on intelligence's appreciation of his worth."

"Even if they rate him as highly as does his daughter, that is still no guarantee that he would be willing to work for us."

"Veronica says he hates the Nazis. He was imprisoned for opposing their war plans."

"According to what you have told me, he was sacked for giving Hitler information the Fuehrer did not wish to hear. But that was before the war started. When the shooting actually begins, men's attitudes are inclined to change. I can tell you that there were quite a few British officers who did not agree with our government's attitude to Nazi Germany before 1939. They are all of them loyally carrying out their duties now, nor would they consider doing otherwise, no matter what the provocation, or the temptation. There is also the point that when Hitler took supreme power, on Hindenburg's death in 1935, he made every soldier in the army, from generals down, take a personal oath of loyalty to him, not Germany. Germans take their oaths very seriously." He smiled at Harry's woebegone expression. "There is, of course, the possibility that if this Sturmer *is* their chief code-breaker, and if he does possess access to all of their codes, and we were able to penetrate his headquarters, we might be able to bring away a good deal of useful information. But once it was realised what had happened, the Germans would of course change all their codes anyway. So that without Sturmer's know-how of breaking them, we would be no further ahead."

"So you think the idea is a non-starter, sir," Lockyer said.

"I didn't say that, Captain. I am merely pointing out some aspects of the situation which need careful consideration. But there is a third consideration, which is more important than either of the others. Your lady friend blithely says we should mount another raid such as this one. Harry, you must realise that this raid was the most absolute piece of cake. The islands were virtually undefended, and there was no strategically obvious reason for us to go there, so the Germans' surprise was complete. It was a trial run, and it worked magnificently. We have not lost a man, save for that idiot Harbord, and he's not badly hurt. We accomplished everything we set out to do. Calais is an entirely different matter. It is a well-fortified, well-defended town, and because it is so close to us its garrison is on their toes all the time. They also have instant access to both reinforcements and air cover. To carry out a raid *and* penetrate several miles inland would be an enormous undertaking. Beyond the current strength of the Commandos. Whether or not it succeeded, the casualties would be high. We would have to be very sure we were getting something of great value in return."

"I have thought of that, sir," Harry said eagerly. "Obviously a frontal assault like yesterday would not be practical. But if a small party were put ashore on the beaches north of the town, it might well be possible for them to penetrate inland without the Germans realising they were there until after they had reached Ardres. Then it might be possible for them to regain the beach and be taken off."

"And if they don't make it?"

"Well. I suppose the old general would have to go, sir. With us."

"Do I gather you are intimating that you would like to lead such a suicide mission yourself?"

"Well, sir, as it's my idea . . ."

Lightman looked at Lockyer.

"It could be done, sir," Lockyer said. "Our MTBs and subs operate in the Channel. It would be possible to put a small group of men ashore on one of the beaches."

"I'm sure it would be possible, Captain. But getting them back off again would be virtually impossible, once the whole area had been aroused. I'm afraid I doubt whether the idea is practicable, but I shall of course place it before higher authority when we regain England. For the time being, it must remain secret to us three."

"And the lady, sir?"

"There is surely no need to tell her anything more than that what she has said to you has been reported."

"Yes, sir. I mean, what will happen to her when we land?"

"She will be taken into custody. But for her own safety she will be kept apart from the other prisoners and refugees until a decision has been taken as to what to do with her, and her information."

"Yes, sir," Harry said, unhappily. "I need some more permission to visit our friend," he told Bingham.

"Another half-hour? You're going to wear yourself out,"

Bingham grinned. "Do I gather things are developing there?"

"Not in the sense you mean," Harry said, and went below.

"Harry!" Veronica held his arm and pulled him into the cabin. "I am going mad, cooped up in here."

"Aren't you being looked after?"

"By some po-faced steward who brings my food three times a day. He will not serve me alcohol. How I would like a glass of schnapps."

"We'll be in England tomorrow morning. Well, Scotland, anyway. I'm not sure they'll have schnapps, but they should have something."

"And what is going to happen to me?"

"You will be looked after."

"You mean I will be sent to a camp. I will kill myself."

"You are not going to be sent to a camp, Veronica."

"You mean they are going to help me?"

"I really cannot say. I have reported what you told me to my superior officer, and he has it under consideration. What is certain is that you will have to be interrogated by our intelligence people. What happens after that depends on you. Convince them that you are telling the truth, and all things are possible."

"And Papa will be rescued?"

"I said, all things are possible."

"You are a dear, sweet boy." She put her arms round his neck and kissed him on the mouth. Then she took his hand and placed it on her breast.

He had never felt anything so compelling. But . . . he held her arms to free himself. "I am also, at the moment, your gaoler. So let's keep it proper."

She still stood against him, looking up at him. "How old are you?"

"Coming up twenty."

"So young, I will bet you have never had a woman."

"You'd lose."

"Well," she said. "That is nice to know. Would you not

116

like to have me?"

"I'd love to have you, Veronica. But not while you're my prisoner."

"I will regard that as a promise," she said. "For when I am no longer your prisoner. Now give me your address."

"Eh?"

"I would like to write to you. You are the only friend I have now."

He supposed she was right. And it could surely do no harm. He did not suppose he would ever see her again. He wrote out his address in Frenthorpe.

Next morning, when the destroyers had entered the bay and dropped anchor, two MPs and a woman policeman came on board to remove Veronica. Harry stayed on the bridge, watching her descending the ladder to the waiting launch.

"Something to put in your memoirs," Bingham suggested.

"Not a lot," Harry said.

"It's been great having you along, Harry. Some adventure. Some success. I wish you many more of them."

Everyone seemed to feel the same way. Officers and men, the Commandos were on top of the world. As the Germans were admitting that the Lofotens had been raided by the Royal Navy – they knew nothing about the existence of the Commandos as yet – and claiming that they had sunk at least one destroyer and killed over a hundred men, secrecy was ended.

"Boast a bit," Lightman told his men. "Make the Germans afraid of us, of where we may turn up next. Stir them up. But first, go home and bask in a little glory. I am proud of you all, and so will all Britain be."

He beckoned Harry to come to his office when the parade was dismissed. "Your friend get off all right?"

"I don't think she was very happy, sir. She was virtually under arrest."

"She *was* under arrest, Harry."

"I hope you are not going to tell me that we were just

117

pretending to go along with her to get her off the ship without a fuss, sir."

"Not at all, Harry. But she has to remain in custody while her claims are investigated and her father's worth evaluated. I am forwarding a resumé of the entire matter to our superiors at the War Office, and they will make a judgement, and on the young lady's eventual fate. But I can't say I'm the least optimistic: it's simply too big a job." He frowned at Harry's expression. "Look, Harry, you have nothing to be ashamed of. You rescued the young woman from a fiery grave and discovered you had caught a tartar. Could have happened to anyone. You have behaved perfectly correctly ever since. If you haven't, in any small way, I don't wish to know about it, the lady hasn't complained. Now go home and grab some leave and forget the war for a week or two."

"Yes, sir. But if there is to be a raid on Calais, I wish to be involved."

Lightman grinned. "Our first volunteer. I will make a note of that, Harry. And you will be involved. You have my word."

Belinda Forester was in the ante-chamber. "Home the hero," she remarked. "With baggage. You shouldn't be let out without a minder."

"Don't you start."

"Whatever I start, Lieutenant Curtis, I finish. In the course of time."

Now what the devil did she mean by that? he wondered.

"By Jove," John Curtis commented. "All that secret stuff . . . an entire secret army raiding the Nazis on their doorstep – great stuff."

"Wasn't it very dangerous?" Alison asked. "I mean, you must have been terribly outnumbered."

"No, Mother, it wasn't the least dangerous," Harry said. "We outnumbered them, and they were taken entirely by surprise."

"The newspapers say you didn't lose a man," John Curtis said.

"And for once, they're not exaggerating."

"But you killed a whole lot of Germans."

"Now there they are going over the top. We killed seven Germans."

"Seven's better than none."

"Did you kill anyone, Harry?" his mother asked.

Harry looked at her. "Yes, Mother," he said. "I killed someone."

It was frightening, he thought, how every time he came home, or even saw his parents, he felt more of a stranger. His father had been a soldier in the Great War, but because of his poor eyesight he had never seen combat; he had never even been sent to France but had served as a clerk for the four years. His mother had been a Land Girl, the great adventure of her life. He did not know if either of them had ever seen a dead body – apart presumably from people like his grandparents, who had died comfortably in their beds – much less someone being blown apart by a sub-machine-gun.

While he . . . when he had received embarkation leave before going to France in October 1939, he had been totally innocent, the boy they had watched growing up for eighteen years, an eager young puppy. When next they had met, in June 1940, he had already swum out of their orbit, their understanding. By then he had seen too many men killed, dead or dying, wounded. Worse even than those horrors, he had known defeat.

He doubted his mother and father realised what had happened to their son; they had only been concerned that he should recover from his wound. But when he had returned home last December, he had receded still further. He had eaten of the forbidden apple, and the world was his oyster. He actually felt he owed Armistead, and through Armistead, Niki, a great deal. They had shaken him out of the Dunkirk-induced depression, the almost pathological anxiety to hit back at the Germans. The early training with the Commandos had completed the

119

rebirth. He had felt a true man, for the first time in his life, a man who could cope with both women and the enemy, and conquer, both women and the enemy. He had, he remembered, been suffering from a serious case of hubris.

Niki's death, and the temporary disbandment of the Leopards, had brought him back to reality, an understanding that man may consider himself to be whatever he chooses, but Fate will find him out, will determine whether his self-assessment was true or false. Yet the recall to the secret army had again sent his spirits soaring. Where it would end . . . thus he had killed three men. The first had been unarmed. He had, in effect, committed murder. No one could possibly blame him for firing at the figure in the corridor, and no one had, there had been no way he could have known whether or not the sailor had been armed. Instead everyone was full of praise for his rescue of the woman. Which had but compounded the mental torment into which he had again been plunged. The sight of so much beauty, naked in another man's bed, the feel of her against him as he had climbed out of the window, her obvious attraction to him, the way she had virtually offered herself . . . and the fact that she had appeared almost as a reincarnation of Niki, even if with a decidedly different background, to be sure.

He needed to pull himself together. He simply could not fall in love with an enemy alien, no matter how attractive she might make herself, or who she might remind him of. So why was he pushing this Calais adventure? It would not, of course, come off. Lightman had made that very clear. But if it did, and he went on it . . . it would be virtually a suicide mission. Was that his aim in life? To earn the appreciation of a woman he would never see again and who he did not truly trust? Or just a desire to engage the enemy in a stand-up fight, instead of murdering them in cold blood?

"I've invited Yvonne to tea," Alison said.

"Oh," Harry said. "Well, then, I'd better go and have a bath and change."

Getting into his blazer was a bit difficult: he had put on weight, not around his waist but in muscle at his shoulders, a result of all the training of the past six months. Still, as long as he didn't attempt to button it up it looked all right.

"Gosh, you look fit," Yvonne remarked. "Or did I say that the last time?"

"I think you probably did," Harry agreed. "It's good to know I'm maintaining my form."

She was prettier than he remembered, although perhaps he was merely in the mood to consider all women pretty. But this was what he needed, England, Home and Beauty. Even before the end of the war?

"I've been reading all about the raid," Yvonne confessed. "It sounds terribly exciting. Terribly dangerous."

"It wasn't really. We were in and out before the Germans knew what had hit them."

"Will you get a medal?"

"They'd have to hand out five hundred of them."

They finished their tea, and he took her for a walk in the garden, Jupiter leaping about their feet.

"Does Gillian know you're back?" she asked, innocently.

"I should think everyone knows I'm back, by now."

"But you haven't been to see her?"

"Why should I do that?"

They had reached the fringe of the orchard, well away from the house.

"I just wondered," she said, pink spots in her cheeks.

Obviously someone had seen him either entering or leaving Gillian's house back in December, and word had got around – at least as far as the library. Damn, but this was a small community.

"Would it upset you if I did see her?" he asked.

"Oh, it's nothing to do with me." She then contradicted herself. "It's just that . . . well, that day in the library . . ."

Now she was thoroughly flushed.

"Does a kiss constitute an engagement?" he asked.

Then where *would* that leave Gillian?

"Well, of course it doesn't. I . . . I think I had better be going home."

"Would you like to be engaged?"

What was he *doing*? Trying to rid his mind of all its impure elements, as a medieval knight might have plunged his hand into a bucket of boiling water?

She had turned away. Now she turned back. "To you?"

"Well, yes."

She was frowning. "Are you serious?"

"Wouldn't you like me to be?"

"Well . . ." her tongue came out and circled her lips. "You mean you want to marry me?"

No, he thought, I don't want to be married to you, spend the rest of my life with you. But he wanted that stability. England, Home and Beauty.

"If I didn't," he said. "I wouldn't have asked you."

Armistead would be turning in his grave, only he hadn't got there yet.

"Oh, Harry," she said, and was in his arms.

He wasn't altogether sure who had made the first move, but she felt good, and as before, tasted sweet. She gave a little shudder when their tongues touched, and a moment later was pulling her head away.

"I never thought it would be like this."

"What?"

"A proposal of marriage."

"You mean I should be on bended knee with a bouquet of flowers in my hand."

"Oh, Harry! Of course I didn't mean that. It's just that . . . well . . ."

"I'll come home with you now, and talk to your dad, shall I?"

"Oh, Harry!" She was starting to sound like a cracked record.

"But you do realise it's not possible for a while."

"How long a while?" Suddenly she was suspicious.

"Well . . . I'm only twenty."

"So am I. But we'll both be twenty-one in a couple of months."

"Yes. The fact is, civilian rules don't apply in the Army. They don't like their officers to get married under the age of thirty."

"Thirty?" she cried. "That's ten years. Surely you can get permission to do it sooner than that?"

"I'll have to ask my CO. He's a decent bloke, but, well . . . it would mean bending the rules a bit. More than a bit. At least, we should wait until the war is over."

She sat on the rustic bench. "And when will *that* be?"

"God knows. But it can't last more than a year or two."

Her shoulders humped. "You don't really want to marry me at all," she muttered.

He sat beside her. "Of course I do, Yvonne. Maybe I shouldn't have asked you, right now. It's just that, well . . ."

She raised her head, and to his dismay he saw there were tears in her eyes. He kissed her, but this time her lips remained closed.

"*Would* you like me to come and talk with your dad?" he asked. "I'll explain the situation, and tomorrow we can go out and buy the ring, and . . . we'll have a party!" A sudden inspiration. "Mother and Dad will be so pleased."

She continued to stare at him. "If we're to be engaged, will you stop seeing other women?"

"Other women? Oh, you mean Gillian? Well, of course. I mean, I have to see her, from time to time. This is a small village. But I won't go to see her again, I promise."

A slip. But she didn't seem to notice. "Have you ever . . . kissed her?" she asked.

Talk about euphemisms. "Ah . . . well . . ."

"I think that is absolutely disgusting," Yvonne declared. "She's old enough to be . . . well . . ."

"Our schoolmistress. One's perceptions of age-relationships change, as one grows older. Let's go and talk with your dad."

He stood up, and she caught his hand. "You won't ever kiss her again, Harry. Or any other woman. Not now we're engaged." It was not a request.

What have I got myself into? he wondered.

123

As far as his parents were concerned, and hers, it was total delight. They immediately got together to plan the engagement party, although he kept reiterating that there was no prospect of an early marriage. He duly bought Yvonne a ring, the best he could afford on his meagre salary, although she seemed delighted, and the engagement party was arranged for the end of the week. Everyone in the village was invited.

"I'm not sure Gillian should be invited," Harry ventured, having scanned the list.

"Good Heavens, why not?" asked his mother. "She taught both you and Yvonne when you were children. She'd be dreadfully insulted if she was left out."

"I don't think Yvonne likes her."

"Oh, really," Alison said. "They've known each other all their lives."

So Gillian was invited, but she declined. And when Harry walked past the school during break the next day, and she was in the yard with the children, she pointedly turned her back.

Surely she could not have anticipated he would marry *her*? Harry wondered. Presumably, in her eyes, he was even more of a cad.

Anyway, the deed was done, and he was now on the straight and narrow. It only remained to obtain permission from Lightman. Presumably he did not need permission to become officially engaged, but he did need to follow that up as quickly as possible. Unfortunately, he did not have a home address for the colonel, so, as he explained to both his parents and the Clearsteds, there was no prospect of choosing a date for the wedding until after he had rejoined the regiment at the end of his furlough.

Which did not seem to please them at all.

It was the day of the party, when the house was full of caterers – rationing and all, Worcester and its environs were still beyond the normal activities of the German bombers, whatever might have happened the previous year at Coventry and nearby Birmingham, and it was still possible to recreate an almost peacetime atmosphere – that Harry received a telephone call.

"Harry?" Lightman asked. "I wish you to report to London, immediately."

Blessed relief. "Of course, sir. I'll be down tomorrow."

"Isn't there a night train?"

"Ah . . . yes. The seven o'clock. That's in one hour."

"Excellent. Be on it."

"But—"

"This is urgent. I suppose I can tell you on the phone. That damned woman you picked up in Norway. She's escaped."

Seven

Preparations

"Ah . . ." For a moment Harry couldn't take it in. "How did she do that?"

"Rather a messy business. She seems to have seduced a guard, made off with his money, and various other things."

"Why did she do this? Has the project fallen through?"

"The damned thing is that it's been approved, and on a scale far larger than either you or I envisaged. But she didn't know this, of course, and perhaps she thought we were moving too slowly."

"She'll be coming here," Harry said, thoughtfully. "I gave her my address. She wanted to write to me," he added hastily. "And she has nowhere else to go."

"We thought that might be the case. I have to tell you that in addition to his papers, she also stole the guard's gun. It may well be that she feels you have abandoned her, and is seeking some kind of revenge. That's why we want you out of there. This project is now absolutely top secret, and we don't want anyone connected with it, in this case you, to have any publicity whatsoever, especially publicity connected with Sturmer's daughter, which will certainly be the case if she turns up on your doorstep shouting for help or shooting from the hip. Understood?"

"Yes, sir. But . . . if I'm not here, and she turns up on my doorstep shouting for help or shooting from the hip, won't there

126

be publicity anyway? And what about my people? I can't risk their lives being endangered."

"Fraulein Sturmer is not going to reach your doorstep, Harry. Although she may get close. The important thing is that when she is, ah, recaptured, you will not be in the vicinity. You will be on the train for London."

Once again it took a couple of seconds for the penny to drop. "When you say she will not reach my doorstep, you mean just that, don't you, sir?"

"Harry, the decision as to how Fraulein Sturmer is to be dealt with has been taken at the very highest level. I know you created this scenario, but I am afraid it is now entirely out of your hands. Your duty is to return here at the earliest possible moment, and more importantly, to be out of Frenthorpe before this woman can get there. The appointed people will take it from there. Get to London, bag a place in a Tube Station overnight, and be in my office at dawn tomorrow morning." The phone went dead.

Harry remained staring at it for several seconds. He told himself the essential thing was not to over-react. He was fighting a war, under the command of Lightman, who he both admired and respected. Wasn't it John Hampden who had said, moderation in war is imbecility? Veronica Sturmer had indeed brought them information of great importance, and her information could save many hundreds, perhaps thousands, of British and Allied lives. But she had nothing more to offer, and she had become a risk which could endanger the entire operation. Therefore . . . but the idea still made him feel sick. His record, thus far, was to shoot three men, virtually in the back in each case, and send an innocent woman to her death. Well, perhaps she wasn't entirely innocent, but surely she wasn't guilty enough to die.

"Not bad news?" Alison asked.

"I'm afraid so. They want me back in London."

"Oh, dear. When must you leave?"

"On the next train. That's at seven o'clock." He looked at his watch: it was just past six. "I have to rush."

"But the engagement party! The guests are invited for seven."

"I'm going to have to miss it."

"Harry! You can't!"

"Mother, I have been ordered to be in London tonight. The last train leaves at seven. I have to be on it."

"Yvonne will go through the roof."

"Remind her there's a war on."

He went upstairs to pack, parted the black-out curtain to look out of the window at the empty street, darkening now as the light faded. Presumably Lightman's people – or whoever was now running the show – were already in place. He wished he could tell his mother and father not to be alarmed by anything they might hear, or even see, outside their house tonight. But that would be to disobey orders. What a mess. All caused by his single act of gallantry – and Niki's memory.

But in any event, he would never have been able to allow the woman, any woman, to burn.

He carried his kitbag downstairs, met his father in the hall.

"This is a bit much, isn't it, Harry? The invasion hasn't started, has it?"

"Not so far as I know, Dad."

"Then what possible reason can they have for dragging you off like this? Do they know you're having an engagement party?"

"No, they don't."

"You mean you didn't tell them?"

"I don't think they'd be remotely interested," Harry said.

Alison emerged from the lounge. "Yvonne would like a word."

"You didn't tell her?"

"I felt obliged to, Harry. One simply cannot have an engagement party without the person who is getting engaged."

Harry sighed, and went to the telephone.

"Harry? What on earth is happening? Your mother says you've been called away."

"I'm afraid so."

"But why tonight? Surely you can wait until morning?"

"I'm sorry. It has to be tonight."

There was a moment's silence. Then she said, "You never did intend to go through with it, did you?"

"Now, Yvonne—"

"You are a brute and a deceiving bastard! I've half a mind to sue you for breach of promise. Go away, and don't bother to come back."

The phone was slammed down with sufficient force to deafen him for a moment.

His mother and father were standing in the doorway.

"I fancy she's not very happy," John Curtis said.

"There's the understatement of the year," Harry said. "Look, I really am most terribly sorry about all this. I'll do my damndest to make things up with Yvonne when I get back."

"All this food, and booze . . ."

"Well, the booze can go back, can't it? As for the food . . . have a feast. I must go."

He kissed his mother, shook hands with his father, and hurried out of the house. He told himself that it was time to put domestic disasters behind him, until he came back. If he came back. It was also necessary to put all thought of Veronica Sturmer behind him, as well. Lightman had said the raid was going ahead, on a bigger scale than either of them had envisaged. That was all that was important.

It was a brisk five-minute walk to the station. The doors were closed and the black-out curtains drawn, but inside the ticket office and waiting room was a cosy pool of light. There were several people already there, waiting for the train. Harry bought his ticket, and then turned up the collar on his greatcoat and went outside on to the platform; he wasn't in the mood to be engaged in conversation, and there were only a couple of minutes to wait.

He walked to the end of the platform, and then back again, and a quiet voice said, "Harry!"

His head jerked, and then he made her out, a shadowy figure in a dark coat and headscarf. "How did you get here?"

"That is my business," she said.

He watched her hands; Lightman had said she had a gun, which was more than he did, at this moment, at least readily available; his revolver was packed in his kitbag.

"You mean you have escaped custody," he said. He had to pretend ignorance of the true facts, at least until he had neutralised her.

"They were tricking me," she said. "They never had any intention of helping me. I overheard one of the guards saying, we'll soon be rid of her. She's going where she belongs."

"I can't believe that," Harry protested.

"So I came to you for help," she said. "You're the only friend I have, in England. Will you help me, Harry?"

"Ah . . . help you to do what?"

"Keep me out of those camps. Help me get my father out of France."

"Veronica, I am a very humble army lieutenant. My father is a bank manager, not a general. I think you did a very silly thing, breaking out. Now the entire British police force, as well as the army police force, will be looking for you."

"So you will not help me."

"Believe me, I wish I could." His head was spinning. How does one tell a beautiful woman for whom one has a considerable weakness that she was going to be shot on sight, like a mad dog? Dare he do that? "How did you know I would be at the station?"

"I followed you from your home."

"You have been at my home?"

"Oh, do not worry, no one saw me. I was just making up my mind to come in, when you left. So I followed you here."

Which meant that Lightman's people were *not* yet in position. What the hell was he to do? What he *should* do was arrest her and march her to the nearest police station. But he didn't like the idea of that on several counts. There was the matter of the gun she was carrying. And it would certainly cause a fuss and the very publicity Lightman was so anxious to avoid. And it could only end with her being sent back to prison and then shot.

Which was likely to happen anyway.

The train whistled as it pulled into the station.

"I must go!"

"Please," she said. "Do not take it. Do not abandon me."

He had turned away from her. Now he turned back. Her right hand was in her handbag.

"I have been summoned to London."

"Because of me?"

"I have no idea. But I'm beginning to think it could be possible."

"Then I will take you."

"Oh, yes? How do you propose to do that?"

He nearly asked, on the back of your broomstick? But decided against it.

"I have an automobile. It is parked only a short walk away."

"You have a motor car? How did you get that?"

"I stole it."

"Oh, my God! Don't you realise that is against the law?"

"Everything is against the law in this country. *I* am against the law."

Doors were slamming, and the train was moving off.

"Damn," he commented.

"I will drive you to London," she said again.

"You realise that when we get there, I am going to have to turn you in?"

"Come."

She took her hand out of her handbag to hold his. Now would be the time to overpower her and take away the gun. But he didn't want to do that. He had a feeling that once he got to grips with her he wouldn't ever wish to let her go. And of course there remained the objection of noise and publicity – unless he acted the Commando and laid her out, which might well cause her serious injury. In any event, she was now his only means of transport.

The car, as she had promised, was only a few blocks away. Harry was surprised. "This is a Wolseley," he said . . .

131

"Is that what it is? When I lived in Berlin, I used to drive my father's Mercedes."

"Have you enough petrol to get us to London?"

"Not in the car. But I took a packet of coupons from the beastly guard. We'll use those."

She started the engine. Because of the requirements of the black-out, the lights had been painted over, and gave only the faintest illumination, but she still drove very fast.

"I hope we don't kill anybody," he remarked.

"Everyone should be indoors," she pointed out.

They negotiated their way out of the village and on to the open road. Veronica drove expertly. Harry began to wonder just how many things she did expertly.

"How did you tackle that guard, anyway?" he asked.

"I seduced him," she said simply.

"Just like that?"

"It is not a difficult thing, to seduce a man, when you are a beautiful woman and the man is hungry for sex."

"And this man was hungry."

"All men become hungry, when they look at me. Even you became hungry, Harry."

"But you didn't succeed in seducing me," he riposted.

She laughed. "I did not try very hard. Would you like me to seduce you?"

"Concentrate on the road."

"I think we should stop and have dinner," she said. "I am starving."

"Don't you realise the police will be looking for this car by now?"

"Not up here, yet," she said. "We have time for dinner."

As always, her coolness was as amazing as the rest of her. And no one at the hotel at which they stopped found anything odd in a handsome young couple, the man in uniform, dining together.

"I think we should take a room," Veronica said. "And spend the night."

"They wouldn't go for it," Harry said. "We're not married."

"They do not know that. We can sign in as a married couple."

"You don't have any luggage."

"You do. My clothes could be in your bag."

The temptation was enormous. "Grab a bed in a tube station," Lightman had suggested, blithely. He didn't have to report until first thing tomorrow morning.

He should be back in Frenthorpe, celebrating his engagement to Yvonne. But he had ended that.

Back to square one. If he spent the night with this woman, would he ever be able to hand her over to be imprisoned or shot?

He had to put it to her. "If we did stay I'd still have to turn you in, when we get to town."

She smiled. "That's tomorrow. Let's talk about it, tomorrow." She summoned the *maitre d'hotel.* "My husband and I rather feel we would like to spend the night here. Driving in this utter darkness is dangerous."

"Oh, indeed, madam."

"So have you a double room? With bath, please."

"I will find out, madam." His gaze drooped to her left hand, but Veronica had pulled on her gloves.

The hotel was sufficiently empty to be glad of the custom, and to serve the bottle of champagne Veronica ordered.

"How do we pay for all this?" Harry muttered.

"I have money."

"Stolen from the guard."

She gave a little shrug, and the champagne having been delivered, closed and locked the door, while Harry uncorked the bottle and filled the two flutes.

She brushed her glass against his. "Here is to a long and lovely night."

"Veronica . . ."

"No, no," she said. "Tonight we talk only of tonight." She stood against him and kissed him, slowly and deeply. "Now I am going to have a hot bath," she said, and began to undress.

As he remembered from his first glimpse of her in the

German naval commander's bed, her body was superb. Niki had been a splendid woman, but certain aspects of age had been visible. Gillian had been overweight; Yvonne . . . well, he really had no idea of Yvonne, nor was he likely to, now. But Veronica was faultless, crying out to be held, to be caressed, to be loved.

She smiled at his expression. "You can touch," she said. "That's why I'm here."

He took her in his arms, kissed her some more, stroked her shoulders, squeezed her buttocks, cupped her breasts, held her pubes. And realised that he had, after all, been seduced and with the greatest ease.

"You will like me more when I have had a bath," she said.

He watched her go into the bathroom; she left the door open. Presumably he was now an accessory after the fact of whatever crimes she had committed. There had to be quite a list. He was also virtually her prisoner. That had to be reversed, immediately. Her handbag lay on the bed. He picked it up, noiselessly beneath the rush of the water, opened it, and took out the service revolver. This he placed in his own bag, alongside his own.

"Harry!" she called. "What is this mark?"

He went into the bathroom, peered at the yellow line drawn round the tub, two inches from the bottom; the water was already surging up to it,

"It's to do with rationing," he explained. "You're not supposed to use more water than that."

"How can one possibly bathe in two inches of water?"

"One sort of scoops it over oneself."

"That is barbaric. Very well!" She switched off the taps. "You will have to bathe me."

Another hitherto unexperienced delight. He undressed and joined her in the tub.

"Why will they not carry out my plan?" she asked as they knelt against each other and he soaped her breasts

"I thought we weren't going to talk about that until tomorrow?"

134

"I have changed my mind."

Harry considered as he continued to wash her. If she was going to be securely locked away – or shot – tomorrow, he didn't suppose it could do any harm, and it might make her feel better.

"The reason for the delay," he said, "is that there were considerable difficulties and the risk of very heavy casualties. It would have been far more difficult, dangerous, and costly, than the raid on Lofoten."

"But the prize would be much greater too."

"Your dad? I must tell you that there was also some doubt as to the genuineness of your information, and as to whether or not your dad, even if we got him out, would be willing to co-operate with us."

"He would not, without me," she said.

Harry got out of the bath and dried himself. Could that possibly be a lifeline?

"However," he said. "The reason I am going to London in such haste is that I understand they are going for it. Or they were, until you did a bunk."

"So you think they may go ahead if you take me back?"

"It's an idea. As to what they are going to do with you . . . you've gone and upset the whole military establishment."

She joined him in the bedroom, opened her handbag, and regarded it for several seconds. "You are a very cautious man," she remarked. "Did you really think I would shoot you?"

"As you say, I'm a very cautious man."

"You saved my life. I do not shoot men who save my life." Which Harry felt was a statement that could do with some amplification. But there was no time, as she got into bed beside him. "They cannot go ahead, without me," she asserted.

"I don't think that's how they see it at all."

"You don't understand." She kissed him, nestled against him, put her hand down to bring him up. "Papa will never leave Germany, or cease working for the Germans, without me."

Harry was finding it very difficult to concentrate. "Well, of course, he will be told you are safe in England . . ."

"Do you think he will believe what you tell him?"

"My dearest girl, if we go in and snatch him, he's not going to have the opportunity to believe us or not, and when he gets here, you'll be waiting for him."

Which was a definite out, he thought,

"It will not happen like that. He is a German officer. He may be against the regime, but he will kill himself rather than be captured. Unless I am there."

"You can't be serious. You want to come with us? If we go, I mean? Don't you realise it is virtually a suicide mission?"

"I must rescue my father," she said. "Besides, if you do not take me, it *will* be a suicide mission. I have been to his headquarters. I know where everything is, how many guards there are and where they are posted. Without me, you will be stumbling in the dark. Now let us make love. I have wanted to do this since first I have seen you."

Snap, he thought. And surrendered.

"I thought I told you under no circumstances again to become involved with this woman?" Lightman asked.

Harry remained at attention before the desk, not having been invited to stand at ease. "She became involved with me, sir. You instructed me to avoid any publicity. So I thought the best thing to do was go along with her. And bring her to London with me."

"You seem to have the knack of doing the right thing in the wrong way," Lightman commented. "Where is she now?"

"In an hotel room, waiting for me to return."

"You really suppose she'll be there when you go back?"

"Yes, sir. She has no one else to turn to. She understands that she is in some trouble."

"Some trouble," Lightman commented, picking up the charge sheet and studying it. "She's no longer armed, I hope."

"No, sir. I took away her gun."

"Yes. Well, we'll have to put her into more secure custody this time. What is the name of the hotel?" He picked up his phone.

"With respect, sir," Harry said.

Lightman looked up.

"Veronica . . . Fraulein Sturmer . . . seems to feel that our mission will not succeed without her presence."

Lightman replaced the phone and leaned back in his chair. "You have told her that we are going ahead?"

"No, sir. I told her that the matter was still under consideration, because of the difficulties involved. She volunteered the information that her father would not leave his post in France unless she was there to persuade him."

"And you believe this?"

"Yes, sir, I do. You yourself said that however much General Sturmer may hate the Nazi regime, once it became a shooting war he would be loyal to Germany. Unless his daughter can persuade him otherwise."

Lightman stroked his chin. "There are certain aspects of this situation which suggest an enormous scam."

"She also points out that we will need her guidance, certainly if we are going to carry out the mission in a limited time. She knows her father's headquarters, exactly where it is situated in the town, its interior lay-out, the positioning of the guards . . ."

"And you believe this too?"

"Well, sir, if she is prepared to come with us, she is putting her own life on the line."

"Yes," Lightman said. "I am not sure the powers-that-be will go for that idea at all, but I think it needs to be made clear to the young lady that if anything, anything at all, turns out to be not as she has told it, she will be regarded as either a traitor or a spy or a double agent, and will be executed on the spot. I also think you should know, Harry, that the appointed executioner will be you."

Harry gulped. "Yes, sir. But for the time being, the other charges . . ."

"Her case will be reviewed when this operation has been successfully completed. Now sit down and listen to me."

Harry sat in front of the desk.

"It seems the bigwigs at the War Office know all about Hans Sturmer," Lightman said. "And regard the possibility of getting him on to our side as worth a great deal of time and effort, and even a few lives. But they understand that a straightforward raid on his headquarters is extremely unlikely to work. Not even, I would say, under the guidance of Fraulein Sturmer. Have you ever used a parachute?"

"No, sir."

"I shouldn't think your lady friend has either. You have one week to master the technique."

"One week, sir?"

"Time is short. It has been decided that we, the Commandos, will carry out a raid on Calais. Such a raid will have some military justification, as Calais is an embarkation point for the invasion of Britain, should that ever happen. There are certainly a large number of barges waiting there. It would be very helpful to our defence if those barges were to be destroyed, as would whatever damage we can inflict on the port installations. We shall be using regulars as well, and will have a force of over a thousand men, backed up by the Navy and, of course, with air support. We estimate that we can risk being ashore for one hour. Then we will have to withdraw, before the Germans can bring overwhelming force against us.

"Now, one hour before we go in, there will be a heavy air raid on Ardres. We happen to know that the area has largely been cleared of civilians, so we would hope to keep their casualties to a minimum. In the midst of this raid a small group will be dropped by parachute in the immediate vicinity of Ardres. They will commence their assault on the Communications Centre immediately. Hopefully they, and in this context I mean you, will achieve complete surprise. You will attack the Centre, guided, if the brass will go for it, by Fraulein Sturmer, destroy the equipment, obtain possession of all the coding and de-coding material you can, and come out, with General Sturmer. At this time you will also destroy the entire building. The Germans will have to work out whether that was just an act of war or whether it was their codes we were after –

138

the important thing is for them not to know we took anything away, and that includes the general.

"Now, of course, the alarm will be raised, and troops will presumably come pouring out of Calais to round you up. However, as they do that, there will be a second heavy air raid, on the area between Calais and Ardres, which will hopefully dislocate movement on the ground and at the same time we will come in from the sea. The German command will have to make a decision as to whether you are the diversionary attack, and our goal the port and the barges, or whether it is the other way around. In any event, as ours will be the major assault, it is our assumption that the main German body will be directed to defending the town and the harbour. It should thus be possible for you and your group to return to us in sufficient time to be evacuated when we leave."

"You mean we return through the German lines," Harry said, thoughtfully.

"There won't be any German lines, as such, Harry. We intend to create such mayhem the entire town will be in chaos. I'm not going to pretend it'll be easy for you to get out, but then it was never going to be. You have, of course, the right to withdraw."

"Of course I will not do that, sir. This is my baby."

"Quite. However, there are one or two other aspects of the situation, requirements if you like, which you need in mind. The first, as I have mentioned, is that at the slightest sign of treachery or double-dealing on the part of your lady friend, she is to be eliminated. This is assuming that she is allowed to be part of the operation at all. Is that clearly understood?"

Harry swallowed. "Yes, sir."

"The second is that should you and your people be unable to rejoin us, while you have permission to surrender – you will all be in uniform so there can be no funny business such as treating you as spies – the general and his daughter must not be allowed to fall back into German hands. That would be to inform the Germans what we were really after, and the fair Veronica already knows too much about our Commando organisation and methods. So again, if in your judgement the completion of your mission at any time becomes impossible, the Sturmers must go before you surrender."

"Yes, sir," Harry muttered.

"I'm sorry, Harry, but it has to be your judgement, as you will be the senior officer on the spot." He grinned. "Except for Sturmer, of course."

"Yes, sir."

"Right. There is a vehicle waiting to take you to parachute training."

"With Fraulein Sturmer, I assume."

"Oh, indeed. Because I am assuming the War Office will go for it. If they do not, she will simply be returned under safe arrest. However, presuming we are both right, you are not to let her out of your sight until this operation has been completed." Another grin. "I shouldn't think that will be too onerous a duty. But Harry, please don't go making the mistake of falling in love with this woman, at least not until the mission is completed."

"Yes, sir."

"One last thing. This mission is and has got to remain absolutely top secret, there are too many lives at stake. At the present time, only the generals who set it up, you, and I know about it. Our people, whether they are going in by sea or by air, will not be told where we are going or why until the moment of embarkation. They will in any event not be told about the Sturmers. Equally, Fraulein Sturmer must not know the details."

"As she created the idea, sir, she will certainly know what we are hoping to accomplish."

"She will know that we are sending a very small force of paratroopers to get her father. She cannot, and must not, know how you intend to get out, or that there will be any support, especially on such a scale. However, to be absolutely safe, it is a part of your brief to make sure that she has absolutely no contact with anyone outside the training centre before the operation. It might be useful for you to let her know that you are under orders to execute her without hesitation if there is a reception committee waiting for you, or any suggestion that the Germans have somehow got hold of information about our plans. Carry on, Lieutenant."

Belinda was seated at her desk in the outer office. "So off you go into the blue," she remarked. "I assume you speak French?"

He pointed at her. "You are not supposed to know anything about it."

She wrinkled her nose, most attractively. "When Dick Lightman says something is known only to him, he means us," she remarked. "What's going to happen to your bit?"

"If you're interested, she's coming with us."

"Ooh, la-la," she said. "Do leave her behind."

"Don't you like her?"

She blew him a kiss. "I like you more."

He wished he could be sure when she was pulling his leg.

"You mean it is going to happen?" Veronica asked, as they sat together in the back of the staff car being driven to the RAF base where they would train. "Do you know, I did not really believe it ever would."

"High Commands move just as mysteriously as God," he pointed out.

"And by parachute! I have never jumped in a parachute."

"That's where we're going now, to train for it."

"How exciting. Is this going to be a very big force?"

"No. Just a platoon."

"But you will be in command?"

"I'm afraid so."

She brooded on this for some seconds. Then she said, "At least I am no longer a wanted woman."

"Let's say you're on a suspended sentence for your gaolbreak. I don't know if charges will be preferred over the car theft. But if this mission is a success, it's possible all the charges will be dropped."

"Oh, it will be a success," she said.

"I hope so. You do realise that if it isn't, we shall all be dead."

She turned her head to look at him. "I understand that, Harry."

He simply could not bring himself to tell her that he was her appointed executioner.

"I have never had so many bumps and bruises in my life," Veronica complained at the end of the week. "How much longer does this go on?"

They had in fact made only two jumps from aircraft, having worked their way up from falling ten feet to a hundred in the training shed. Yet the amount of work they had had to do, all day, had been considerable. Harry was glad of that as Veronica was so exhausted every night she revealed no desire to do any socialising, certainly not to the extent of leaving the camp, which he would have had to refuse. She was not even very interested in sex, but he had his suspicions that she never had been, had used her enormous allure principally as a weapon to obtain what she wanted. That might have been a slap in the face for Harry the Great Lover, but it also enabled him to look at her in the abstract way that would be necessary if he had to carry out his final orders.

He still didn't know if he would be able to.

But at last they were on their way. Their training sergeant had pronounced them, if not totally proficient, at least capable enough not to kill themselves. And the orders had arrived that her guidance could be accepted. "Not much longer at all," he said. "We leave here tonight."

She gave a squeal of excitement, and hugged him.

"I've a present for you," he said, and gave her a steel helmet.

The airfield was in south-east England, quite close to Dover, where, Harry assumed, the main strike force was already assembled. They arrived just after midnight, in utter darkness, but even so could discern the various bomb craters and crashed aircraft.

Lightman was there to greet them. "You remember Fraulein Sturmer, sir," Harry said.

"How could I forget? Will you wait over there, Fraulein?"

Veronica obeyed, staring at the transport aircraft waiting on the tarmac, the group of soldiers standing by the open doors. They stared at her with equal interest, although as she was wearing battledress with her hair tucked up beneath the helmet it in the darkness it was difficult to deduce even that she was a woman.

"Now, Harry," Lightman said. "Timings. These need to be fairly exact. Time?"

Harry looked at his watch, "Twenty-four thirty-seven."

"Twenty-four thirty-eight. Adjust. We're using my time."

Harry obeyed.

"You will board at zero one-fifteen. The bombing raid takes off at zero one-thirty. You will take off then as well and tag along behind. The bombers will be over their target at zero one forty-five. You will be immediately behind them. Your men should be assembled and in position by zero two zero zero. At this time we shall be leaving Dover. You will assault the Communications Centre at zero two-fifteen. You have half an hour, both to obtain possession of the general, loot the place of anything valuable, and then destroy it. At zero two forty-five, the second air raid will take place. They will not be targeting the centre, or Ardres at all, but rather Calais, and the road between the port and Ardres. At this time, also, we will be attacking the harbour and securing a bridgehead. The moment the raid is over, you will return to Calais. It is possible that you may be able to do this fairly quickly, but in any event it must not take you more than half an hour. We will expect you at some time between zero two-thirty and zero three zero zero. We will be pulling back out at that time. Understood?"

"Yes, sir."

"Very good. Now come and meet your men." He led Harry towards the group. "This is Sergeant-Major Copley. Lieutenant Curtis."

"Sir!" The sergeant-major stood to attention. He was a very big man and wore a moustache.

"All of these men were at Lofoten," Lightman said. "So they are fully experienced. They are also volunteers for this mission, and have been trained as parachutists. The beginnings of our airborne section, you might say. It would be very nice if you could bring as many of them back as possible."

"Yes, sir. Do they know were they are going?" Harry looked at the sergeant-major.

"No, sir," Copley said. "They have volunteered for a mission of national importance, which will be extremely dangerous."

"Have you replacements?"

"I have twenty men, sir." Copley's tone was disparaging, he did not think there would be any need for replacements.

"I should like to meet them all. With your permission, sir?" Harry asked.

Lightman nodded, and Harry went across to where the men were gathered, followed by the sergeant-major and the colonel, and found himself facing Jonathan Ebury.

"Jon, you old son of a gun." Harry shook hands. "How come?"

"The word went out that they required an explosives expert to volunteer, so I did. What are we going to blow up?"

"Hopefully, lots of things. Just give me a little while with the men. Sergeant-Major!"

"Atten . . . TION!"

The men clicked to attention. Veronica almost did so as well.

"Lieutenant Curtis is our commanding officer for this mission," Copley said. "He will now address you."

"At ease," Harry said, and went down the line of men, the sergeant-major at his shoulder, being introduced to each in turn. Several he already knew, including the two medical orderlies, and five had taken part in the assault on the German headquarters in Svolvaer. He was pleased about that – they would know, and they would tell their comrades, that he was an officer who led from the front.

144

When he had shaken hands with the last man, he took his place in front of them. "First let me say that it is an honour and a privilege to command you. Now, you are all volunteers, but any one of you is entitled to change his mind. I can now tell you that we are going to be dropped five miles inland from Calais, at a place called Ardres. Some of you may have heard of it."

"Isn't that where Henry VIII met the French King Francis at the Field of the Cloth of Gold, sir?" someone asked.

"Brilliant," Harry said. "We are not going there to joust, however, We are going to destroy a very important German Communications Centre. Now, we will go in as part of an air raid, and arrangements have been made to bring us back out. I won't tell you anything more than that, because then you won't be able to tell the Germans anything, should any of you be captured. We will have the advantage of complete surprise. However, I do not wish anyone to be under any mis-apprehension about the risks involved. These are considerable. I would not put the individual survival chance at higher than fifty per cent, and there is the possibility that we will all wind up in a German prisoner-of-war camp. Thus if any man wishes to withdraw he may do so, now, without prejudice to his reputation or his future in the Army."

He waited for several seconds. No man moved.

"Very good," he said. "And as I expected, Sergeant-Major."

The sergeant-major read out five names. These were appar-ently his reserves.

"You men may either remain here until this morning," Harry said. "By which time the operation will have been completed, or . . ." he looked at the colonel.

"You may accompany me," Lightman said, "when you will be included in the assault force."

"We would like to accompany you, sir," said a spokesman.

"Very good. We will leave now. Lieutenant Curtis, I wish you every success."

He shook hands and then led his recruits to his command car, and they drove into the night.

"I need light," Harry said.

145

"Over here, sir." The sergeant-major led Harry, Jonathan and Veronica to one of the Nissen huts, where they were admitted by an RAF ground crew. Inside were four men wearing flying gear, drinking coffee. "Flight-Lieutenant Nichols, Pilot Officer Graham, Flight-Sergeant Peters," he introduced. "And Flight-Sergeant Noon. He's your despatcher, sir."

Again Harry shook hands with each man in turn. Like everyone else they looked curiously at Veronica. She had taken off her hat.

"I just need to brief my people," Harry said.

Nichols nodded. "We'll go through our checks." He looked at his watch. "Fifteen minutes."

"That'll do."

The aircrew left, and Harry beckoned Veronica, while he spread the plan on the table. "You have the floor," he told her. "We will be dropped approximately half-a-mile from the village."

"That will take how long?" she asked.

"Ten minutes after we are reassembled from the drop."

"Then, you see, we follow this path here . . ." she prodded the map, while the men looked over her shoulder. "This is a dairy, on the right, and there is the convent. The centre is at the end of this street. Here." She spread out her second plan. "This gate is made of wrought-iron and will be locked." She glanced at Ebury. "It will have to be blown in. There will be two sentries outside the gate, and one inside. They will have to be dealt with. Then there is an open yard, and then the building itself. There is a sentry on the door. Inside, you see, this corridor leads into the ground floor and general operations room. This is where the main codes and coding machines will be found. It is manned on a twenty-four hour basis, but in the middle of the night there will only be four men on duty. Upstairs are the living quarters, occupied by the general and his staff." She traced the stairs with her finger, and looked up at Harry.

"We have to be in and out within half an hour," Harry said. "We must be on our way back to the coast by three o'clock. Any questions?"

"Do we walk out, sir?" asked the sergeant-major.

"We'll use vehicles, if these can be found," Harry said, and in turn looked at Veronica.

"There are normally vehicles parked in the yard, inside the gate," she said. "But you intend to drive out? The alarm will have been raised."

"There will be a diversion to assist us. Now, establishment."

"There is a permanent staff of twelve in the building. But these are technicians rather than soldiers. The building itself is guarded by twenty men, under a lieutenant. They are housed in this annexe here . . ." she indicated the plan. "Normally, there are only the four sentries on duty at night. However, they will have been alerted by the air raid."

"And will be concentrating on the sky rather than the ground," Harry said. "At least until we commence our assault. We go in hard, gentlemen. With the exception of General Sturmer himself, who we wish to take prisoner, you will eliminate anyone wearing uniform found within the headquarters perimeter."

Veronica licked her lips.

"Now," Harry went on, "after the completion of the mission, we shall endeavour to make our way back to the coast as a group. However, should this be impracticable, or should anyone be separated from the main body, the code word for rejoining the Commando units which will be operating in the town will be Paymaster-General. Use this when challenged by any English-speaking soldier. Understood?"

Ebury and the sergeant-major nodded.

"I hope I'm going to be given a whang at something bigger than a steel gate," Ebury remarked.

"Keep your fingers crossed," Harry suggested. "Now you may board the aircraft."

The two men went into the night.

"What is this about a diversion?" Veronica asked. "You did not mention this to me."

"Men like to have their secrets."

147

"This is very big," she remarked. "Bigger than I had hoped. I had not realised it. What are we really going to do?"

"We," Harry said, "are going to rescue your daddy, God willing."

Eight

The aircraft climbed steeply. The ports were blacked out, but Harry was given a jump seat behind the pilots, and he looked out at a considerable number of other planes, flying in formation. The para carrier was at the very rear.

"We go in the moment the raid is over," the pilot said. "Hopefully while there is still considerable confusion on the ground."

Below them the country was dark, but within a few minutes they could see whitecaps. As they did so, they also saw lights in front of them, the flaring glow of explosions and the criss-cross pattern of searchlights.

It was only ten minutes from their airfield to Calais!

"Stand by," the pilot said, and Harry went aft to join his men. And his woman.

He sat beside her. "Is all well?" she asked.

"So far." He looked at Jonathan, who sat with his haversack on his lap. That haversack contained both explosives and detonators, with which he was going to have to jump. But the little man gave him the thumbs-up. "Stand-by, Sergeant-Major."

"Sir!"

The order was given, and the paratroops stood up and took their places.

Harry went to the front. "You jump immediately behind me," he told Veronica. "Scared?"

She grinned. "Not when I am immediately behind you."

He wondered if *he* was scared? Not of the jump, or the following action, he did not suppose. But he was scared of being in command, for the first time. So, all he could do was lead from the front. Jonathan was the one who really needed, and apparently had, the guts.

The despatcher stood beside him. The red light was winking above his head. The aircraft had been steadily dropping for some minutes; now it evened out, and the door opened.

"Good luck," the despatcher said, and Harry fell forward into space.

He supposed it was a good thing that he had only just completed his training, because this felt just like one of those jumps, save that those had been made in daylight. This could well have been, for he looked down on several large fires, which he presumed were in and around Ardres. That was about a mile away, he reckoned, and was glad the breeze was no stronger: it was blowing from the south-west, towards the burning village.

He looked up, but could see nothing above his canopy, and a moment later the ground was rushing at him. He landed on his feet and went down, breaking his fall as he had been taught, rolling several times before coming to a halt, rising to his feet again to gather in the chute and found himself gazing at a cow.

"For God's sake don't moo," he said.

Now the other parachutes were clustering down. He freed himself, found Veronica. She was panting and groaning.

"Are you hurt?"

"I'll manage," she said, holding on to him to stand up.

"Sergeant-Major?"

"Sir! All present and correct."

"Jonathan?"

"I'm here."

"With your little bag of tricks, I hope."

The noise from the village was tremendous, sirens wailing, various alarms going off. In all the confusion no one seemed to have noticed them. Harry checked his watch. It was a quarter to two.

"Let's go." He glanced at Veronica. "You okay?"

"I have hurt my ankle. I will be all right."

"Stay close. We have to move it. And put on your helmet."

It was slung round her neck.

He set off at the double, crossing the field, watched by several scandalised cows, and gained a narrow lane with high banks.

"That way." Veronica pointed as she limped behind him.

Harry turned left as directed and went up the lane, which ended in a road crossing it at right angles. They crouched in the ditch while several vehicles roared by.

"Emergency services," Veronica said.

Harry hoped she was right, as the trucks were making for Ardres. The village was now very close, the houses illuminated by the fires. The noise continued to be enormous, but all of these factors were in their favour, he reckoned.

Once the trucks and fire engines were past, the little band hurried up the road, and reached the outskirts of the village.

"Down there," Veronica said.

They turned down the narrow street, and someone shouted at them, in German. The man was standing at the crossroads in front of them, unslinging his rifle. Harry fired a burst from his tommy-gun, and the soldier went down.

"Did you have to?" Veronica asked.

"Yes," he said. "Which way?"

"To the right, and then across the street."

As with earlier, there was so much noise no one seemed to have registered the shots, and a few moments later they were across the street and darting down an alleyway.

"There it is," Veronica said.

At the end of the alley there was a high wall and a large closed gate. But no sentries visible.

"Jonathan," Harry said, and Ebury hurried forward, panting as uual.

As he unslung his haversack to reach the explosives, a sentry

151

appeared from where he had been sheltering from the bombing. Now he uttered an exclamation in German, and fired his rifle. One of the paras went down with a thud, but by then several of them, including Harry, had returned fire, and the man fell against the wall.

"Who's down?" Harry asked.

"Squires, sir," the sergeant-major said.

"Patch him up. He'll have to stay here until we come out. Let her go, Jonathan."

Ebury had already fixed the plastic explosive, and now he came back to them, trailing his wire.

"Down," he said, and pressed the plunger.

The bang was surprisingly quiet, swallowed in the general cacophony with which they were surrounded. But the gate was sagging open. Harry scrambled up and led his men forward; the sergeant-major and one of the medics remained, tending the wounded Squires.

Beyond the gate there was, as Veronica had promised, a large open yard, in which were parked several vehicles. There was also the second sentry, who like the first had been taking shelter from the air raid, and now emerged, to go down immediately under a hail of fire.

"Corporal Richie," Harry said. "Select two trucks and mount a guard. Let's go."

He moved towards the building on the far side of the yard, but this now came to life. Several upstairs windows, in both the main building and the annexe, opened to reveal men firing rifles.

"Take cover!" Harry bawled, but himself ran forward, reaching the foot of the steps before hurling himself down, and in the same movement throwing a grenade, which landed against the closed door and blew it open. Here again the sentry was missing.

To his consternation a body landed beside him, and he realised Veronica had followed him.

"Do you want to get yourself killed?" he asked.

"I want to make sure Papa is not killed," she replied.

Dust spurted around them but in the darkness the Germans could not see them clearly.

Harry blew his whistle, then rose to his knees and hurled a second grenade. This completed the demolishment of the door, and he ran up the steps. There was no light in the building, but he saw movement in the entry hall and sent a tommy-gun blast into the gloom, listening to a stifled exclamation and the sound of a body falling. He looked back at Veronica, immediately behind him, and at Ebury and the rest of the squad coming through the door.

"In there, Jonathan," he said. "Gather up all the code books and sheets you can find, then lay a trail to blow this building up. Leave me three men."

Jonathan waved his men forward, using a flashlight. He was greeted with some fire, but this was immediately returned.

Harry went to the stairs, started up, and was confronted by a soldier armed with a rifle. He gave him a burst and found himself lying down. As on Dunkirk beach, he felt nothing.

"Harry!" Veronica screamed.

"Just a scratch," he said, hoping he was right. He forced himself up and went up the stairs, hobbling and firing. At the top his magazine was empty, and he stopped to replace it with a spare taken from his haversack, now suddenly aware of pain. The other bloody leg, he thought.

His men were at his shoulder, also firing, but the floor seemed clear for the moment. They faced a corridor off which there were several doors, and now one of these opened, slowly.

"Don't shoot!" Veronica shrieked. "Papa!" She broke into a torrent of German.

The door slammed shut.

"Break it down," Harry commanded, and slid down the wall to sit as two of his men ran forward.

"Let's have a look, sir," said the third man, Corporal Green – the other medic. Now he expertly split Harry's battledress pants to expose the wound, using a flashlight held in his teeth.

The other two Commandos were hurling themselves against

the door. Veronica stood behind them, still shouting in German. All the shooting from downstairs had now ceased.

In the distance, though, were more sirens.

"How is it?" Harry asked.

"I've seen worse," Green commented. "Look, sir, I'll have to bind this up as best I can until we can get you to proper treatment. You're losing blood."

"Do it," Harry agreed.

He looked along the corridor, to see a man in a general's uniform emerging, hands held high. Veronica ran forward to embrace her father, and they shouted at each other in German.

"Evacuate," Harry said.

Green finished binding his leg. "Can you stand, sir?"

"I'll have to." Harry held on to the corporal to reach his feet.

"Harry!" Veronica gazed at the torn pants, the already bloodstained bandage. "You *are* hurt!"

"Just a scratch," he said again. "General Sturmer?" He saluted.

"Lieutenant Curtis is our commander, Papa," Veronica said in English.

"This is madness," Sturmer said, also in English.

"Not if we get out," Harry said.

His men were already waiting at the head of the stairs. Harry started down, behind Veronica and her father, and lost his footing. He was in fact feeling quite dazed, which he put down to a combination of shock and loss of blood, combined with the now severe pain in his leg. He actually fell into the general, and had to be grasped by Veronica.

Ebury was in the entry hall, his men carrying several sacks of material.

"Stand by to take command, Jonathan," Harry said.

"Shit," Ebury commented. "How bad is it?"

"I don't know. But my judgement may go. Are your explosives set?"

"Five minutes," Ebury said.

"Then evacuate."

154

Two of the Commandos carried Harry across the yard to where Corporal Richie waited with the two commandeered trucks. Harry found himself next to a groaning Private Squires.

"Casualties?" he asked.

"One dead, sir. Four wounded, including yourself. The other two are in the other truck."

Sergeant-Major Copley was commanding the gate with three more men. "Company," he called.

"Hold them up, Sergeant-Major," Harry said.

The firing from outside the gate became general.

"You will not get out," Sturmer said. "You will all be killed."

"What time is it?" Harry asked.

"Twenty-nine minutes past two."

"Wait for it."

Even as he spoke, they could hear the drone of airplane engines, and a few minutes later the bombs started to fall. Once again the sirens wailed.

"They will blow us out of existence," Sturmer grumbled.

He seemed a confoundedly pessimistic fellow, Harry thought.

"They're not aiming at us," he said.

The bombs came down with great *whoompfs*, and the firing from the gate died down.

"Get your men together, Jonathan," Harry muttered.

Jonathan blew his whistle, and the Commandos hurried back from the gate. Now the noise was immense, and more buildings had burst into flames, while from behind them there came a dull explosion, which rocked the vehicles. They looked over their shoulders at the exploding windows of the Communications Centre, the red flames reaching up to the roof.

"Nice work, Jonathan," Harry said.

"All my gear!" the general moaned. "My equipment! My books!"

"We've brought a few with us," Harry assured him. "Move it, Jonathan."

"Let's go," Jonathan shouted. "No stopping!"

The two trucks roared at and through the shattered gate, the

155

Commandos firing their automatic weapons to either side. The Germans had again sought shelter from the bombs, now they could not regroup in time before the trucks were through and roaring down the street, swerving left and right to avoid falling debris from the burning buildings. Then they were out of the village and racing along the road towards Calais.

"They will stop you in the town," Sturmer said "This is suicide."

"Look," Harry told him. "And listen."

As he spoke the night sky in front of them lit up, and there was a huge new explosion of sound.

Sturmer attempted to stand up to see better, and Veronica had to claw him back down.

It took them only a few minutes to gain the outskirts of the port, driving beside the canal. But here they suddenly ran into a challenge from a roadblock. The first truck, commanded by the sergeant-major, drove straight at it, guns blazing, and burst through. The second received a hail of fire. The driver died instantly, and slumped across the wheel. Corporal Green reached across him in an attempt to regain control, but it was too late. The truck swerved sideways, hit the embankment, and entered the canal upside down.

It had all happened so quickly Harry had no time to take a deep breath before he was thrown out of the truck into the water. He remembered that French canals were seldom more than five feet deep, and thrust down with his legs even as he felt water start to flood his lungs. As he had used both legs, the pain was intense, seeming to shoot up his entire side into his shoulder, but his head broke the surface and he was able to cough and spit and take deep gasps of air.

He looked up, at the embankment, which was lined with German soldiers, pointing their rifles, and shouting. The only word he understood was *"Achtung!"*

Veronica had also regained the surface, and was shouting in German. Harry discovered Sturmer splashing about beside him. But there was no sign of Squires.

"Private Squires!" he called. "Jonathan. Corporal Richie. Corporal Green."

"Here, sir."

The rest of his men gained the surface. Only the driver and Squires were missing, although the rest all had at least minor injuries.

"I think Squires has bought it, sir," Green said.

"They are telling us to come out of the water and surrender," Veronica was saying. "You must surrender, or they will kill you."

It went against the grain, but Harry supposed he had no choice. They had lost all their tommy-guns, and although he still had his revolver he didn't suppose it would be very effective against several rifles. Although, as he did still have his revolver, and was not going to get out, it was his duty to shoot both Sturmer and Veronica. But orders or not, that went against the grain too . . . and there was no certainty that he *wouldn't* still be able to get out – and with the Sturmers.

"All right, chaps," he said. "Hands up. *Kamerad!*" he called.

The officer commanding the Germans shouted instructions.

"He says we must come out of the water, one at a time," Veronica interpreted.

"Okay. You go first."

Veronica reached up and two of the soldiers pulled her out. As she had, remarkably, retained her steel helmet and was wearing British battledress, they did not appear to realise she was a woman. Her father was next, to the astonishment of the Germans, who had not expected to pull one of their own generals from the canal. Sturmer immediately launched into voluble explanations. So much for that, Harry thought. The attack had been a total failure, apart from the destruction of the Communication Centre, at the cost of God alone knew how many lives.

He and his men were pulled out of the water and disarmed.

"What is your father telling them?" Harry asked Veronica.

"That you kidnapped him and destroyed his headquarters."

"That's great."

157

"Is it not the truth?"

"Oh, surely. Whose side are you on, now?"

She made a moué. "You must trust me."

He hoped he could.

The German officer was shouting at them.

"He says we must stop talking," Veronica said, as they were pushed into the small command hut. Harry's leg gave way and he sat down. Veronica chattered at their captors in German.

"Are you all right?" Ebury asked, kneeling beside him.

"No," Harry said.

The Germans had dragged the bags of books and papers from the canal, supervised by an excited Sturmer. Now these, as well as the remaining Commandos, were pushed into the hut.

"Look, tell these people that our officer needs help," Ebury said to Veronica.

She translated, and the German officer bent over Harry. The noise from outside continued to be enormous, and he asked a question.

"He wishes to know what is happening in the port?" Veronica asked.

"Tell him I wish I knew," Harry said through gritted teeth.

Veronica addressed the officer again, who riposted with some more questions, realising for the first time not only that she was a woman but that while she was speaking fluent German she was wearing British battledress. Now her father joined in, and there was a great deal of shouting. Harry looked at his men, a total of six, including the two corporals, either standing or sitting on the far side of the room, watched by two armed Germans. But they were alert, and they were Commandos.

"Bit of a mess," Ebury remarked.

"You could say that."

One of the Germans had been using the telephone, and now a man wearing a red cross on the sleeve of his tunic came in. He asked several questions, and was directed to Harry. He bent over him, widened the split in his pants, and began removing the bandage.

"Go easy, Doc," Harry said. "Or you'll have me shouting for help."

The pain was intense.

The officer was standing on his other side, asking questions again.

Veronica knelt beside Harry, who was doing his best to concentrate as the doctor's fingers probed the wound.

"He wishes to know how many paratroops were dropped, and what were your orders," Veronica said.

"And what have you told him?"

"That I know nothing. That you took my father and I prisoner when you attacked the communications centre."

"And daddy is going along with this?"

"For the moment. He is confused."

"And how have you explained your uniform?"

She gave one of her moués. "I told him I was naked in bed and you gave me this to wear. Well . . . I was naked in bed when first we met."

"And he accepts that we carry out our raids with spare uniforms in our kitbags, which just happen to fit German women?"

"He is confused too," Veronica explained. "No one knows for sure what is happening."

The officer was now impatiently snapping his fingers.

"Tell him that we are part of a paratroop battalion, five hundred strong. That our orders were to attack and destroy the Communications Centre, and then to attack the inward defences of Calais. That we intend to capture the town and hold it as a beachhead for an invasion, which will follow in a few hour's time. That he is almost certainly surrounded and should surrender to me right away."

Veronica stared at him with her mouth open. He had an idea that she actually believed him. Which was brilliant, because she related what he had said to the officer, whose jaw also dropped. Then he ran to the phone and began twisting the handle.

The German medic was bandaging Harry's wound again, speaking to Veronica as he did so.

"He says you must go to hospital. He says there is still a bullet in there, and he does not have the instruments or the facilities to take it out. Anyway, you will need anaesthetic."

"If I go to hospital, that's it," Harry told her. "And for you, whenever your friend gets around to considering all the holes in your story. Will Daddy back you?"

Veronica looked at her father, who was standing against the wall, water dripping from his clothes, looking morose. He clearly understood that he was in as compromising a situation as his daughter, when their captors got around to evaluating the situation.

For the moment the captain was shouting into the telephone.

The doctor stood up, snapping his fingers.

"He says you must go with him," Veronica said.

"Tell him I cannot walk," Harry said.

It was obvious that if he was going to get them out of this mess he would have to do it himself. And it had to be done now, before any more German soldiers arrived. Besides, they had only about twenty minutes left to gain the docks before the Commandos were due to pull out.

The doctor was speaking again.

"He says two of your men may carry you," Veronica said.

Harry checked the room. There were two soldiers pointing their guns at the captured paratroops. There was another man on the door, and he reckoned there were about four more outside on the embankment. There was the medic, who had a holstered pistol on his belt, there was the captain, still shouting into the telephone, and there was the operator, standing beside him.

"Jonathan," he said.

Ebury, kneeling on his other side, looked up and then at the medic.

"I'll need two of you," Harry said.

Veronica addressed the medic. Who gave orders to the guards. Corporal Green came across to join them.

"You're supposed to be carrying me to hospital," Harry told them. "But I don't think that is what we want to have happen,

160

is it? When I say go, Jonathan, you take the captain. Corporal, you go for the telegrapher. Will the lads respond?"

"Oh, yes, sir," Green said enthusiastically.

"Right. Remember, it's all or nothing." He glanced at Veronica. "That goes for you too, or you're liable to wind up against a wall being shot for treason."

She licked her lips. "I'll tell Papa."

"No, you won't," Harry said. "I'm not sure he's on our side, yet. Just pray he reacts properly. Ready. Go!"

The medic was still standing above him, half turned away, waiting for him to be picked up. Harry clasped both hands and swung them into the back of his knees. The medic gave a strangled gasp and fell backwards, hitting the floor heavily. As he did so, Harry rolled on top of him and unclipped the holster, drawing the Luger and opening fire in the same instant. His first bullet went wide, his second slammed into the nearest of the two guards.

That man fell. The second turned, rifle thrust forward, and was hit by several bodies as the Commandos launched themselves at him. He went down in a flurry of arms and legs, as did the man on the door, who was attacked in the same instant. Both the captain and the telegrapher turned back from the phone, and were hit by Ebury and Green. They too went down.

The door was pulled open, and a soldier appeared there. Harry shot him through the chest, and he fell backwards.

"Close it!" Harry shouted, and the door was shut just as several shots burst into it.

Ebury was dragging the captain to his feet, having secured his pistol. The telegrapher was in the hands of Green. General Sturmer remained standing against the wall, having made no attempt to take part in the fracas.

Neither had Veronica, who had moved to stand beside her father.

The captain was spluttering.

"What's he saying?" Harry asked.

"He says you will all be killed. He has summoned tank support, and they are on their way."

"Then we'll have to get a move on. Private Small, how many men are outside, do you reckon?"

Small was the man who had slammed the door.

"I don't think more than three, sir."

"Armed with rifles," Ebury pointed out.

"Well, we have three rifles and three pistols. Corporal Green, tie these beggars up."

The medic was sitting up, looking dazed, and also spluttering.

"He says you will lose that leg if you are not treated soon," Veronica said.

"I'm working on it. You too, Doc."

The five surviving Germans were made to sit in the middle of the room and were secured together by their various belts.

"Now," Harry said. "We are going to leave this place. Corporal Green, you'll have to act as my crutch. Jonathan, you bring up the rear."

"I say, old man, I should lead the charge."

"I need you," Harry said. "To keep an eye on our prisoners, and also to bring as many of those sacks as you can carry."

"I am not a prisoner," Veronica objected.

"I think you and Daddy had better so consider yourselves," Harry said. "Just in case we're recaptured."

She gulped at that possibility.

"Stand-by," Harry said, being assisted to the door by the corporal. "Douse the light."

The light went off, and Harry drew a deep breath. He was well aware that even in the darkness the first man out was likely to stop a bullet, but this had to be done if any of them were going to get away. And he assumed he was fairly close to death anyway. He reached for the door, and was checked by a sudden burst of firing from outside. None of it was directed at the command post.

He pulled the door open, and he and Green stumbled out, to gaze at the bodies scattered about . . . and at Sergeant-Major Copley and his men, looming out of the darkness.

"We came back as soon as we realised you weren't with us, sir," the sergeant-major explained. "But it took time. The place is crawling with Jerries." He peered at his officer, who was still being supported by Corporal Green. "Are you all right, sir?"

"He's hit," the corporal said.

"Have you transport?" Harry asked.

"We abandoned it about half-a-mile away, sir. Found it easier to get through the streets on foot. There's all hell going on down by the docks."

"That's where we have to reach. I want two volunteers."

All of his men stepped forward.

"I'll take the two biggest. Corporals Richie and Green. You may have to carry me."

"Sir!" They stood one to either side.

Harry also selected a rifle to use as a crutch, but he didn't know how far he was going to get without fainting. "Now," he said. "Our destination is the docks. We'll do best to split up, but remember the password, Paymaster-General – there's no point in getting out of this hole to be shot by our own side. Jonathan, you're in charge of those bags, take the main body to help you, and deliver them. Sergeant-Major, your responsibility is to deliver the general."

"And you, sir."

"The corporals and I will find our own way out. Obviously we'll travel more slowly than the rest of you. Leave us two tommy-guns."

They looked unhappy, but he knew they would obey him.

"What about me?" Veronica inquired.

"I think you should stick with your dad."

"Tanks, sir," Copley said.

Even above the wailing of the sirens, the explosions and gunfire coming from the waterfront, they could hear the clanking of the treads.

"Go," Harry commanded. "Go, go, go."

Jonathan waved the Commandos forward and they dashed down the street.

"Come along, sir," Copley said, and looked hopefully at Veronica.

She spoke to her father, who still seemed to be in a daze. But

Harry was beginning to wonder if it *was* a daze, or if the general was not doing some very deep thinking.

"Take him along," he commanded.

Veronica held her father's arm and hurried him down the street, Copley on his other side.

"Let's go," Harry told the two corporals.

They had him on his feet, the rifle butt wedged into his shoulder, and now helped him limp and hop behind the others. The German medic had done a very good job of binding up the wound, but Harry knew he was still losing blood, while the entire right side of his body was a mass of pain, making him feel quite sick.

The medic had said he could lose the leg. That simply wasn't on. It *couldn't* be on.

At the corner they paused to look back, and watched the first tank roll down the embankment behind them. It stopped at the sight of the dead bodies, and men climbed out of its hatch.

"We could drop those fellows, sir," Corporal Richie suggested.

"And what about the ones behind?" Harry asked, as several more of the huge vehicles came into view. "Let's get out of here before they free those fellows in the hut."

They hurried down the street as fast as they could, aware that they had only a few minutes start,

"Do you know which way we go, sir?" Green asked.

"Into the breeze. It's off the water."

They turned a corner, and checked as in front of them, crossing the next street, was a body of German soldiers, on the double, hurrying towards the sound of the fighting. They were bringing up more and more reinforcements to combat the supposed 'invasion'. Harry could only hope they would hold some of their troops on the landward side of the town, to repel the reputed paratroops.

The houses to either side were shuttered and in darkness, it was impossible to tell whether or not they were occupied. If they were, the people inside were very sensibly keeping their heads down. Quite a number of the houses were in any event badly damaged. Harry reckoned that would be from the defence of the town by the British back in 1940, a defence which had ended in surrender.

The last of the Germans disappeared and they resumed their journey, and were again checked by a shot, close at hand. They looked left and right, rounded the next corner, and Richie pointed. "Shit!"

He had excellent eyesight, even in the darkness. But now Harry also made out the body lying on the far side of the road. He hobbled across behind the corporals, and they stooped beside Copley.

"Took me by surprise," the sergeant-major muttered. "I was looking at those Jerries . . ."

"Which one?" Harry asked through gritted teeth. He was aware of an overwhelming fury.

"It was the general. I didn't know he still had a gun." Copley began to cough.

"And the woman?"

"I think she tried to stop him."

"But she went off with him. How bad is it, Green?"

The corporal had opened Copley's battledress tunic, and then his shirt. Now he raised his head, his face grim.

"I'm done," Copley said. "I know that, sir. You get out."

Harry hesitated, but there was nothing he could do for the dying man. Save avenge him.

"They can't be far," he said.

"They'll have gone behind those Jerries," Richie said. He looked back up the street; now they could hear the clank of the tank treads. "We'd better get out of here, sir."

"Get one for me," Copley said, his breathing now very heavy.

"Good luck, Sergeant-Major." Harry and the corporals hobbled round the corner, gazed down an empty street. The shooting was now quite close, and Harry guessed they were again close to the canal, which debouched into the docks themselves. Then he heard voices, from quite close at hand, shouting . . . and one of them was a woman.

The corporals had heard it too.

"Leave this with us, sir," Richie said.

"I want them alive," Harry said.

Richie grinned. "We'll bring them."

He and Green crept up to the corner, tommy-guns thrust forward. Harry followed them slowly, using both wall and rifle to keep himself upright. On the next street a three-man patrol was questioning the general and Veronica, obviously as confused as had been the men at the command post.

"*Achtung!*" Richie shouted.

The Germans turned, and the corporals opened fire. Veronica screamed and hurled herself down, dragging her father with her. The patrol died instantly from the hail of bullets.

Harry limped forward. The corporals were standing above the two prisoners, tommy-guns aimed.

"You bastard!" Harry said.

The general stood up. "It was my duty," he declared.

Harry looked at Veronica.

She licked her lips. "There was nothing I could do," she said. "He took me by surprise as much as the sergeant-major. I didn't know he was armed."

"But you ran off with him."

"What was I to *do*? He is my father."

"Tanks," Richie remarked.

"Right. Hands behind your back, General," Harry commanded. "Corporal Green."

Green pulled the belt from one of the dead soldiers and secured the general's wrists.

"This is an insult to an officer and a gentleman," the general protested.

"Just be glad you're still in one piece," Harry told him.

"Please don't hurt him," Veronica said.

"As for you, I've a good mind to leave you here."

"Please," she begged. "I have not betrayed you."

"They're close, sir," Richie said.

"Then let's go. Oh, you come along too," he told Veronica.

It took them an exhausting ten minutes to make their way

through the narrow streets, having to stop every so often and shelter from German troops hurrying to and fro.

"You utter a sound, General, and I will blow your brains away," Harry warned.

But once again the general seemed to have subsided into a daze, although Harry now had no doubt that this was an act.

But at last they reached the bridge across the canal. This was covered by German machine-gun fire and equally by firing from the far side, where the Commandos had established their bridgehead. Behind them were huge clouds of smoke and flame from the various port installations they had destroyed, as well as the barges they had set on fire. But clearly they were on the point of withdrawing. Already aircraft were swooping and snarling overhead as the RAF provided cover for the waiting fast launches and MTBs.

"Into the water," Harry said. "Up there."

He pointed towards the railway line about half a mile to their right, and they made their way towards it. The corporals carried him to a deserted area – the Germans were concentrating on holding the bridge, clearly supposing the invaders had tanks and would want to get them across. He was lowered into the water, the others followed, and they waded forward.

"Halt!" someone shouted in English, in the same instant firing into the water in front of them.

"Paymaster-General," Harry called.

A moment later they were being dragged out the other side.

"By Golly," Harbord said. "We didn't think you were going to make it."

Part Three

The Hit

But Thy most dreaded instrument
In working out a pure intent
Is man, arrayed for mutual slaughter,
Yea, Carnage is Thy daughter.
                              William Wordsworth

Nine

"Mr Curtis," said Sister Murton. "You are turning into a bad penny."

"Put it down to France," Harry suggested. "Every time I go there, I get shot in the leg."

"Well," she said, "you only have two legs. If I were you, I'd be worrying about where you might be hit the next time."

"You mean there is going to be a next time?" Harry asked.

As on the previous occasion he had been wounded, he remembered very little of what had happened after he had regained contact with the Commandos. By then he had lost a great deal of blood, and reality had become mixed up with dreams and nightmares, faces and images. He wasn't even sure how long ago the raid had been.

"Oh, we'll patch you up," Sister said. "There's talk of a medal. You have to be able to stand if you're to go to Buckingham Palace."

A medal! But there was no use in asking Sister how things had turned out. Dr Jackman was a little more helpful.

"Apparently it was a great success," he said. "A couple of hundred barges destroyed, together with all the main port installations, and the Germans thrown into a right mess."

"Casualties?" Harry asked.

"Light. I think thirty-four men were killed, nine missing, and roughly a hundred wounded. Including yourself, of course."

171

Out of about a thousand men, Harry thought. He wondered what the doctor would consider heavy casualties.

"Am I going to lose the leg, doctor?" he asked.

"We'll save the leg," Jackman assured him.

The next day Lightman came to see him. "I'm told you'll mend," he said. "Then it's a desk."

"If I can walk again, I can fight again, sir."

"That's brilliant," Lightman said. "Of course we'd like you back. If you'd like to do that."

"I would like to come back, sir, as soon as I am able. Can you tell me if the raid was a success? I gather casualties were heavy."

"They were acceptable for a sortie like that. Yes, it was a success. So much so that the top brass are getting quite ambitious. I've done my best to remind them that it was just a raid, and that its primary object was, and must remain, top secret. But they, and we, are getting a lot of good publicity over the audacity of the assault, and the destruction of those barges."

"And General Sturmer?"

"I'm afraid he's not being entirely co-operative, at the moment. But we'll bring him round."

"He is guilty of murder."

"That's a technical point, Harry. He was in uniform, as was Sergeant-Major Copley, and they were mutually engaged in a battle. We'd have a hard time making that one stick, even if we wanted to. And in any event, it would be rather counter-productive to have gone to all that trouble, and suffered those casualties, to lay hands on the general, and then immediately hang him for murder."

"And . . . ah . . ."

"The young lady is being treated as a prisoner of war."

But a peculiar expression had crossed Lightman's face. Harry found it disturbing.

"We promised her better than that, sir."

"Yes, we did. I have made representations, and her case is being considered. But it is a little difficult to know what to do with her. Of course, if Papa would co-operate, things might be different."

"If you could persuade them to trust her, she could be very useful."

"As you say, if. However, Harry, now that we have correlated the various reports of the action, her attitude seems to have been ambiguous, to say the least. Ebury reports that she didn't actually assist in breaking out of the German guard post, and Corporal Green has some doubts as to how big a role she played in the murder of Sergeant-Major Copley."

"She said she was taken by surprise, that she didn't know her father had a gun."

"That's what she would say, to us, isn't it?"

"But she did guide us to the Communications Centre," Harry argued.

"That was primarily to get her father out. She could well have changed sides again when he made it plain he was not going to co-operate. As I say, the whole situation is being evaluated. If it is possible to use her, then we shall do so. Your business is to stop worrying about enemy aliens, and concentrate on getting fit." He stood up. "Oh, by the way, you've been promoted to captain."

"Good lord," Harry said. He wasn't yet twenty.

As Lightman appreciated. "Keep on at this rate, a rank a year, and you'll be a general before you're twenty-five. You're also going to get a gong. I recommended it. The MC."

"Thank you, sir."

"My pleasure. You did a brilliant job. Ebury will get one as well, and there will be medals for your corporals, as well as a posthumous one for Sergeant-Major Copley."

"Again, thank you, sir."

"So . . . I'll be in touch."

"I would like to see her, sir. If that is possible."

Lightman frowned at him. "Are you sure that's a good idea?"

"I think it is."

Lightman hesitated, then shrugged. "I'll see if it can be arranged."

*　　*　　*

173

His parents came to see him, predictably agitated.

"The newspapers are saying it was a high risk operation," John Curtis said.

Neither of them knew anything of the real reason behind the raid, of course.

"Well, I suppose it was," Harry agreed. "But it had to be done. And I'm getting an extra pip. And a gong. That can't be bad."

"But you *are* going to get a staff job now?" Alison asked, anxiously. "I mean, twice wounded . . ."

"The quacks tell me I'll soon be right as rain," Harry assured her.

"Well . . ." she looked embarrassed, and glanced at his father.

He licked his lips. "Yvonne would like to visit you."

"You mean she's back on board?"

"Well . . . she understands now why you had to leave in such a hurry. She's very proud of you, actually."

"She never did return the ring," Harry mused.

He didn't really want to see her again. He knew now that he would never marry her, that he had fallen in love with Veronica, however temporarily angry he had been with her over the death of Sergeant-Major Copley, without being absolutely sure she could be trusted. Or would ever love him back. Veronica had her own very personal agenda, which she was following, whatever the difficulties placed in her way.

But he was an officer and a gentleman. At least whenever he was in England.

"If that's what she wants to do," he said.

Yvonne came a week later. By then Harry was feeling a good deal stronger, although his leg was still both painful and inactive, and he had been moved from intensive care to a general ward. She gave him a tentative kiss on the forehead and squeezed his hand, then sat in the chair beside the bed, embarrassed by the number of men, and nurses, and visitors, with whom they were surrounded. It was a large ward, filled with wounded officers, each of whom had a wife or mother or sister or girlfriend at his bedside.

"Are you going to be all right?" Yvonne asked, twisting her hands together as she drew off her gloves. "You don't look very well."

"I am not very well, at this moment," he agreed, observing that she was still wearing his ring. "But that's mainly blood loss. I'm coming along."

"And then you'll have a nice long leave," she said, hopefully.

"Well . . . as long as is necessary, I suppose. There is a war on, you know."

"But you're not going to fight again, surely?"

She had obviously been discussing things with Mother.

"If I can, I mean to."

She frowned at him. "And now you're a captain," she remarked.

"All the more reason to be up and doing."

There was a brief silence, while she did some more finger-twisting. "The fact is," she said at last, "I've been thinking about joining up."

"I'm sure they could use you."

Her frown was back. She hadn't expected him to agree so readily. "But, you see, if you were going to have a long furlough, or well, even a short one, I'd postpone it . . . joining up, I mean, until afterwards. I mean, I'd want to be in Frenthorpe when you were there."

"Even when they let me out of here, I'm not going to be good for very much, for quite a while," he pointed out.

"Good for . . ." she flushed. "I don't know what you mean." Because she obviously did.

"We could be talking about a year or more," Harry said.

"Oh." She considered. "But I suppose, even if I joined the ATS or whatever, they'd give me leave to get married."

"They probably would. Who's the lucky chap?"

Her head jerked.

"I might know him," Harry suggested.

"How can you be so . . . so nasty."

"Yvonne," Harry said patiently. "I am not being the least bit nasty. When last we spoke, you terminated our engagement, rather positively."

"I was angry at the way you were behaving."

"Were you indeed."

"But now that I realise it wasn't your fault . . ."

"You'd like the engagement to be on again. I'm sorry, it can't be on again. I'm a soldier, and I do what my commanding officers tell me to do. So you're likely to be made angry a whole lot of times before the war is over."

"I understand about that, now."

"And I have said it won't work," Harry told her.

She gazed at him for several seconds, then stood up. "I'll look forward to seeing you in Frenthorpe, when you come home," she said.

"Women can be hell," said Tim Hodgson in the next bed, as she walked out.

She was setting up to be a problem, Harry knew. But he was able to forget about her a week later when Veronica appeared. She looked even more gorgeous than he remembered, wearing a trim suit and a hat with a curled up brim.

"I never thought I'd be allowed to do this," she said, and kissed him on the lips, while his hand sought hers.

"How have they been treating you?" He was surprised that she had been allowed to come alone, without a policeman at her elbow.

She sat beside the bed. "I think good, in the circumstances."

"I understand Daddy is being difficult."

She made a moué. "He is coming round."

"And all the while you've been locked up?"

"Oh, no. Well, only in a manner of speaking. I am in the care of some very tough women."

"I'm glad they're women."

"Oh, yes?" She smiled. "Even if I obviously turn them on? Just joking," she added hastily.

He wondered if she was.

"But I have also been working," she said.

"At what?"

"I have been being interviewed, evaluated, questioned . . . I think they wished to find out if I can be trusted."

"And can you?"

"Do you not think so?"

"What I think is hardly relevant."

"Well," she said, "now they think so too. I am being sent for special training."

"Good lord! Where?"

"A place called Blissett Hall. It is very hush-hush."

"Blissett Hall," he said thoughtfully.

"You have heard of this place?"

"As a matter of fact, I have. But . . ." he frowned as memory drifted back. "It's where they train special agents."

"I have been told this. I am to be a special agent."

"Just like that? Have you any idea what is involved?"

"I am told the training is very tough. I am prepared for this."

"I meant, have you any idea what they will do with you when you are trained?"

She nodded. "This has been explained to me. They will send me to France."

"And you are prepared to risk that?"

"They say I am ideal for the job. I speak both German and French fluently. I *am* German, so I can act the part convincingly. I have proved that I have the nerve. And I can parachute jump. You taught me to do that."

"But if you are taken by the Germans . . ."

"I know. I will be shot."

"And before that?"

She shrugged. "It must be my business not to be caught."

He held her hand. "Why are you doing this?"

"I have taken a side. In great affairs, one must take sides. Besides," she smiled, "the alternative is a prison camp for the duration, and that could be a long time."

"Did anyone ever tell you that you are a very brave woman?"

"You are the first. But I am no more brave than anyone else, Harry. Now I must go."

"I would like to see you again."

"I would like that too, if it is possible. But they tell me that once you go into this place, Blissett Hall, they do not let you out until your training is complete."

"And when will that be?"

"I have no idea. So I will have to say, *auf wiedersehen* for the time being."

He still held her hand. "Listen," he said. "I love you."

She regarded him for some seconds; it was impossible to determine her expression. Then she said, "That is the nicest thing anyone has ever said to me."

"But you don't feel like saying it back."

"I have not dared to think about things like love, for a long time. Let us talk about it again, when you are well again, and I have completed my training."

It occurred to Harry that he was making a right mess of his emotional life, however well he might be doing in his military career.

But it was, in any event, a horrific time for a soldier to be confined to bed. It seemed that the whole world was being convulsed, and swallowed, by the Nazis that summer. In the spring, within days of the Calais raid, came the debacle in Greece and Crete, which virtually turned the Mediterannean into an Italo-German lake. At the same time there was the destruction of the battlecruiser *Hood* by the German battleship *Bismarck*, and although *Bismarck* herself was sunk only a few days later, there was the disturbing thought that she had at least one sister, *Tirpitz*, awaiting completion, when she too might break out into the Atlantic.

But all of this was submerged when in July Germany invaded Russia.

"You're fretting," Sister Murton admonished, as Harry sat

178

in his wheelchair in the grounds by the lake, staring at the water. "Look at your hands. Tight little fists. You must relax, Captain."

"When am I going to walk?" Harry asked.

He was attending physio classes every day, but his leg remained weak.

"It'll happen," Sister assured him.

If only he had some idea of what the Commandos were doing. Obviously much of what they *might* be doing was secret, but he wished someone would come to see him just to keep him in the picture, and he was very relieved when in fact Jonathan Ebury appeared towards the end of the summer.

Harry was walking now, slowly, using what might have been the same pair of crutches as the previous year. Which did not mean he was feeling any less frustrated and irritable. Predictably he had heard nothing from Veronica and it was now several months since he had last seen her. He could only imagine what she might be undergoing at Blissett Hall. His only regular visitors were his parents, and they were usually rather gloomy, both at the way the war was going, and at the situation with Yvonne. He didn't seem able to get it through to them either that he did not intend to marry the girl.

But seeing Jonathan again was a treat. The explosives expert had also been promoted captain, and was chubbily cheerful as ever.

"So what have you been up to?" Harry asked.

"Training," Jonathan said.

"No action?"

"Not that I've noticed. But one feels it's coming. We're doing a lot of amphibious assault stuff, working with destroyers, attacking Scottish fishing villages. We've even had some tanks working with us. I think that Calais do really fired the brass up."

"And I'm stuck here on my tod," Harry said bitterly.

"You'll be out in time," Jonathan promised him.

Harry could only hope he was right. Slowly he regained the use of his leg as he walked up and down the grounds, Sister

Murton as his side. But it was October before Dr Jackman declared him fit. "When I say fit, I mean fit to leave hospital," he explained. "You are to have two months convalescence leave. But first, there'll be some interviews."

"Not Mr Roberts again," Harry protested.

Jackman gave one of his wintry smiles. "No, I don't think Mr Roberts will be necessary this time, Captain. But the brass wishes to have a word."

Next morning he was packed and waiting, and found himself looking at Belinda.

"Well, hello," he said.

"You could at least say that you are pleased to see me."

"You are a sight for sore eyes," he assured her. "But then, you always are."

"Flattery could get you anything," she said. "How are you?" She peered at him. "You don't look all that strong."

"I'm not all that strong. But I'm improving. Have you come to take me to Lightman?"

"Could be." She carried his bag to the car, which she was apparently driving herself. "How's your girlfriend?" she asked as they drove out of the hospital grounds.

"I was hoping you'd be able to tell me that."

"I only know she was sent to Blissett."

"Shouldn't she have completed training by now?"

"I wouldn't know." She drove expertly, concentrating on the road. They might never have shared that moment of the knickers together.

"So tell me, how is the war going?"

"Bloody awful, is the short answer. The Germans will be in Moscow in a week or two."

"And then?"

"It's generally supposed the Russians will fade away, into Siberia and make a separate peace, and we'll be back on our own."

"And us? I mean the Commandos. Jon Ebury gave me the impression we may have something on."

"Something." They had entered a town, and as she slowed

180

for the traffic, she glanced at him. "Just how keen are you on the German Fraulein?"

"Half-Norwegian," he reminded her. "I think she's terrific."

"Have you had her?"

"Is that any business of yours?"

"I think it might be. I've always felt you and I had some unfinished business."

"Would you like to finish it?"

"If I didn't, I wouldn't have raised the subject. But I don't go for the word finish too much. We'll talk about it later." She swung into the yard of a pub. "Come inside and I'll buy you a drink."

He followed her, and as he had suspected might be the case, found himself facing Lightman, seated in a corner of the saloon bar, wearing civilian clothes, and drinking beer.

"Sit," the colonel invited. "I thought we might have an informal chat."

Harry sat, and Belinda procured them drinks. Hers was a half.

"All well?" Lightman asked. "You've lost a lot of weight."

"I'm mending. The quack says I'm to have two months off. But—"

"You'd rather get back to work. The question is, are you coming back to us?"

"I'd like to. As soon as I'm fit again."

"We'll be glad to have you. When *will* you be fit again?"

"I feel fit now."

"I think we'll have to go along with that two months."

"I'd like to be in on the next big show, sir."

"You don't have to, you know, Harry. You've done enough for glory."

"I'm not thinking of glory, sir."

"I'm sure you're not. Well, I'll pencil you in."

"Am I allowed to ask for what?"

Lightman grinned. "No, you are not."

"Well, sir, am I allowed to ask how things are going? I mean,

I know they're going badly in Russia, and not too well in North Africa, but . . ."

Lightman sighed, again serious. "I'm afraid we've come a cropper there. I'm not talking about the Eighth Army. I'm talking about us. You know that our real problem in North Africa is Rommel. He is a brilliant tactician, make no mistake about that. One also has the feeling that he could be a brilliant strategist, were he ever to be given the opportunity to plan his own strategy, and the resources to carry it out. The brass feel that if the German-Italian Army in Cyrenaica were commanded by somebody else, we might have a good chance of winning, just as Wavell won when he was opposed only by the Italians. So . . . we were told to take Rommel out."

Harry raised his eyebrows.

"I know," Lightman said. "It's not the way the British have usually waged war in the past. But these are desperate times. Assassination of enemy leaders, where it can successfully be carried out, has become part of the game."

Harry swallowed. But as he had thought about Veronica, moderation in war . . . "And have we succeeded, sir?"

"We have had a complete disaster. Fortunately, only a handful of personnel was involved. Commander Keyes VC, was in charge. He and his group attacked Rommel's headquarters, at Beda Littoria, just west of Tobruk, last Monday night. Unfortunately, Rommel wasn't there, and his guards were. Our people were wiped out."

Harry gulped. "All of them?"

"It seems likely. Keyes we know is dead. A couple of the Commandos may have got away, into the desert. But I wouldn't give much for their chances."

"Shit," Harry muttered, and glanced at Belinda. "I do apologise."

"Feel free," she said. "That's what I said when I heard the news."

"However," Lightman said, "that misfortune cannot be allowed to affect our future. We have big plans afoot. You know the accommodation address in London. Report there the very moment you feel up to resuming training. But Harry, you, we, have to be sure about this."

"I will be, sir."

"Very good. Forester will drive you to the station."

Harry shook hands, and followed Belinda into the car park.

"I'd say he's pretty upset."

"And you'd be right. Commander Keyes was a personal friend." He sat beside her and she started the engine. "So, the station. I'll have to make you out a travel voucher. Where do you want to go?"

"I don't really know," he said.

She glanced at him. "Don't you have a home? Family? Friends? There's a rumour going about that you're engaged to be married. Not to the Fraulein, I hope."

"Not to the Fraulein," he said. "But it's still a problem."

The fact was, with Mother and Father apparently firmly in Yvonne's camp, the only thing he really wanted to see at home at this moment was Jupiter.

"Ah," Belinda said. "Would you like to tell Mother?"

"It'd take too long."

"How long is too long?"

"Are you serious?"

She hesitated for just a moment. "Yes, I'm serious."

"But . . ." he glanced at the ring on her left hand.

"History."

"He isn't . . . ?"

"No, no, he's very much alive. I meant the marriage is history." She had seen his glance. "I wear the ring for protection. When I want to be protected. Listen. I am supposed to drive you to the station, issue the necessary vouchers, and place you on a train for wherever it is you wish to go. Then I return to the pub, pick up the boss, and drive him up to London. Then I have the weekend off. So instead of the station, I drive you to a little country hotel which I know, and which is only a couple of miles from here, leave you there, and get back to you this evening? That'll give us all the time in the world for you to tell me your troubles, and maybe get one or two other things off your chest, or wherever, as well. Well, virtually two days. Certainly two nights."

"I may need them. I have no idea if I'm in any state to perform."

She turned right instead of left at the corner. "I'm not bothered about that. If it happens, it happens. I just want to be with someone I can talk to, and who might like to talk to me. Being a driver-cum-adjutant in a top secret environment doesn't leave too much time for close friends, unless they happen to be in the same environment. Right?"

It had never occurred to him that others could be as lonely as himself. "Right," he said.

She touched her lips with her fingers, and reached across to touch his lips in turn. "And if you want to close your eyes and pretend I'm Veronica, go right ahead."

"I've read her file," Belinda said.

She lay on her back and smoked a cigarette. This was backwards; they hadn't had sex – yet. But Harry suspected they were going to, in some shape or form.

She was naked, and entrancing in her general smallness, when compared with the three other women he had known. It was all very neat and perfectly proportioned. Small breasts matched slender thighs. If her legs were short that was because her body was short. The close-cropped black hair matched the small head and the piquant features. Only the surprisingly thick mat of pubic hair seemed disproportionate.

While he, on his elbow beside her, was acutely aware of his weakness, of the two terrible scars on his thighs, of the inertia between. But it was stirring.

"She really seems too good to be true," Belinda said, and glanced at him. "Or don't you want to hear things like that?"

"It seems to be a fairly widely-held opinion."

"Which you do not share."

"Maybe I just know her better than most people."

184

"There's no answer to that." She stubbed out her cigarette and rolled on her side, against him. "Would you like to make it permanent?"

"I think I would." He touched her forehead with his forefinger, traced down the bridge of her nose.

"But . . . ?"

"I'm not sure she feels the same way."

"That's a waste. What about this other woman?"

"Family friend. Kindergarten together. One of those apparent inevitabilities."

"Brought to fruition by the war?"

"Only in a very limited direction."

"Well bred, is she?"

"Far too well bred."

"She'd probably make you the better wife."

"Right now, I'm not sure that's what I'm looking for."

"Oh, quite." She did the same for him, drawing her finger down his nose.

"Tell me about you."

"There's nothing to tell."

"But . . . you say you and your husband are separated . . ."

"And we'll be divorced in the course of time. Nothing dramatic. He just upped and left me. Well, I suppose, by joining the army, I upped and left him. Certainly when Lightman chose me as his girl."

"And are you? Lightman's girl?"

"From time to time. He's quite happily married. But he's in the same position as you, me, everyone else in the regiment. He can't talk about his work, even to his wife, and he doesn't see her very often, anyway. And obviously there are occasions when he and I are stuck together in some remote part of Britain . . . what the hell? He's a vigorous sexual animal. So am I, when aroused."

"Will you tell him about us?"

"Will there be anything to tell?" Her finger was back, stroking down his chest. Now he was on his back, and she was on her elbow. "What would you like to do to me?"

"I'd like to stroke you all over. Front and back and inbetween."

"Sounds like fun." Her finger continued on its way, down his belly to reach its goal. "And we can pause for a break, halfway."

Ten

Belinda was like a breath of fresh air, a woman who regretted nothing, wanted nothing, save the company of a congenial man. He wondered how many men she found congenial, apart from Lightman and himself? He hoped it wasn't *too* many. As if it was any of his business. When he was with Belinda, he had to think like Belinda. When he was away from her . . . well, why not still think like Belinda?

He returned home on Monday in that frame of mind, was nearly knocked over by Jupiter, and Mother was waiting in the hall to greet him.

"Oh, Harry! How long will it be this time?"

"Actually, a couple of weeks at least."

"Oh, splendid. Then we'll be able—"

"No," he said. "No engagement parties. No parties at all, on my behalf. I've come home to get fit. That means a lot of walking and a quiet life."

"But Yvonne . . ."

"Is history," he said, quoting Belinda.

Yvonne quickly learned he was back, of course, and came to call, but he was so cold she left, and next day his ring was returned.

"Oh, Harry," Mother said.

That also soon became public knowledge in the village, and when he walked past the kindergarten school a couple of days later, Gillian smiled at him. But she too was history.

Any chance of proper relaxation was in any event ended

after the first week of December, with the news of the Japanese attacks on Pearl Harbour and Malaysia and the Phillipines.

"Now we're fighting the whole world," John Curtis said sombrely.

"Correction, Dad," Harry said. "Now the Axis and Japan are fighting the whole world."

Which merely made him the more anxious to get back to the regiment. It was not until after Christmas, when his weight and strength had entirely returned and he was seriously thinking of returning to duty, that he learned that the Commandos had carried out two more large raids, once again on the Lofoten Islands. He couldn't make head nor tail of that, but a week later Lightman called, driven as usual by Belinda, who remained totally po-faced as they shook hands.

He reckoned she hadn't told the colonel of their week-end.

"Happened to be in the district," Lightman said. "And thought I'd drop in and see how you're getting on."

"I'm just about ready to go, sir. But I seem to be missing a lot of action."

"Don't you believe it," Lightman said. "Mind you, this was more of a show than the last time. Jerry has fortified the islands. Well, he's put in a couple of big guns. But that's really why we went back."

"To take out a couple of big guns on the Lofoten Islands?"

"To practice our landing techniques in the face of the big guns. It was an exercise to prepare us for . . . whatever lies ahead. As I told you, the brass is planning something really big for this summer. So, come back to us as soon as you can."

He and Belinda stayed to lunch, to the delight of Alison, happy to see her son on such good terms with his colonel. They left in the afternoon. There had been no opportunity to be alone with Belinda, but Harry supposed that was a good thing. It had happened, they had both enjoyed it, and now it needed to be forgotten.

It would have had to be forgotten in any event, as only a few days later, when he was on the point of packing up for London and then training camp, the doorbell rang, and he found himself gazing at Veronica.

For a moment Harry couldn't believe his eyes. It was certainly Veronica, but her expression had a glow he had not seen before, and she was obviously tremendously fit. She still wore her hair long, and she was dressed in a civilian suit, with stockings and high-heeled shoes, and a broad-brimmed hat. She carried a small valise.

"May I come in?" she asked.

"Oh, my dear girl!" He allowed her into the hall, then took her hat from her head to hold her in his arms. She was wearing lipstick. It was a long time since he had kissed a woman wearing lipstick – not since Niki.

"I suppose you had forgotten all about me," she remarked.

"There's an unlikely projection. More likely you'd forgotten about me."

"Well," she said. "I couldn't write."

"Oh, absolutely. I'm just being impatient. But now . . ."

"I have come to say goodbye."

"Eh?"

"I have completed my training, and have been assigned."

"To?"

"I have no idea. And if I did, I would not be allowed to tell you. I've been given two days leave before I must report. So . . ."

"Two days? You mean you can stay here for two days?"

"If you would like me to."

"Like you to? Oh, my darling . . ." he kissed her again.

"Ahem," Alison said from the drawing-room doorway.

"Oh. Ah." Harry turned, still holding Veronica's hand. "This is Veronica, Mother."

Alison came forward. "I don't think we've met," she said, frostily.

"No, we have not, Mrs Curtis," Veronica said. "I am Veronica Sturmer."

Alison's expression became more frosty yet.

"Veronica is Norwegian," Harry explained, hastily. "She came back with us from the Lofoten Islands, last March."

"I see. Well, welcome Miss . . . Sturmer? Is that a Norwegian name?"

"I have a German father," Veronica said, without embarrassment.

"Oh. Ah. Well . . ." Alison looked at her son.

"If you are wondering why Veronica isn't in an internment camp," Harry said, "that is because she is a British soldier. Who happens at this moment to be on embarkation leave before going overseas. She would like to spend the last couple of days with us. With me," he added for good measure.

That she had come to him, at such a time, had banished all his doubts, sent him on to such an euphoric high that he would even antagonise Mother.

"You mean she wishes to stay here?" Alison asked, crossing t's.

"With your permission, yes."

"I'll make up the spare room."

Harry hesitated. But the spare room was immediately across the upstairs hall from his own, and he didn't want to upset his mother *too* much.

"We'll help you," he said.

Veronica went out of her way to be both charming and co-operative to Alison, who had thawed somewhat by the time John Curtis came in. He was, predictably, enchanted by the lovely young woman, and both the Curtises were enthralled by the story of how Harry had rescued her from the burning headquarters building in Svolvaer, and equally by the story of the raid on Ardres, of which they had hitherto had no details.

"I can see that you have done a good deal of adventuring together," John said. But he had seen more than that, and after lunch took Harry into the garden for a chat while they threw the ball for Jupiter. "Would I be wrong is supposing that this rather striking young woman is the reason you went off Yvonne?"

"Only in a manner of speaking. I was never really *on* Yvonne."

"You asked her to marry you."

"Yes, I did. And I regret it, on every count. I was feeling, well . . . insecure, I suppose."

John Curtis looked at his son. "*You* were feeling insecure?"

"I do, from time to time, believe it or not. And no sooner had she said yes than she was laying down the law. And then, along came Veronica. You can hardly compare the two."

What he was telling his father was not chronologically correct, but the truth about his feelings at that time was impossibly complicated.

"Allowing always that beauty is so often skin deep," John Curtis observed. "I apologise. I shouldn't have said that. But I suppose I am allowed to ask where we go from here?"

"I intend to marry her, if we both survive the war."

"Ah. I'm not sure your mother will go for a German daughter-in-law."

"Veronica is Norwegian. She has a passport to prove it. And it won't be Mother marrying her, it will be me. If you feel Mother doesn't want her under this roof, then I shall find her an hotel. And I will go with her."

John Curtis gazed at his son. He was well aware that the somewhat effete schoolboy athlete he remembered only four years ago had entirely changed, into a man who had been taught to kill and who had put that knowledge to work. A man who, if all the signs were right, would one day in the not too distant future be at least the commander of a regiment, if not a brigade. A man who would make his own decisions, unaffected and certainly not deterred by others' opinions, even those of his nearest and dearest.

He wondered how many of those decisions would be wrong ones? Every man had to be allowed a few of those in his life. But some mistakes were far more serious, and potentially disastrous, than others.

On the other hand, Harry had said that they intended to

wait until the war was over. It was up to those who had his welfare at heart to be patient.

"We certainly do not wish you to move out," he said. "I'll have a chat with your mother."

"They do not like me," Veronica suggested, as she lay in his arms that night.

"Well, my people have been at war with your people twice this century. I suppose a little bit of prejudice had to creep in. They'll get over it. Certainly after the war."

"By which time you anticipate that Germany will have once again been defeated."

"Of course. Don't you? In two years Germany hasn't been able to defeat Britain. Do you seriously think she can beat Britain, Russia, and the United States?"

"Russia will be out of the war by the summer."

"She was supposed to be out of the war by Christmas. And even if she is out by summer, the Americans won't be. And when you say out of the war, you mean Russia will have been militarily defeated. Holding the country down is going to take more troops than I think even Mr Hitler possesses. So . . ."

"We must not quarrel about it," she said. "We must never quarrel. I worry about you so. You are almost well again, no?"

"Actually, I'm almost well again, yes."

"And you are going back to the Commandos?"

"You bet. There are big things on this year."

"Tell me."

"Now, sweetheart, you know I can't do that. Even supposing I knew, which I don't."

"But you know it is something big."

"So Lightman says."

"Another raid on France?"

"Could be anywhere."

"I think you know, and will not tell me," she grumbled. "You do not trust me. After all we have been through together, you do not trust me."

192

"Of course I trust you," he protested. "But I really and truly do not know."

"You see," she said, snuggling against him. "I am being flown into occupied France."

"I know. And I wish to God you weren't."

"Ah, it will be . . . what do you say?"

"A piece of cake. But it won't, you know. When I think what the Germans will do to you if they catch you . . ."

"They are not going to catch me," she said. "But I cannot help but think how wonderful it would be if . . . well, I do not know exactly where I am going to be, but I do know it will be somewhere in the west, Normandy, or Brittany, or even Gascony. Near to the sea. Wouldn't it be magnificent if I were to be stationed close to where your raid is to take place? Then perhaps we could meet up."

"Darling," Harry said. "The odds against that happening must be about fifty million to one."

"Not if I knew where the raid was to take place. Then I might be able to arrange to be in the vicinity."

"Well, we'll have to accept the long odds, because I do not know where we are going, or even if it is in France at all."

Veronica's feeling that Harry mistrusted her was the only blot on a delightful two days. Otherwise she was the most loving and sympathetic of companions. They went for long walks together, stopping and resting whenever Harry became tired or his leg began to hurt. They made no plans, preferring to dwell on their so disparate pasts, an essential roadway to getting to know each other. He gained the impression that in her youth she had been an enthusiastic Nazi, but then, so apparently had been all her friends and schoolmates, so she could hardly be blamed for that. Nor was he prepared to blame her for her occasional lapses into supposing that Germany could still come out of the war satisfactorily, by means of a negotiated peace which would leave her in possession of most of her conquests.

Yet she was about to risk her life to bring about the defeat of her own people. He found this ambivalence in her character fascinating.

And domestically she was even more of a charmer, willingly helping Alison about the house, clearing and washing dishes, even peeling potatoes. By the time she left, two days later, she had quite won the older Curtises over, and they were nearly as tearful as Veronica herself when the time came to say goodbye.

"When will you be back?" Alison asked, holding her close.

"I don't know," Veronica admitted.

"And you shouldn't be asking questions like that, Mother," Harry pointed out. But he asked the question himself when he took Veronica to the station. "You *are* going to come back?"

"Oh, yes," she said confidently. "My tour of duty is only for six months, then they will bring me back."

"How?"

She smiled. "I have no idea. This is what I have been promised. So . . . I will come to you in the summer."

"I'll be here, somewhere," he promised her.

How does one live a life of comparative ease, fairly secure even from rogue bombers, when the woman one loves has gone off to hell? With perhaps torture and death at the end of it. In any normal circumstances the situation would have been intolerable. But this was war, and toleration was there because he would soon be back in action himself, fighting, if not at her side, certainly in the same direction. He renewed his get fit efforts with an even greater determination, using weights to bring his legs back to their full strength.

To his great pleasure, the following week Paul was home. It was the first time the brothers had seen each other in more than two years. Paul had only a brief furlough, and then was away to sea again. He was a lieutenant-commander now, and in charge of an escort destroyer in the Atlantic.

Then came the great occasion of the visit to London,

accompanied by his mother and father, to receive his Military Cross from the hands of the King himself.

The following week, home again, there was a knock on the door, and he opened it to Belinda Forester.

"I never feel you're actually pleased to see me," Belinda said.

"That's because I'm always pleased to see you," Harry replied.

It was over a fortnight since Veronica had left, and Belinda was as pretty as ever. He supposed he was the luckiest man in the world to have two such mistresses, although he did not suppose Belinda could strictly be classed as *his* mistress . . . and he had a suspicion she had not come down here for any nooky. She was wearing uniform, carrying a briefcase, and looking very efficient.

"May I come in?" she asked.

"Oh, I'm sorry." Hastily he stepped aside. "I was lost in the view."

"You say the sweetest things. When do I get to see your medal?"

"When next I'm in uniform."

"Which will be soon, I hope." Belinda took off her cap, laid it on the table, and fluffed out her hair, then faced the lounge door, where Alison had appeared.

"Ah . . . Captain Forester, Mother," Harry said. "My mother."

"My pleasure, Mrs Curtis. We met last year, when I was down with Colonel Lightman."

"I remember," Alison said, a trifle uncertainly. "Is the colonel with you today?"

"I'm afraid not. This a flying official visit. You'll forgive me, Mrs Curtis, but I need to be alone with your son."

"Oh. Ah . . ." Alison looked at Harry.

"We'll take a walk in the garden," Harry said, and opened the door of the conservatory. "This is Jupiter," he explained, as the dog bounded up to them.

"I remember him. What a lovely fellow." Belinda handed

him her briefcase while she stooped to stroke the dog. "I gather your lady friend has departed?"

"Just how did you know she'd been here?"

Belinda retrieved her briefcase. "She told me."

"You've seen Veronica?"

"She came to the office to say goodbye. I have to say that she has a lot of guts."

Harry guided her to the rustic bench, sat beside her. "And she came to see you? I find that very strange."

"Actually . . ." Belinda gazed at him, "she came to see Dick. That's Colonel Lightman. I just happened to be there."

"And she knew where to find you? And Dick?"

"Why, yes. Didn't you tell her?"

"I don't know myself. I only know the accommodation address."

"Ah. Well, I suppose Dick must have told her."

"Are you trying to tell me that Lightman has been seeing Veronica?"

"I suppose he regards her as his protegée."

"He told me once he didn't think she could be trusted."

Belinda smiled. "What Dick Lightman says, and what he thinks, are two completely different things. And what he intends to do, about either his words or his thoughts, is completely different again."

"You are saying that Lightman has been having it off with Veronica? I don't believe you."

Belinda shrugged. "You can believe what you like, Captain Curtis. What I am telling you for a fact is that he paid several visits to Blissett Hall last autumn. I don't think it was to discuss the war situation with the commanding officer."

"I thought Blissett was so top secret no one is allowed in or out."

"No one is, unless you happen to be a senior officer in a regiment like the Commandos." She frowned at him. "I've upset you."

"You're bloody right you've upset me. I was going to marry that girl."

196

"Was?"

"Well . . ."

"For God's sake, Harry. Grow up. Did you seriously think you were the only bloke she'd ever dropped her knickers for? Wasn't there a German naval officer *in situ* when you arrived?"

"That was forced."

"What woman wasn't, when she's telling another man about it?"

He glared at her. "I ought to . . ."

She grinned. "Put me across your knee? I'd have you on a charge. You may be a captain yourself now, but I still have seniority."

"And you came all the way down here to tell me this?"

"Actually no. I am to make an assessment of your fitness. We're moving towards something big."

"Lightman mentioned it when you were last down."

"That's right. Now time is getting short. We want you back in full training immediately. Are you up to it?"

"I think so."

"We need to be sure. Show me your legs."

"Here?"

She glanced at the house. "I suppose we'd better retreat into the shrubbery, or your mother will think I'm raping you." She got up and led the way through the orchard until the house was out of sight. "Here will do."

Harry looked left and right, feeling like a guilty schoolboy, and dropped his pants. It was a fine day, but at the end of January the air was close to freezing, and he could not stop himself from shivering. "You know what they look like," he suggested.

"Complete with two matching scars," she said. "Very neat." She placed her valise on the ground, hitched up her skirt above her knees, and knelt on the valise. Then she grasped his thigh, firmly, and squeezed. As he remembered, she had very strong fingers.

"Ow!"

"Does that hurt?"

"Well, of course it hurts. Wait till I do it back to you."

"I'd turn black and blue. What I meant was, does it hurt inside. The pain would be sharp."

"Not really."

"Hm. Take your pants right off."

"Now we're getting somewhere. What about yours?"

"Just jog," she said. "On the spot."

Harry obeyed, while she watched the muscles rippling in his thighs. She kept him going for several minutes, until his cheeks were flushed and his breathing heavy.

At last she said, "Stop." She opened her valise, took out a stethoscope, and listened at his chest.

"I never knew you were a doctor," he said.

"I'm not. But I was a nurse before I joined up. You look, and sound, okay, Harry. Get dressed."

"Seems a shame to waste a nice afternoon."

"We'd freeze, and I have other calls to make." She handed him an envelope. "Travel documents. You'll report to Colonel Lightman at that address at zero eight zero zero tomorrow morning. Please be on time."

"You mean I don't get to travel with you?"

"I don't think that would be a good idea," she said.

"So it's goodbye again," Alison said, holding Harry close.

"Just for a couple of weeks."

"And you've no idea where you're going?" John Curtis asked.

"Haven't a clue."

"Harry," Alison said. "That woman . . . the captain . . ."

"We're just good friends," Harry assured her.

Actually, he was relieved to be travelling alone. He needed to think. About so many aspects of the situation.

As Belinda had pointed out, it was both senseless and childish to feel resentment against Dick Lightman. Lightman was a bold, vigorous man with a pronounced libido. Harry had always used him as a role model as to what a successful

198

Commando officer should be like. He had also made it
perfectly clear from the very beginning that he regarded
Veronica Sturmer as little better than a whore. Nor could
he possibly have the slightest idea that Harry might be in
love with her. No doubt he assumed they had slept together,
but with nothing more than a physical relationship in mind.
If she had made herself available to him, it would have been
completely out of character for the colonel not to take up the
opportunity.

It was the woman who was distressing, on every possible
count. Again, he told himself, she had never actually said
yes to his proposal of marriage. He had presumed that had
been because she wanted to see how the war would go, how
her father would be treated, whether she would be accepted
by the British establishment. Now he had to wonder if she
had put him off simply while she ascertained if there was
nothing better. Yet, knowing Lightman, the colonel would
certainly have left her in no doubt that he was not going to
leave his wife and family for her. And when, having been
given two days embarkation leave, she had chosen to spend
them with him rather than with her father, he had supposed
she had made up her mind.

But she had obviously had more than two days leave. Just
as he had deceived his parents back in December of 1940.
Talk about being hoisted on his own petard! And after leaving
Frenthorpe, Veronica had hurried away, again not to see her
father, but to call on Lightman, at his office. Was she so
much in love with the man? Or, reversing the coin, had she
been so disappointed in *his* performance?

So where did that leave him? He was about to go into
battle again, presumably under Lightman. There was no
leader he would rather have. But did he still want to marry
Veronica?

"Harry!" Lightman shook hands. "Glad to have you back.
Forester says you're fit for duty."

"Yes, sir." Harry could not prevent himself from looking

at the large table on the far side of the room, covered by a sheet.

"Our target," Lightman said, coming round the desk to raise the sheet and pull it away. On the table there had been constructed a model of a French town and harbour, but it was more than a harbour, it was an estuary, through which a broad river turned to the south, between two lines of sandbanks, before exiting into the sea. The port was on the north back, before the turn, and was a place of some size, containing several large docks. "Any idea where that is?"

Harry stood beside him, studied the shape of the coast to either side of the river entrance, the direction of the river itself. "St Nazaire."

Lightman raised his eyebrows. "Very good. You weren't supposed to be able to recognise it that readily. Hm. But that's our target, all right."

"With what in mind, sir? Is this the invasion?"

"Good God, no. We don't have the men for that yet. No, this is strictly a raid. But one with a very definite purpose." He indicated the docks. "That is the largest dry dock in Europe. It is, in fact, the only dry dock on the Atlantic coast which can take a ship as big as *Tirpitz*."

"Is she coming out, sir?"

"We think so. She is certainly completed, and the Navy think she is likely to repeat the *Bismarck* manoeuvre of last year. You'll remember what a near thing that was. But the point is, we did manage to damage her quite severely. She was attempting to get into Brest for repairs when we finally caught up with her. But even if she had escaped and made Brest, while it would have been very good publicity for the Germans, there are insufficient facilities in Brest to effect a proper repair on a ship that big, certainly as regards underwater damage. So she would probably have been marooned there for the rest of the war. Now we must assume that the Nazis have learned from that episode. Our agents in occupied France have informed us that there has been a good deal of work on the dry dock in St Nazaire, and it seems plain that the plan is to have *Tirpitz* break out, disrupt our convoys, and then use St Nazaire as a base for any repairs that may become necessary. I need hardly remind you that with America now in the war, the Yanks will be ferrying more and more material, and indeed, men, across the Atlantic, to build up our forces for the invasion. Loose a ship like *Tirpitz* on that lot, and there could be very serious consequences. The whole invasion could be put back a year or so. So our business is to go in and destroy that dry dock. Simple as that. Incidentally, St Nazaire is being developed as a major U-boat base. We'll take those out at the same time."

"Yes, sir," Harry said. Our agents in Occupied France, he thought. One of whom has shared both of our beds. "It won't be quite the same thing as shooting up a few barges in Calais, though, will it? Blowing up a dry dock requires serious explosives."

Lightman tapped his nose. "We have some ideas."

"And getting there won't be quite so easy, either. That's a long way, through enemy-controlled waters."

"Four hundred miles," Lightman said. "But we have some ideas on that too. This is a high risk operation, Harry. But then, everything we do is a high risk operation. I'm looking for volunteers."

"Of course I volunteer, sir."

"I never doubted it for a moment. You'll command C Company. As I said, this is strictly a raid, and at a long distance, so we're only using as many men as will be absolutely necessary. Just three companies. With Naval support, of course. You'll use one of the south coast fishing ports, in your case Lyme Regis, for training. It's a matter of approaching the shore in motor launches, disembarking your men, and getting them into the town as rapidly as possible. Speed and hitting power. You'll also have a model like this one available, to pinpoint your objectives. Understood?"

"Yes, sir. Are you going to lead us, sir? As it is such a small force?"

"Sadly, no. I wish I were. Your CO will be Colonel Newman. One of the very best. Oh, by the way, you'll find some old friends in C Company. Good luck. I'll be down to see how you're getting on in a couple of weeks."

"And the day, sir?"

"You'll be informed. But it's pretty close. You'll train each day as if it could be tomorrow. One day you'll be right. And please remember, the info about our target is top secret."

Eleven

Belinda was in the outer office, waiting with the usual envelope of passes and travel vouchers.

"I may come down to see how you're getting on as well," she suggested. "Would you like that?"

"I think I might. Tell me something, Belinda, how long has the old man had that model in his room?"

"Oh, several weeks now. This thing has taken a lot of planning."

"So it would have been there when Veronica visited him."

"I suppose it was."

"Covered by that sheet?"

"I really have no idea. But surely it wouldn't have mattered whether it was or not? There is no way anyone could have recognised it."

"I did," Harry pointed out.

Now why had he said that? he wondered. It had left Belinda frowning. He wondered if she would tell Lightman?

But Veronica was on their side, risking her life to help the Allied cause. The problem was, he had supposed she was on *his* side, giving her all to him and only him. The fact was, childish or not, he was damnably jealous. And angry as well. Yet he still wanted to possess her, desperately.

It was a pleasure to get back to the men with whom he had served previously. There were quite a few recruits, but sufficient familiar faces as well.

"Sergeant-Major!" He shook hands with Johnson.

"Welcome back, sir. All fit?"

"I think so. Sergeant Green!"

"Good to see you, sir." Green had been promoted.

"And going places," Harbord said enthusiastically, eyeing the third pip on Harry's shoulder. "I'm your number one."

"Glad to have you along."

"Any idea where we're heading?"

"None at all," Harry lied glibly.

He had them hard at work the next morning. They boarded their motor launches in the little harbour, were taken out to sea for half-a-mile, before turning back for the assault. It was still bitterly cold, and the sea was more often than not fairly rough, but gradually the Commandos overcame their sea-sickness, which Harry considered very important as they were undertaking another lengthy sea journey.

The launches would roar at the beaches, stopping in the shallow surf, keels bumping on the sand, while the Commandos leapt out and splashed ashore.

"I'm going to get chilblains for sure," Harbord complained.

The junior lieutenant, Avery, did get chilblains, but refused to report sick.

Afternoons were spent studying the model of the town and the docks, making up and checking timetables for moving from the waterfront to their appointed target, in the case of C Company this was the submarine pens. Gradually the confidence of professional expertise built up.

Then they practised re-embarking under fire from the shore, while the inhabitants of the little port stood on their esplanade and watched in amused wonder at the military antics.

Lightman duly came down after a fortnight, accompanied by Belinda, to watch C Company being put through its paces.

"They look pretty good," he remarked. "Transport will be here tomorrow morning, and you will be taken to the port of embarkation."

"Which is?"

"You'll find out when you get there."

The concentration on secrecy was vaguely disturbing, yet at the same time reassuring; if they didn't know from where they were leaving, how could the Germans?

"I suppose *you* know where it is," Harry murmured to Belinda, having manoeuvered to stand beside her.

"Of course."

"Will you be there to see us off?"

"Of course," she said again. "I only wish I was coming with you."

They assembled in Falmouth, some three hundred Commandos. Waiting for them was a flotilla of destroyers. Harry had hoped that amongst the ships' officers might be his old friend Bingham, but he was not to be seen. However, both Tate and Ebury were amongst the other officers, greeting Harry with considerable affection.

Colonel Newman addressed them.

"You know our objective," he said. "And what we have to do there. Now I must tell you how it is going to be done. We shall leave here at dawn tomorrow morning, laying a course south-west into the Atlantic. This is hopefully to avoid discovery by any enemy aircraft or submarines, and equally, if we *are* spotted, to make sure he does not realise where we are going. Tomorrow night we shall start to close the shore. And by the next night we shall be in position south-west of Belleisle. At this point you will be discharged from your destroyers into your motor launches, and you will make for the shore. The destroyers will return to sea, and hope to pick us up again when we leave.

"We will be led in the assault by one ship, *HMS Campbelltown*, Commander Beattie. She is, as they say, expendable. Her business will be to ram the dock gates and lay down sufficient high explosive to destroy them beyond repair. I am sure you understand that this will be an act requiring courage and determination of the highest order, and will need to be so supported.

"Our rendezvous at the mouth of the Loire will be with the submarine *Sturgeon*, which is already in position and waiting

205

for us. The assault is timed for zero one-thirty, and will be preceded by an air attack.

"Once ashore, you will carry out your various demolition duties as quickly and efficiently as possible, and then regain your motor launches and return to your parent vessels. We will, of course, have the crew of *Campbelltown* with us.

"Now, this whole exercise may appear hazardous in the extreme, and make no mistake about it, it is. However, remember always the positive factors which are in our favour. Firstly, you are probably the most highly trained body of fighting men in the world, and the best equipped. Each of you knows what he has to do and how to do it. Secondly, we will be faced with the reverse of that coin. St Nazaire is garrisoned by second-line troops. There are no panzers in the vicinity, no Waffen SS units on which they can call. There will be some submarines in the pens, and we understand there are a few old destroyers situated in the port itself, but these too are manned by reservists. We shall go in, hit them very hard, and get out again, before they realise what's happening. Third is a corollary of that, and is our greatest asset: surprise. They have no idea what we are planning, and where we are going. St Nazaire is rather a long way away. It will never occur to the Nazis that we would attack it.

"Of course, it goes without saying that if we are spotted at sea, the mission will have to be aborted. However, we have reasonable hopes that this will be avoided. The weather forecast for the next week is for low cloud and rain. That is why the mission has been brought forward. I'm afraid this forecast also indicates strong winds and rough seas, but I am sure you can put up with this, knowing that the chances of our detection are thereby substantially reduced. Now, the Supreme Commander, Combined Operations, wishes to have a word. Gentlemen, Rear-Admiral Lord Louis Mountbatten."

The assembled force stood to attention as the tall, spare

figure in the naval uniform took Colonel Newman's place on the podium. "At ease," he said.

This was the first time Harry had seen Lord Louis: his appointment to the command of Combined Operations was a very recent one. But he knew the royal cousin had had a distinguished career with the Royal Navy, concluding with the sinking of the destroyer he had been commanding, *Kelly*, by air attack during the evacuation of Crete. He was certainly not an armchair admiral.

Now Harry studied the strong, aquiline features as Mountbatten addressed them in clipped tones.

"Colonel Newman has rightfully pointed out that we have a great deal going for us in this operation," he said. "However, I wish no man to be under any misapprehension that this *is* a hazardous project. We must expect casualties, and these may be heavy. But you are undertaking a duty which we believe is of the greatest importance to the Allied cause, and indeed, to our eventual victory. We must deny the enemy the use of bases from which he might hope to control the Atlantic, or certainly seriously disrupt our traffic on the ocean at a time when the build-up of American men and material is vital to the establishment of a situation where the invasion of Europe can become a practical proposition. The destruction of the docks and U-boat pens at St Nazaire is absolutely esential to this build-up. No matter what happens, no matter what casualties are incurred, if those docks and U-boat pens are destroyed, your mission will have been an unqualified success, and you will deserve, and receive, the grateful thanks not only of this nation, but of the whole free world. Thank you, and good luck."

"Stirring stuff," Belinda said, as they gathered in the bar for a farewell drink. All the officers had by then been introduced to the admiral, and the spirit was very gung-ho.

"One can imagine Alexander the Great saying something like that to his Companions before the Battle of Arbela," Harry agreed.

"He had more at stake. But . . . how do you feel?"

Harry shrugged. "Same as always before going into action. Suspended."

She nodded. "I can understand that. I'd take it very kindly if you came back."

He raised his eyebrows.

"I mean it," she said. "I don't know why, but you've become quite my favourite man."

"On the strength of one weekend?"

"You are a male chauvinist pig, Captain Curtis. Women don't rate relationships on the basis of sex. Most women, anyway. Would you believe that I just happen to like you? So you consider yourself bespoke. That's my bad luck."

Harry was embarrassed. He was genuinely fond of this woman. But as she had said, he was bespoke . . . and for the second time in his life wondering if he was following the right course.

"You know," Belinda said. "I have been given a room all to myself, for tonight. Interested?"

"What about His Nibs?"

"He's living it up with the brass."

"Ah. I'm more than interested, Belinda. But I'm leading my men into battle, tomorrow, however long it may take us actually to get there. I think my place is with them."

"Duty," she said. "Always duty. You'll go far, Harry Curtis, if you don't get your stupid head blown off. Well, then presuming that when you come back your lady friend will also have completed her tour of duty, this could be goodbye . . . save for perhaps the occasional distant wave."

"Shit!" he muttered. "Belinda . . ."

"We don't want to start weeping all over each other in public," she said. "Come outside."

They stepped into the cold night air, and were in each other's arms. Her kisses were desperate, searching . . . as were her hands. But then, so were his. He roamed over her back, massaged her bottom, caressed her breasts, unbuttoned her uniform jacket to get inside.

208

"Just remember," she said. "Supposing you do come back, that I'm always here."

"At least we're heading south," Harbord remarked as he and Harry and Avery walked the quarterdeck of their destroyer. "No brass monkeys this time."

As it was still late March, the dusk was early, and was already shrouding the sea. Which Harry thought was all to the good, as the blacked out flotilla of destroyers faded into the gloom, denoted only by their wakes and the bones in their teeth. They had left Falmouth at dawn, and thus far had had a totally uneventful voyage, although the five ships, accompanied by an MTB, must be making a big target from the sky.

"Did you go up to Lofoten the second time?" he asked.

"Oh, yes," Harbord said. "Piece of cake. Managed to avoid getting hit, that time. But no beautiful women. I suppose they were all moved out."

"There was only one," Harry said.

"Will this be a piece of cake, sir?" Avery asked. He had not seen action before.

"Somehow I don't think so," Harry said.

Avery was distinctly nervous. Harry felt sorry for him, because in addition to apprehension the seas were quite lumpy, and the lieutenant had to leave the table halfway through dinner.

"You think he'll be all right?" Harbord asked.

"I expect so. We must keep him busy, tomorrow."

By dawn they were south of Ushant, some distance away to the east. The clouds remained low, cutting aerial visibility, but the wind had dropped, and the seas had gone down.

"Couldn't be better," Lieutenant-Commander Moore said. "We'll be in and out before they know what's hit them."

Avery emerged, pale-faced but determined, and Harry had both the boy and Harbord accompany him below decks to inspect the Commandos. They made sure all the fighting gear was in order – they were carrying Bren guns as well as the tommies – and, far more important, had a chat with each man.

Several had been sick during the night, and some of these still looked peaky, but morale was high, and became higher yet as the officers sat with them and discussed the coming assault.

"They're a good bunch, sir," Sergeant-Major Johnson said. "They'll do you proud."

Because he was the man with the reputation, the man to whom they all looked for leadership. Harry still found that surprising. In many ways he still felt like a schoolboy, about to go out to bat. He still found it unreal that he should have crammed so much into the past three years. And this time? In and out before the enemy knew what had hit them, the captain said.

It had worked before.

During the day the wind continued to drop, and so did the sea, and by that evening it was dead calm. Everyone cheered up. They had come so far without being spotted. It seemed all was going according to plan.

"Well, gentlemen," Lieutenant-Commander Moore said at dinner. "I will give you a toast: the Commandos."

His officers rose, glasses held high. Although drinks were always available in the wardroom, officers generally did not indulge when at sea, but tonight was an exception, for a single glass of wine.

Harry responded. "The Navy!"

Then it was time to move.

Harry stood beside Moore on the bridge, peering into the darkness. On the quarterdeck, his men were being assembled by the two lieutenants and Sergeant-Major Johnson. He assumed the same was happening on the other carrier destroyers. Out in front, *Campbelltown* continued on her way, for her date with destiny.

"There!" Moore said.

The eastern horizon was entirely dark, but now Harry saw a pinpoint of light, glowing and then fading, before glowing again.

"That's *Sturgeon*," Moore said. "She's been on station for the past couple of days, marking the position. Well, old man, if you'd like to stand by."

They shook hands, and Harry slid down the ladders to go aft and join the company.

The destroyers were reducing speed, and soon afterwards they could make out the dark shape of the submarine, resting on the surface. Beyond her, to the east, all remained dark.

"Launch," Moore said from the bridge, and the four motor boats were swung over the side. The Commandos immediately commenced boarding. Harry remained on deck to the last, making sure everyone got down safely, and with his equipment. He was commanding the lead launch, Harbord, Avery and the sergeant-major the other three. Each boat was manned by a crew of three, under a petty officer; Harry's, as it was the immediate headquarters, was commanded by a sub-lieutenant, a boy even younger than Harry himself, named Clark.

Now, the engines no more than a low grumble, they heard the roar of aircraft above their heads. As usual, the RAF were spot on time. Before Harry had himself embarked, the invisible eastern horizon was suddenly illuminated by explosions, and punctuations of light as the German anti-aircraft batteries opened up.

"Cast off," Sub-Lieutenant Clark commanded, and the launches were pushed away from the sides of the ship.

The submarine was flashing her light again.

"She's saying good luck and goodbye, sir," Clark told Harry, standing beside him at the wheel of the launch.

The submarine glided into the darkness and disappeared.

The launches took up their positions in two lines abeam, behind *Campbelltown*, all moving slowly, Harry discovering that his company was in the lead, while the MTB, containing both Colonel Newman and the flotilla captain, Commander Ryder, moved up and down the rows, checking each boat in turn, wishing them all good luck and God speed, before taking up its position, in front of the launches and immediately behind the destroyer.

Harry looked over his shoulder, saw the destroyers, like the submarine, fading into the darkness. The difference was that they would, hopefully, be there in the morning to take them off.

Now *Campbelltown* increased speed, and the launches did likewise. The bombers continued to range over the port, which was now clearly marked by the fires and the ack-ack guns. The shore to the south, however, remained in darkness.

"They don't have a clue we're here," Clark muttered.

Harry could only hope he was right, and that the officers on board the destroyer knew where they were going; he had no idea where they were.

A light winked in front of them, on the destroyer's stern, he estimated.

"Reduce speed," Clark said, and did so. "We must be nearly there."

"Look there, sir," said Sergeant Green, standing immediately behind Harry.

Harry looked to their right, and saw a line of white. There was another on their left hand now as well, some distance away.

"Surf," Clark said. "We're in the river."

And still they were travelling in total darkness, total concealment.

"Piece of cake," Green muttered. "Piece of cake."

"Let's hope we're not early," Clark said, for the RAF was continuing to swoop and strafe and drop bombs.

Harry looked at his watch; it was just after one, and they were supposed to be at the docks at half-past.

The river was narrowing now, and even in the darkness they could make out the banks to either side; speed was reduced further. Harry, peering ahead, thought he saw the destroyer shudder and almost come to a halt. Jesus, he thought, if she runs aground . . . but a moment later she forged ahead again. The tide was falling, and she wasn't going to get back out, but then, she had never been intended to get back out.

Now the bombing stopped. The aircraft disappeared as suddenly as they had come. Fires continued to burn, and one or two of the ack-ack guns continued to fire. Harry wondered if any of the planes had been shot down.

Now, total darkness . . . and then, without warning, total light. The searchlights were mounted in groups on either bank,

212

and they lit up the entire little flotilla, moving from launch to launch, but concentrating on *Campbelltown*, illuminating her so completely that Harry could make out the figure of Commander Beattie, standing on the bridge.

"Shit!" Green muttered.

"They *did* know we were coming," Clark said.

For a moment Harry's brain seemed to have gone dead with the enormity of it, the knowledge that they had sailed, voluntarily, into a trap.

Then the guns opened up. The shooting was a little wild for the first few moments, then it was awesome in its accuracy as both heavy guns and machine-guns raked the flotilla from each bank. Harry stared in horror at the destroyer, into which shell after shell was smashing; she was loaded with high explosive and could go up at any moment. But she didn't, was heading straight for the now visible dock gates, White Ensign streaming in the night air.

It was time to be concerned closer to home. The shells were landing all over the river, sending up huge plumes of white water, causing the launches to roll and buck. None had actually been hit, so far as he could see. The machine-guns were far more dangerous, their bullets slicing through the thin hulls of the motorboats. He heard shout and groans from his men, crouching below him.

He could do nothing for them at that moment, as they followed the destroyer. *Campbelltown* had increased speed. And now she smashed into the lock gates at virtually full velocity. Harry had been told that the gates were thirty-five feet thick. The destroyer went into them so hard that before she came to a halt her bows were level with the inner panels.

All this while she had been raked by the German fire. She was carrying a sizeable contingent of Commandos herself, and these were lying on her decks, firing their Bren guns into the darkness. Now they had to evacuate the vessel as rapidly as possible, still being cut to pieces by the enemy guns.

Harry looked at his watch. The time was zero one three three, which was three minutes after schedule, but he didn't suppose that was too bad in the circumstances.

It seemed an interminable time after *Campbelltown* had struck before the launches reached the dock, but it could not have been more than a few minutes. In that time he saw the last of the men still alive get off the destroyer, and from the explosions and firing knew they were fulfilling their secondary duties of blowing up the pumping station and the machinery operating the gates, while at the same time the coastal battery mounted on the dock, which had been firing into the destroyer at almost point blank range, fell silent. Then there were a couple of short, sharp detonations as the scuttling charges were set off, and *Campbelltown* began to sink, still in the dock entrance.

She had not yet completed her part in the operation though, Harry knew cemented into her hull were a further five tons of high explosive, on a time fuse, to go off in a few hours

It was time for the second wave. The MTB surged ahead and loosed its torpedoes against the gates to the U-boat pens. The launches raced behind her to get their men ashore, but now they were fully exposed to the firing, which had turned from the destroyer to these lesser objectives. One launch took a direct hit, and disintegrated. Harry saw men tossed this way and that, some jumping into the river. But now there was a new hazard, as petrol from the launches' fuel tanks spread across the water, and to the general cacophony was added the screams of burning men.

"Nearly there," Lieutenant Clark said, as calmly as ever.

But even as he spoke, the launch gave a great shudder, and burst into flames.

"Abandon ship," the lieutenant said. "Quickly now."

"Into that?" Green watched the flames spreading across the water with horror.

"It's only a few feet to the shore," Clark told him.

"Over you go, lads," Harry told his men as they moved to the gunwale, causing the launch to roll dangerously – but the whole bow section was now in flames.

"Show them how, Sergeant," Harry called.

214

Green took a deep breath and leapt over the side, tommy-gun held high. He went down, but came up immediately. "I can stand."

Then he gave a gulp and turned round, to sink again as machine-gun bullets sliced into him.

"Ashore." Harry bawled. "Make the shore."

The men obeyed him, trying to ignore the firing. Harry slid down the short ladder into the hull. There were several dead men, and six wounded. "Can you move?" Harry asked.

There were only groans and stricken eyes.

"You have to get out," Harry shouted. "Or you'll burn alive."

Or choke, he realised, as they were surrounded by swirling smoke.

Clark and the naval ratings joined him, and they began pulling the wounded men out.

"They'll probably drown anyway," Clark panted.

"They'll have a chance," Harry said, heaving his man to the gunwale. "Look, there's the land."

As he spoke there was a *wumpff*, and the launch exploded.

For a moment Harry lost consciousness. He recovered as his head dipped beneath the water, and when he came up discovered that, like the sergeant, he could stand. He had lost the man he had been carrying, as well as his tin hat, and he didn't know what else besides – but he was still wearing his belts, and amazingly both his haversack and his tommy-gun were still slung round his neck. All around him there was pandemonium, boats exploding, guns firing, men shouting and screaming and drowning. What had happened to the other boats in his company he did not know, and Clark and the naval ratings had disappeared.

The water was burning only a few feet away from him. He floundered to the shore, knowing he owed his life to the fact that the Germans, perhaps as awe-struck as anyone by the total destruction of the flotilla, were no longer shooting at the water. He reached the concrete emplacements of the dockside, and was dragged clear by Avery.

"Shit," the lieutenant kept saying. "Oh, shit!"

Again Harry looked around for Lieutenant Clark and his crew, but could not see them. Gallant men, he thought. But there were quite a few men ashore, bedraggled and probably traumatised – but most still had their weapons. He crawled up the sloping embankment to join them, realising that his battledress was torn to ribbons, held in place only by the webbing of his equipment. They lay on their stomachs, pinned down by the hail of fire above their heads.

"Anyone seen Lieutenant Harbord or his people? Sergeant-Major Johnson?" he asked.

They merely stared at him.

"Right," he said. He had a mental picture of where they were and what they were to do, born of many hours studying the maps they had been given as well as the model, and he intended to carry out his orders, no matter that the thought of their betrayal as well as the physical effects of being blown up had him feeling physically sick – his various aches and pains were irrelevant. "Our target is to the left. That means getting up this slope on to the dock and running like hell. The wounded will have to lie where they fall, we'll pick them up later. On a count of three." He drew a deep breath. "One, two, three!"

He leapt to his feet, unslinging his tommy-gun as he did so, only then wondering if it would fire after its immersion in the river. But it chattered reassuringly as he gained the top of the slope and squeezed the trigger. His men scrambled behind him, and to his right he heard a cheer and saw Harbord's people also emerging over the top of the embankment, some fifty yards away. Behind him was Sergeant-Major Johnson and his section.

Harry waved his hand. "Take the pens," he shouted, and himself ran at the control hut for the gates, expecting at any moment to be cut down. But there was no defensive fire, and to his amazement he saw several men leave the hut and run desperately for the shelter of the pens themselves.

"They're running away!" Avery shouted.

Harry reached the station, threw the door open, hurled

himself inside. There was one man remaining, sitting on the floor and pawing at his bleeding head. "Do not shoot," he begged in English. "*Kamerad*! You are the invasion, no?"

"Whatever turns you on," Harry told him, and reached into his haversack for his grenades. "Get out."

The German crawled to the door, was seized by the collar and jerked outside by the waiting Commandos. Harry pulled the pins on two of the grenades, rolled them beneath the machinery, and got outside himself, just before the building was rocked by the explosions. Then he waved his men forward to support the attack on the pens. Several of these contained U-boats, but there were only skeleton crews and a few guards, and these were already in a state of panic. Those that did not flee or dive below went down in a hail of bullets while grenades began exploding.

Harbord panted up to him. "No opposition."

"Set the charges to blow these up," Harry told him. "Who's that?"

Another man was looming out of the darkness. "Sergeant Cray, sir. Orders from Colonel Newman. Mission accomplished. Blow the pens then withdraw to the boats and get to sea."

"Very good," Harry said. "Let's get to it."

They laid their charges, concentrating as best they could while all around them the night was exploding into noise and violence, as the guns on the river bank continued to fire. Harry didn't suppose Jonathan Ebury, who he knew was somewhere in this attack force, would think much of their efforts, but they got the explosives into place, and fell back towards the dock, Avery and a corporal paying out the wire. Harry pressed the plunger, and the front of the pens collapsed in a huge roar. The U-boats inside would be there for a few weeks to come, he estimated.

He led his men back to the dock, and stared at a scene of utter catastrophe. It was still some hours from dawn, yet the river was bright as day from the burning boats and oil. All the launches which had actually got into the estuary before the firing had begun had been sunk. Those men who had survived had drifted downstream on life rafts and were calling for help, Harry even thought he heard someone singing. The shore batteries and machine-guns continued to blaze away at anything that moved in or on the water. Upstream, the small German destroyers had managed to get out of the main port to join in the fight, and one of these was also on fire, but she must have been hit by her own people, Harry deduced.

"Shit!" Avery muttered.

"What now?" Harbord asked. "Looks like we've bought it. There's no way out."

"So we stay ashore and fight," Harry said, his brain a cloud of raging fury that such a disaster could have overtaken them.

"Captain Curtis!" It was Colonel Newman himself, emerging from the gloom with what remained of his staff.

Harry stood to attention. "Sir!"

"We can't stay here. The Germans will bring up reinforcements. Take your men through the town and fight your way out the other side. Then go to ground in the country. This is a prominent French resistance area. Hopefully they will find you and assist you."

"Yes, sir," Harry said. "And you?"

"I'll be doing the same thing, but I reckon we have more chance of making it in small groups. Good luck and God speed," Newman said, and shook hands. Then he hurried off to rejoin his command.

"Just like that," Harbord remarked.

"It's a chance. Muster."

He commanded sixty men. Quite a few of them had burns or minor injuries, but they were still capable of fighting. There were also half-a-dozen seriously wounded. These his medics patched up as best they could, but they understood they would have to be left behind.

"Remember," Harry told them. "No heroics. When the Germans come along, just surrender."

Their weaponry wasn't so good. They had lost most of their Brens and used most of their grenades. Harry looked at his watch. It was just coming up to three. "We have to be out of here by dawn," he told his men, knelt, and opened his town plan on the ground. His waterproof flashlight had shattered, but Harbord's was still working. The plan was thoroughly soaked and splodgy, but he could still make out, firstly where they were, and then where the houses ended. "Along this street," he said. "And then that one. On the double, but stay together."

He led them away from the docks. For the moment they were not under fire, although the noise remained tremendous, burning buildings, as a result of the air raid, collapsing with huge crashes, sirens wailing, people shouting and screaming. And the guns on the river still crashing away, although surely they had run out of targets by now.

"Do you think any of our people got out by sea, sir?" Avery asked.

"Not if they got in," Harry said. "But I've an idea not all of the launches actually did that."

He stood at the head of a street in which several houses were burning. A fire engine was at the far end, and men were pumping water at the blaze. There was quite a crowd of civilians standing round them, women and children as well as men, mostly in their nightclothes. Damn, he thought. He hadn't come here to kill civilians. Especially French civilians.

"To the left," Harbord suggested.

Halfway down the street there was a turning.

"They'll know we're here," Avery said.

"I think they already do," Harry said, as heads turned in their direction. "Only return fire. Go, go, go."

He led his men down the street, trotting rather than running, as he suspected they still had a long way to go. People began shouting, but there were no soldiers to open fire, and the Commandos reached the corner without opposition. They turned to the left, found themselves in an undamaged street, so far as could be seen in the darkness.

The noise behind them was increasing, and now they could hear the sound of engines.

"On the double," Harry said.

Their boots clattered on the cobbles as they ran down the street to the next corner. Harry hesitated, uncertain of which direction to take.

"Tanks," Sergeant-Major Johnson said.

They could hear the clatter of the tracks.

"Shit!" Avery said. "Oh, shit!"

"We'll have to take cover," Harry said. To be caught in the open by even one tank would mean their total destruction. He pointed. "Those houses."

He led the way, running up the steps of the first house, while Avery and Harbord and the sergeant-major directed their squads to the next three. The front door of Harry's choice was predictably locked, and was solidly made; thrusting a shoulder against it had no effect whatsoever.

A voice shouted in French. As it was a broad Gascon accent Harry could not understand what he was saying, but presumably the man was asking what they wanted, or telling them to go away. To his surprise, it came from above them, where a window had been thrown up; he would have expected all the inhabitants to be in the cellars.

"*Ouvrir*," he shouted, which was all he could think of on the spur of the moment. "*Nous sommes soldats Anglais.*"

The man muttered something, but the window closed. Next door Avery was also having a difficult time gaining access, but his French was better than Harry's.

The door opened. "British soldiers?" the man asked, in English. "Then it is the invasion?" He sounded delighted.

"I'm afraid not," Harry said. "We need to shelter for a few minutes."

"Shelter? Here? It is not the invasion?" The delight disappeared from his voice. "You come here, you blow up our town, you kill our people, and now you wish us to shelter you?"

"We're all on the same side," Harry reminded him. "Listen, we're coming in. It would be nice if you invited us."

The man hesitated, then stepped back. As he did so, the first tank came round the corner, immediately followed by another.

The huge vehicle stopped for a moment, surveying the street, its commander trying to see in the gloom.

He could at least make out there were quite a few people in front of him. "Halt there!" he bellowed in French.

One of the Commandos fired at him.

"Christ almighty!" gasped Corporal Bellew, next to Harry.

"Inside." Harry gestured them into the narrow hallway, but only half were through before the tank fired. The shell struck the building next door, high up, sending a cascade of slates and plaster down into the street. Not all of Avery's men had got inside either, and several were hit by the falling debris.

"*Mon Dieu!*" Harry's host gasped. "They will destroy my house."

"I'm sorry," Harry said, feeling genuine concern. He had brought calamity on this essentially innocent household. But if it had not been them it would have had to be someone else; he could not allow his command to be massacred. The last of his men was inside, and just in time, as a second shell exploded, it seemed immediately above their heads. Harry fell in the doorway and crawled to safety, while the Frenchman closed and bolted the door, as if he supposed it could keep out a shell.

"Take the front rooms," Harry commanded. "But hold your fire. We can't hurt those tanks, and we don't want them to know how many of us there are."

How many were there, he wondered? About a dozen with him and similar numbers in the other houses. And they were utterly pinned down, at least in front.

He found himself in the midst of a great deal of shouting, as two women of indeterminate ages, both in their dressing gowns and wearing mob caps, emerged from the cellar. He did not think they were saying anything complimentary.

Their husband was apologetic, having decided to make the best of a bad job. "It is war," he said. "Women do not understand about these things."

"Well, tell them to get back in the cellar and maybe they won't get killed," Harry suggested.

The tanks were firing regularly now. The noise, both of the explosions and of collapsing masonry, was tremendous. Then suddenly it stopped. Harry knelt in a window, looked out at the street, which was filling with German soldiers, and smelt burning. If they didn't get out now, they never would.

"What is out the back?" he asked the Frenchman.

"My garden, monsieur."

"And then?"

The Frenchman shrugged. "More gardens. More houses."

"And then another street."

"But of course, monsieur."

"Well, listen, you get down in the cellar with your women. Get as far away from the front of the house as you can. When the Germans come in, tell them that I and my men forced our way in here against your wishes. Understand?"

The Frenchman nodded. "You will fight them?"

"Briefly. It's our job, monsieur."

"Then I would like to shake your hand." He did so, and hurried for the cellar steps.

"Now, then," Harry told his men. "We must do what damage we can, and then withdraw. I want someone to get out the back and carry a message to the other commanders."

One of the privates stepped forward. "Sir!"

"Tell Lieutenants Avery and Harbord, and the sergeant-major, that we must attempt to withdraw from the back of these houses and see if we can find our way out of town. There is still a chance we can make it." He checked his watch: a quarter to four. "Tell them we pull out at zero four zero zero. We assemble in this back yard, and proceed through the houses behind. It is essential that we stick together."

"Yes, sir." The private hurried for the rear of the house.

"Now let's see what we can do to discourage those fellows," Harry told his men, and knelt at a window to peer out. The German force in the street was now nearly battalion strength, he estimated. They were emplacing machine-guns and were in any event backed up by the tanks, of which there were now six.

Now a loud hailer was brought into play. "You in there,"

shouted a voice in English. "There is no escape. Come out with your hands up."

"And you, sir?"

"I'll be along," Harry told him. "You, you and you, stay with me."

The four men crouched below the window sills. They had the Bren gun and their tommies.

The German officer waited a few more seconds. Then he shouted, "If you do not surrender, we will destroy you."

A moment later they listened to a barked command. Instantly the morning exploded in a manner reminiscent of their experience on the river a few hours previously. The tank cannon boomed, the machine-guns chattered, and the infantry poured volley after volley into the houses. Glass shattered, plaster came down, furniture was torn to ribbons. But the house was was made of good stone and cement, and the four Commandos remained unhurt.

The firing was maintained for several seconds, and then stopped.

"Our turn," Harry said, "and then run like hell."

The Bren was pushed into the broken window, and they commenced firing, using their tommy-guns as well. From the shouts and screams they had some success.

"Now," Harry said. "Out!"

Two of the men hefted the Bren, Harry and the other man ran beside them. They had not reached the back door when the firing recommenced, systematically destroying the house, which was now burning quite fiercely on its upper floors. Harry led his men across the back garden to a fence, beyond which the rest of his command was accumulating. To the noise of the firing behind them was added the shouts of people all around them, trying to discover what was going on. There was also more noise of engines in front of them, and Harry began to realise that they were thoroughly trapped.

"Where to?" Harbord panted.

Harry checked his compass. "Over there," he said, pointing to the north-east, determined to keep going as long as possible.

They made their way through several other back gardens, and down various lanes, and reached another street . . . to find it also occupied by tanks and soldiers.

Harry sighed. "Looks like we've had it. Remember, chaps, you're British soldiers. Sergeant-Major, we'll be separated. You understand?"

"Yes, sir."

"Very good. I don't know when we'll meet again, but it's been an honour to serve with you. All of you. Anyone got a white handkerchief?"

Twelve

"H a ha," said the German colonel. He was in a high good humour. "You come, but you see, we were waiting for you."

"You wouldn't care to tell us how?" Harry asked.

It was well into the morning now. As he had known would be the case, Harry, Harbord and Avery had been separated from their men, but they had not been ill-treated. Rather had they been brought to this relatively undamaged command centre, close to the docks, fed breakfast and good coffee, and were now, he presumed, awaiting transport to where they were to be taken. But at least there was no sign of any Gestapo or SS to make life unpleasant.

He hoped the transport came soon; it was getting uncomfortably close to ten o'clock, at which time the immense explosive in *Campbelltown's* bilges was due to go off.

"Ha ha," the colonel said again. "We know everything you do, Englander. This was a very brave, very desperate throw."

"We were sent to knock out your docks," Harry pointed out. "I think we did that."

"You think so? Bah. My engineers and divers are on board your destroyer now. We will get her out of there, if we have to take her apart rivet by rivet. We will have those gates working again in a week."

Harry looked at his watch. "With respect, Colonel, I wouldn't hold your breath."

The Colonel frowned at him, started to turn his head, and

225

was sent tumbling against the wall by the huge blast which swept through the town, every window in the command post dissolving into flying glass. Harry found himself lying on the floor, tasted blood. Avery and Harbord had also been thrown about, as had the other German officer in the room and the two guards.

"*Gott in Himmel!*" exclaimed the colonel, sitting up. "What was that?"

"Five tons of high explosive, sir," Harry explained. "Packed into the hull of the destroyer."

The colonel scrambled to his feet and ran to the door, which had been blown open by the blast, stared at the utter chaos in the outer office. The echo of the explosion was still reverberating, but that apart, the town had fallen absolutely quiet.

"A bit more than a week, I think," Harry suggested.

The colonel turned and glared at him. "That is mass murder. My people—"

"That is war, Herr Colonel," Harry said.

"You think you will get away with this? You are demons. We shall see." He stamped from the room while the guards, hitherto standing about somewhat nonchalantly before being knocked over by the blast, now stood against the walls with drawn pistols pointing at the officers.

"They seem a little upset," Harbord remarked.

Slowly noise returned, softly at first and then billowing into a huge gush of sound, sirens, car horns, shouts, screams.

"What happens now, sir?" Avery asked.

"We wait," Harry said.

More than an hour passed, and then several more men appeared; in their midst were two more British officers.

"Jon Ebury, by all that's great," Harry said.

The little man looked thoroughly battered. And like them his clothes were in rags. With him was Kevin Tate.

"Family reunion," Tate remarked.

"Did *anyone* get out?" Harbord asked.

"I don't think so," Tate said.

"Colonel Newman?"

Tate shook his head. "I think they got him too."

"Shit!" Avery muttered.

Several more men came in, and these Harry did not like
the look of at all. Two of them were in civilian clothes,
with black leather raincoats, belted at the waist, and slouch
hats. At the sight of them the guards instinctively stiff-
ened.

So the Gestapo hadn't been all that far away after all, he
thought.

The two detectives surveyed the five prisoners with expressions
of the utmost contempt. Then one said, "We have been told one
of you is an explosives expert. Who is this?" His English was
perfect.

There was a moment's silence.

"I asked a question," the detective said.

"And it's not one we are required to answer," Harry said.
"We are British officers, wearing uniform. You are entitled to
asks us our names, our ranks, and our numbers. These we will
give you. Nothing else."

The detective glared at him. "You think you can play games
with me, Englander?"

"I am reminding you of the laws of war," Harry said.
"Failure to observe them will involve you in very serious
consequences."

"Bah," said the detective. "The rules of war are made by the
people who win the war. We have our own rules. Now, the
explosives officer."

Harry would have defied him again, but Jonathan touched
him on the arm and shook his head.

"I am the explosives officer," he said.

"Ah! Very good. Your name?"

"Captain Jonathan Ebury."

"Your regiment?"

"I am not required to give you that."

"Ha! Another comedian. None of you is wearing any

regimental insignia. I am not sure that you can still be regarded as being in uniform. If you are not, you can be shot. Do you understand this?"

"I understand that you may well find yourself indicted as a war criminal," Jonathan said.

"Take him into the next room," the detective said.

Two of his men seized Jonathan's arms and marched him through the door.

"If you harm him—" Harry threatened.

"I will deal with you later," the detective said, and followed.

The British officers gazed at each other.

"Bastards," Harbord commented.

From the next room there came a grunt, followed by a half-stifled groan.

"Shit!" Avery shouted. He had been sitting on the floor. Now he suddenly leapt to his feet, in the same instant reaching into his tunic and drawing a service revolver.

"Jesus!" Tate gasped, and grabbed at him, but he was too late. One of the guards shot the boy in the chest. Avery was dead before he struck the floor in a welter of blood.

Harry knelt beside him, and the guard stooped and picked up the revolver, which had fallen from Avery's hand.

The colonel reappeared in the doorway. "That was very stupid," he commented.

"He was murdered," Harbord said.

"My men were entitled to defend themselves," the colonel said.

Harry's shoulders slumped. He knew the man was right.

"What are you doing to Captain Ebury?" he asked.

"I am sorry," the colonel said. "I have no jurisdiction over the Gestapo. And if there are other explosive charges planted by the docks . . ."

There came another groan from the next room.

"I am sorry," the colonel said again. "Please do not do anything else stupid, gentlemen." He turned to leave the room, and checked in surprise as three men entered. They wore black uniforms with high-peaked caps. The insignia was the Death's Head, they carried tommy-guns, as well as holstered pistols on their belts. In their midst, also wearing uniform, was Veronica.

Harry was utterly surprised. Yet it was undoubtedly Veronica, although her hair was pulled back into a tight bun beneath her sidecap, and her face was cold. Nor did it change expression as it looked over them.

She addressed the colonel in German, pointing at Avery's body and, again to Harry's surprise, his reply was both a protest and deferential.

Veronica nodded, unbuttoned her breast pocket, and took out a folded piece of paper. This she handed to the colonel, who studied it with obvious consternation. Then he made a remark.

Veronica shrugged, and turned to face Harry. "You will come with me," she said in English.

"But . . . come where?"

"To Nantes. General von Reitener wishes to speak with you."

"I will not come without my companions," Harry said. He did not know what game she was playing, whether or not she could be trusted – whatever it was, it was very deep. But she was going to play it his way.

"I give the orders here," she said.

"And Captain Ebury," Harry said. "He is currently being tortured by those thugs out there."

She gazed at him for several seconds, then gave another shrug. "Very well. Outside. All of you."

"And Lieutenant Avery?"

Veronica looked at the dead body. "We certainly cannot take him. He will be given a proper burial. Now haste."

Harry hesitated, looked at Harbord and Tate. Harbord of course had met Veronica in Calais, and was clearly as mystified by her appearance as was Harry. Tate had never met her. But she was their only hope.

"I think we'd better do as the lady says," he told them, and led

Alan Savage

them into the outer room. Here Ebury had been tied to a chair, but up till now the detectives had been doing nothing more than hit him. His face was bruised and one eye puffy, but he did not look badly hurt.

Veronica addressed the detectives in German. Like the colonel, they protested, more vehemently. Veronica walked to the desk, picked up the telephone, and held it out. Harry understood the word Reitener again. Whoever this general was, he obviously carried weight. Still protesting, the detectives released Ebury.

"Can you stand, Jon?" Harry asked.

"I can stand." Ebury got to his feet, uncertainly, and identified Veronica for the first time. "I don't understand."

"I think explanations will come later," Harry said.

"Outside," Veronica said. "Haste."

They were nudged by the tommy-guns of her escort, and went outside, where there waited an open command car.

"In the back," Veronica said. "It will be a tight squeeze."

The four officers got into the back, and two of the escort got in with them, sitting facing them on the back of the front seats. The third man got behind the wheel. Veronica sat beside him.

"Are we allowed to know what is going on?" Harry asked.

"When we are out of town," Veronica replied.

They had to drive slowly through the crowded streets, littered with rubble and bomb damage, as well as casualties. But everyone made way for the command car manned by three SS officers and flying the swastika on its bonnet.

"I don't suppose you'd have anything to drink?" Tate ventured.

Veronica opened the glove compartment and took out a bottle of water, which she passed back. All four of them were parched.

"Well," she said. "That was very easy, was it not, Henri?"

"Because it was the easy part," Henri pointed out. "When they telephone Nantes . . ."

"That cannot be until the lines have been repaired," Veronica reminded him. "We have several hours. That wood over there."

They had left the town and were on a country road. Above their heads planes were swooping low, and all around them they could hear the rumble of vehicles as more and more reinforcements were pumped into St Nazaire. But the lane remained empty, and a few minutes later they were in the shelter of the trees. The car stopped, the three Frenchmen, as Harry now understood they were, got out and began to undress, while they also opened the boot and took out their somewhat rough country garb.

"You must put these uniforms on," Veronica told the Englishman. "I know they will not fit very well, but no one is going to look very closely at you, and anyway, they are better than those rags you are wearing."

The officers also got out and began dividing up the clothing.

"There are four of us," Harry pointed out.

"You wanted to bring half the army," she pointed out. "But it may turn out for the best. Mr Ebury, you will remain as a British officer. You will be our prisoner, eh? Please behave like one. And do hurry, gentlemen."

The clothes were not a good fit, especially the boots. Harry couldn't get any on at all. What he did appreciate was the holster on his belt containing a loaded Luger pistol.

"You will be the driver," Veronica said. "So your feet will be out of sight."

"I'm afraid I don't drive," Harry said. "Well, I've had some lessons, but they got overtaken by the war."

"I drive," Tate said. "Where are we going?"

She spread a map on the grass beside the car. "We are here." She prodded the wood. "You see it is only fifty-odd kilometres to Nantes. We have to go to Nantes because that is the nearest bridge across the river. But we will get through without trouble. Nantes is in a state of great confusion, and I have the papers to prove that I am one of General von Reitener's secretaries."

"And are you, General von Reitener's secretary?"

She wrinkled her nose. "Of course."

"And what happens after Nantes?" Tate asked.

"Once we are across the river, we will drive east, in the

direction of Poitiers which is on the border with Vichy France. But before Poitiers there is a little town, Mirabeau. That is a local headquarters for what we call the Route, the way we get British airmen out of France and into Spain. Once we get there, you will be in good hands. They will get you across the border."

"And when will that be?"

"Oh, by this evening, certainly." She inspected them. "Right. Now please, leave everything to me. Just sit still and look very military. Mr Tate, you will drive. Mr Harbord, you will sit beside him. I will sit in the back, with you, Harry, and Mr Ebury will sit between us. We will keep your feet out of sight. Henri . . ." she shook hands with each of the Frenchman. "I will be in touch whenever I can." She inspected the Englishmen again, adjusting their caps and various belts, got into the car. "Now return to the main road, Mr Tate."

The Frenchmen melted into the trees, and Tate turned the car.

"Do not drive fast," Veronica said. "You are a soldier, carrying out a duty."

Tate nodded.

"Now would you care to tell us just how you managed this?" Harry asked. "Did you say you are, actually, this general's secretary?"

"Yes."

"How come? Or have you changed sides?"

"No, Harry, I have not changed sides. I have carried out the orders given me by Colonel Lightman, personally."

"You'll have to explain that."

"You know I was trained as an agent to operate in Occupied France. But with my background, I was too useful to be just an ordinary agent. Colonel Lightman interrogated me at great length . . ."

I can imagine, Harry thought.

". . . and found out all about my background. The Nazis, you see, have never admitted that my father was kidnapped, and may even be working for you. The official story is that he was killed in the air raid on Ardres, when his communications centre was blown up. Again, the official statement was that this was by a bomb. Equally, no one in Berlin knows I was taken prisoner in Lofoten. This has made me a free agent, and of course Lightman knew that Reitener was in command of the Nantes area. When I told him that Reitener is an old friend of my father and my family, and incidentally, was very fond of me as a girl in Berlin, the plan was made. So when I arrived in Nantes, and went to see him, and told him I had come from Berlin and how distraught I was because of my father's death, with my mother also dead, he was very pleased to see me and anxious to help me."

"You became his mistress."

"That was necessary. But, at my suggestion, and so there would not be a scandal, he gave me a job as his private secretary. This was what Lightman wanted. I have had access to a number of top secret files. But his main object was to have me on the spot before this raid was to take place, so that I could keep him informed, via the contacts I had already established with the Resistance, of any changes in the situation here."

"Seems you didn't do a very good job," Ebury remarked.

"Well," Veronica said, "somehow the Germans found out the raid was going to take place."

"How, do you suppose?" Harbord asked, sarcastically.

"I have absolutely no idea."

"Fraulein," Harbord said, "you have just told us that Colonel Lightman told you about this exercise long before it was known to any of us, and you have spent the last few months in France, in and out of this von Reitener's bed."

He was the most tactless fellow, Harry thought.

"That is perfectly true," Veronica said, without rancour. "And I am now risking my life to save yours. I must be a remarkable traitor."

But she was, Harry thought, a remarkable woman. He had thought before that she was following, and always would follow, a very personal agenda, known only to herself. There was also a flaw in what she had just claimed, although it was understood only by himself. She had not intended to risk her life to save *them*, she had risked her life, and was still doing so, to save *him*. Because despite all, she loved him.

Which left him in a very difficult position, as she was their only hope of getting out. Besides, he had to be sure.

"How did you know where we were?" he asked.

"I didn't. I knew you were one of the Commando force, and I also heard very rapidly, because General von Reitener was informed, that several British officers had been captured. So I contacted Henri and we went to St Nazaire to see what could be done. I had a forged order from the general that a certain British prisoner was to be released into my custody."

"The paper you gave to the colonel."

"That's correct. But you were the fourth group of captured officers I visited before I found you. Until then, I did not use the paper, obviously."

"All very neat," Tate commented. "But now you've burned your bridges, Fraulein. When the forgery is discovered . . ."

"I will, as you say, have burned my bridges. I will have to come out with you," she said equably. "I have nearly completed my tour of duty, anyway."

This was not the way British secret agents were taught to behave, Harry reflected. But again, she was not a typical British secret agent.

"Company," Tate remarked.

Harry sat up to look ahead. They had just turned on to a main road, and in front of them was a long column of vehicles, coming towards them and undoubtedly bound for St Nazaire.

"Pull off and let them pass," Veronica said. "If anyone salutes, return it."

"To the cap or stiff arm?"

"To the cap."

Tate pulled off the road, and they waited for the column to rumble by. One or two of the officers acknowledged their presence, the rest were disinterested. It took fifteen minutes for the column to pass, leaving behind it a thin pall of dust.

"That made my heart go pitter-patter," Ebury commented.

"You are perfectly safe," Veronica assured him. "As far as the Germans are concerned, the operation is finished."

An hour later they were in Nantes. It was now lunchtime, and the city was busy. There was a road block before they entered the houses, but Veronica showed her various passes while the men sat rigidly to attention, and they were waved through. Harry got the impression that she was fairly well known to the garrison.

There was so much he needed to think about, so much understanding he needed to attempt. But at the moment it was intensely difficult. Apart from the tension of actually being in the middle of the German army, he was now suffering the inevitable reaction from the violent action of the night, compounded by the fact that he had had no sleep. The same undoubtedly went for his companions. All they could do was sit it out, and wait . . . and try to forget the enormity of the disaster that had overtaken them. Apart, perhaps, from the very last launches who had not actually got into the river before the batteries had opened up, and thus, hopefully, had managed to get back out, unscathed, the entire force had been wiped out, either dead or prisoners.

How the Germans would crow.

Horns blared, policemen shouted, as the traffic thickened.

"For God's sake don't hit anything," Harbord told Tate.

Harry glanced at Veronica, but she was as composed as ever, giving directions in a quiet voice. Tate obeyed them, and a few minutes later they came to the bridge, beneath which the Loire rolled majestically towards the sea.

Here there was another road block, but again Veronica's passes got them through. The city extended south of the river, and there was yet another road block before they at last gained open country. Once clear, Veronica directed them to a village – she obviously knew the area very well – and they stopped so that she could buy bread and cheese and some *saucisson,* as well as a bottle of wine. "Now we can picnic," she said. "But we will not stop driving; they will be working on repairing those telephone lines."

Were they living in a dream world? Harry wondered. Even without the repaired telephone lines, General von Reitener would surely by now be wondering what had happened to his secretary who just also happened to be his mistress.

But Veronica remained confident, and they encountered no more obstacles as they approached Mirabeau at dusk, having driven by the river most of the way, through famous places such as Saumur and Chinon, before swinging south. Now they were close to the border of the German-occupied part of France and hopefully beyond the range of the confusion caused by the action at St Nazaire.

"Pull off over there," Veronica said, as they entered a small wood. "We cannot risk driving this car into the town, as we must assume the lines have been repaired by now, and the number of the car will have been circulated."

Tate turned off the lane and drove through the trees, stopping when they were totally concealed. Veronica opened the boot, to reveal some more French clothing. These were for a woman, and she took off her uniform and changed into the skirt and blouse, tying her hair up in a scarf.

"Now," she said. "I will go into Mirabeau and get help. You will remain here. Please do nothing stupid. Just stay put until I return."

"You can go in and out of the town?" Harbord asked.

"I have French identity papers. But you see, I did not know there were going to be so many of you. I need to contact the local Resistance to arrange things. I will be back by midnight."

"What exactly is the plan?" Ebury asked.

"In the first instance, to get you across the border into Vichy France. It will still be difficult, and dangerous, because if you are caught you would be handed back to the Germans. But most of the Vichy people are really on our side, and they will, if possible, look the other way. Once we are there, we will get you down to the Spanish border."

"I thought the Spanish were on Hitler's side," Ebury remarked.

"Some of them. But we have agents there who will see you into Portugal, and then home."

"You keep saying you, not we," Harbord said.

"Oh, I will be with you," Veronica said.

She gave Harry a long look, and then disappeared into the trees.

"Some gal," Tate remarked.

"Do you trust her?" Harbord asked Harry. "I mean, anyone can see she has something going for you, but still it all adds up, doesn't it?"

"Perhaps," Harry said. "But if she can get us out let's worry about the rest after."

"All those good men," Ebury said.

"I said, we'll worry about that afterwards," Harry told him.

It was now utterly dark, and very cold. The four men sat close together, beside the car, watching and waiting. There was little wind, and the wood was filled with the sounds of the night. They also heard traffic moving on the main road, which was only half a mile away.

"Oh, for a hot bath," Tate said.

"And a gallon of red wine," Harbord suggested. "Do you think we're the only ones who got out?"

"We're not out yet," Harry reminded him. "But I would say we're the only ones who have got this far. Unless one or two individuals managed to reach the woods and link up with the Resistance."

They waited, while the night grew colder yet. Checking their watches merely added to the tension, but they were so exhausted they kept nodding off. Four hours passed before they heard a rustling sound. Instantly they drew their pistols, crouching beside the car.

"It is I," Veronica said.

With her were two men.

"We'd just about given you up," Harbord said.

"It is a bad business," Veronica said.

"What's happened?" Harry asked.

"The house in Mirabeau has been taken by the Germans."

237

"How was that?"

She shrugged. "Betrayal, I suppose."

"So what do we do now?"

"We will try to cross the border tonight. It will not be easy, as it is patrolled. But we must do this. By tomorrow they will be scouring the entire country for us. For me."

It was the first time since Lofoten that Harry had heard her sounding agitated.

"How far is it?" Ebury asked.

"About ten miles. But it is mostly open country. We will make it. I would have you meet Armand and Lucien."

The two Frenchmen shook hands. They were very young, but they carried sub-machine guns.

"They will guide us," Veronica said.

They made their way through the trees to the edge of the wood, overlooking the main road. There was little traffic now, but every so often a truck rumbled by, filled with soldiers. They crouched in the last of the trees until all was quiet, then ran forward and across the road, just gaining the other side when more headlights came into sight.

"Down," Veronica snapped, and they lay full length in what appeared to be a field of cabbages.

Once again the traffic disappeared, and they were able to get up and plod forward. The sky was overcast, and there was not a star to be seen, but Armand and Lucien appeared to know exactly where they were going. Yet progress was slow, as they trudged across fields and climbed over stiles and fences, carefully avoiding any human habitation. By the time Armand waved them to a halt at first light, they were exhausted, and Harry reckoned they hadn't covered more than half the distance.

"We cannot risk the border in daylight," Armand said. "We will have to wait until tonight."

"Wait where?" Veronica asked.

He stood up to survey the countryside. "There is a farm."

"Will they shelter us?"

He grinned. "They will have to, madame."

They crept forward into the yard. A dog barked, and an upstairs window was thrown open. "Who is there?" a man shouted.

Shades of St Nazaire, Harry thought, and hoped this one would have a better outcome.

"We are the Resistance," Armand said. "Open up. Keep out of sight," he told the Englishmen.

There was some grumbling from above, but the window was closed, and a moment later a light flared in the house as a lantern was lit. Then the door was opened; the farmer held the dog by its collar – it was a large animal and continued to bark.

Armand went forward.

"Are you mad?" the farmer inquired. "Do you not know there has been a raid in Mirabeau? There are Germans everywhere."

"That is why we need shelter," Armand explained.

The farmer peered past him. "How many?"

"There are seven of us, six men and a woman. We need to cross the border. We will do that, tonight."

"You wish to stay in my farm all day? You will have me shot. And what of my wife and children?"

"Nothing will happen to them, and you will not be shot," Armand said, patiently. "No one will know we are here. And tonight we will leave again."

The farmer hesitated a last time, then stood back. Armand beckoned the others to follow him in.

"What is this?" the farmer asked, staring at the German uniforms.

"These are English soldiers," Armand said. "This morning they blew up St Nazaire. Now they need to escape."

By now the farmer had been joined by his wife, a small, thin woman, and two wide-eyed children, a boy and a girl. Harry did not suppose either of them was more than ten.

It was time to take command, as he was the senior officer.

"My apologies, monsieur, madame," he said. "I am sorry to have to inflict this ordeal upon you. But we are very tired. If it could be possible to have some sleep . . ."

"Of course," Madame said. "And food, eh?"

"And a hot bath," Tate suggested.

"But of course," Madame said again.

Harry took Veronica aside. "What happens now? You said if we did not get across tonight we would not make it at all."

She nodded. "It will certainly be more difficult. But we can still do it. This area is big for the Resistance. In the morning I will make contact with various people I know and we will arrange something."

"Won't the Germans be looking for you?"

She smiled. "I can make arrangements about that too. Trust me."

They gazed at each other.

"Seems I have no choice," he suggested.

"Rest," she told him. "Regain your strength. I have said I will get you out. I will do this." She kissed him.

They were made as comfortable as possible. Being so close to the Vichy border conditions were much better here than further north or west. There was ample food, Madame made her own bread, and the coffee was excellent. So were the beds to which they were shown after sharing a communal tub. Harry slept heavily, and awoke in the middle of the afternoon, to the sound of traffic. He got up, glanced at Ebury, with whom he was sharing the room and who was still snoring, and went to the window, being careful to stand at the edge.

It was a bright afternoon, and he could see a good distance. He hadn't realised the farm was so close to a main road, and that road was at the moment filled with German transport, moving east.

That didn't look too promising.

He found that his underclothes and shirt had been washed and pressed, and waited in a neat pile on a chair by the bed: he must indeed have been sleeping heavily. He put these on, as well as the ill-fitting breeches, and went downstairs. Madame was in the kitchen, the children were not to be seen. Neither was anyone else, except the dog, who greeted him as a friend.

"They will soon be back," Madame said.

"Who?"

"Well, the children from school, and Mademoiselle Sturmer and her friends from the village."

Harry was aghast. "You let your children go to school?"

"But of course, monsieur. If they had not gone, questions would have been asked."

"Will they not tell their friends about us?"

"I do not think so, monsieur. I told them not to."

Harry scratched his head.

"And in any event," Madame went on, "their friends are our friends. You will not be betrayed."

Harry hoped she was right. "And Mademoiselle Sturmer and her friends?"

"As I said, they have gone into the village. They wish to find out the best way across the border."

Harry could not recall ever feeling so uneasy, so utterly at the mercy of people he did not know. Because he couldn't even claim to *know* Veronica.

He went back upstairs, checked his pistol.

Ebury sat up. "Trouble?"

"I hope not," Harry said, and watched the two young Frenchmen approaching across a field. There was no one else in sight.

He went downstairs. The farmer had also come in.

"We have brought these for you to wear," Armand said, placing a bundle of clothing, which included sabots, on the table.

"You don't think we'd be safer in German uniforms?"

"No. They are looking for men in SS uniforms. They have orders to shoot on sight."

"All the way over here?"

"All southern France," Lucien said. "They know you crossed the river. All bridges have been sealed. But they also know you will try to get into Vichy."

"Where is Mademoiselle Sturmer?"

"I do not know," Armand said. "She went off on her own. She said she had something to do."

"Shit!" Harry muttered.

Ebury and the others had also come downstairs. "Will we make it?"

"Who can say, monsieur. You must try."

"When?" Harbord asked.

"I think as soon as it is properly dark. There are still four miles to go."

Madame fed them immediately, made sure they all ate well. The children came home from school, full of the story of how the Germans were looking for four escaped British officers.

"You didn't tell them where we were, I hope," Tate said, as jocularly as he could.

"No, monsieur," said the boy, seriously.

Just before dusk Veronica came back.

"Where in the name of God have you been?" Harry asked.

She looked as insouciant as always, if a trifle tired and sweat-stained. When she took off her headscarf, he saw, to his consternation, that at some time during the night or the early morning, she had cut off her hair, and then shaved her head, leaving it almost bald. The absence of hair made her appear a quite different person, even if it enhanced the bold good looks of her face.

"By God, Miss Sturmer, you certainly don't do things by halves," Harbord commented.

"I think you need to remember that I have been making arrangements," she said. "You know the Germans have sealed the border, in this area."

Harry nodded. "So are we stuck?"

"No. I can get you across. Now listen to me very carefully, all of you. It cannot be done tonight, but it can be done at dawn tomorrow morning. By then the Germans will have relaxed somewhat. But security will still be tight. However, every morning at dawn one of our people drives his truck across the border to pick up fresh meat for the German garrison in Tours. He is well-known to the border patrols. You will be concealed in the truck. On his outward journey he takes garden produce for sale in Poitiers, and it is in this that you will be hidden, Now, this is what you need to remember. There is almost no chance of you not being found. The moment you are found, any one of you, draw your pistols and shoot your way out."

"That will be committing suicide," Harbord objected.

"Hopefully not. I have sent a message across the border to our people there, and they will be waiting. At the first shot, or any other alarm, they will attack the guards surrounding the truck, and hopefully rescue you."

"Why should they risk their lives for us?" Harbord asked.

"They will be risking their lives to attack the Germans, Mr Harbord. Just as you did in St Nazaire. That your rescue may be a by-product is not the most important thing."

"But surely there will be repercussions," Ebury said.

"Of course. There always are. Now go and sort out this clothing and prepare to leave. Harry."

She waited by the door to the small living-room. Harry went in and she closed the door.

"You see I am doing everything I can for you," she said.

"Why? When it will mean destroying your own position here?"

"You once told me that you loved me. And I told you that no one had ever said that to me before. Do you not still love me?"

"I want to, believe me."

"Ah. Is it that you have found out about Colonel Lightman? He had me in his power."

"Like that naval commander, Conrad."

"Why, yes," she agreed.

"And you are a woman who yields to superior power."

"Until the situation can be reversed, yes."

"You could have told me about it."

"Would that have served any useful purpose?"

He sighed. "I suppose not."

"Or are you still thinking that I betrayed you?"

"I don't want to, believe me. But somebody did. At the same time, if you did . . . why are you risking all to help us escape?"

"I am helping you to escape. Do you think you will ever find out the truth?"

"Ask me that again when we're out of here."

She made a moué. "I would like to make love to you, one last time. But I do not suppose you are in the mood."

"I don't think I am."

"Well, then, at least kiss me."

He held her close. Her lips were warm and wet, her body as enticing as ever.

"Now go and prepare," she said.

They left the farmhouse at eight o'clock. It was another overcast and dark night.

"What do you reckon?" Harbord muttered.

"We're in her hands, again," Harry said. "We have to go along with her."

They had checked their weapons, and the clothes they had been given were a surprisingly good fit. They bade farewell to the farmer and his wife and children, and then crept into the night. As soon as they were well away from the farm Armand and Lucien took their leave, silently clasping the Commandos' hands before fading into the darkness.

"Will they be all right?" Harry asked.

"If they can get back to Mirabeau," Veronica said. "But they know the country. They will make it."

The five of them crept across the fields towards the little town. There was a curfew, but few patrols about, and Veronica knew exactly where she was taking them. They made their way around the back streets and thence into the yard where the truck was parked. It had already been filled with vegetables, which were covered by pieces of sacking. Carefully they inserted themselves amongst the cabbages and cauliflowers, working their way down to lie on the floor.

"You understand," Veronica whispered. "That although he is one of us, the truck driver will deny any knowledge of you or how you got in here. If you are taken alive, you must not betray him."

They nodded their agreement, and settled down to wait. Harry supposed it had to be the longest night of his life. There was so much still to be resolved, to be understood

. . . but nothing could be considered until they were across the border. Supposing they got there.

At last the first light. By then the Commandos and the woman were thoroughly cramped and uncomfortable. They listened to the sound of feet on the cobbles of the yard, and then two men got into the truck, chatting to each other as if they had not a care in the world.

Perhaps they are hoping we are not really here, Harry thought.

The engine started, and the truck drove out of the yard. It was stopped on the outskirts of the village, but resumed after a few minutes and a brief chat with the German patrol. Then it was on the main road and rumbling towards the border. Harry listened to the occasional traffic passing them or going the other way. It was still very early in the morning, and there were a disturbing number of people about. He had to suppose they were all Germans except for this truck.

The truck began to slow. "We are nearly there," Veronica whispered. "Be ready, but do not move unless you have to."

The truck stopped, and the border guards engaged the driver in conversation. They obviously knew him, but they had their duty to do, and after a few moments two of them came round the back and lifted the canvas backboard to peer into the interior. They continued chatting, paying very little attention to the vegetables, although one of them did some prodding with a stick. Then without warning Harbord sat up and shot the German in the chest.

"Shit!" Ebury gasped.

"You blithering idiot!" Tate shouted.

The second German was unslinging his tommy-gun. There was nothing for it now. Harry shot him in turn.

"Out," Veronica shouted. "Get out. Run for the trees."

The officers leapt down, Harry waited for Veronica, jerking her from the tail of the truck, and they landed together on their hands and knees.

He gave a quick glance left and right. The truck was actually on the border crossing, the barrier having been raised. From the German post several men were emerging, automatic weapons levelled. On the French side blue-uniformed *douanes* were peering from their own post, obviously wishing to avoid having to take action. The two truckers had thrown themselves from their cab and were lying face down on the ground, hands over their heads.

Ebury, Tate and Harbord were already across the border and running towards the trees about a quarter of a mile away. The Germans were shouting at them to stop, and when they did not, opened fire. This meant they were shooting into French territory, but Harry did not suppose that was going to bother them very much.

And now, from the trees, there came answering fire. Veronica's reinforcements.

"Are you all right?" he asked.

"We must run for it," she said. "We are helpless here."

The trees looked a long way away, and all of the other three had gone down. Whether they were taking shelter or had been hit he couldn't tell. But to stay by the truck was to commit suicide: he could hear the wail of a siren to indicate that reinforcements were on their way.

"All together, then," he said, and they rose and sidled along the side of the truck. Harry paused by the bonnet to send several shots at the customs house, which was in any event being riddled with bullets from the wood. They left the shelter and ran up the road, through the open barrier, and then veered to their left, towards the nearest trees. Bullets sang about them and it was impossible to tell whether the shots were coming or going. Harry had a wildly exhilarating feeling that they were going to make it, then Veronica gave a half-grunt, half-moan, and fell to her knees.

He grabbed her shoulders to urge her on again, and when she fell full length scooped her from the ground and heaved her round his shoulders. As he did so he felt an impact himself, but there was no blood of his own. He realised she had been hit again.

He staggered forward, still surrounded by flying lead, and fell into a shallow ditch, where the other three were also crouching. Tate was on his back, and was clearly dead. Ebury appeared to be in a state of exhausted shock. Harbord was kneeling, reloading his pistol from Tate's. He looked up as Harry slid down beside him, Veronica rolling from his shoulders to lie on the ground.

"Is she dead?" Harbord asked.

Harry felt for a pulse and found one. There was a lot of blood. "Not yet. We must get her to the trees."

From where people were shouting at them, telling them to hurry up.

"Can you make it?" Harry asked Ebury.

The little man nodded.

"Listen," Harbord said. "That fellow touched me. He knew I was there."

"I'm sure he did," Harry agreed. "Let's go."

He scooped Veronica into his arms, stood up, and began staggering the last hundred yards to the wood. As he did so, the Resistance men in front of him again opened fire. But the Germans were firing too. He reached the trees, dropped into shelter, looked round and saw Ebury immediately behind him. Fifty yards back, Harbord had fallen.

A bearded man appeared through the trees. "There is transport waiting," he said. "We must be out of here before the Germans get permission to come across."

Harry nodded. "The woman is badly hurt," he said.

"We will see to her."

Harry looked back again, to where Harbord was trying to crawl to them.

"Leave the bastard," Ebury said. "He made this happen."

"He's still my officer," Harry said. He glanced at Veronica and the man bending over her, but she was unconscious. He drew a deep breath, left the trees, and ran towards the wounded man. As before he was surrounded by buzzing bees, but he reached Harbord unhurt. Third time lucky, he thought, as he got an arm round the lieutenant and began half carrying him.

"In the leg," Harbord gasped. "In the leg."

"After a while, you get used to it," Harry told him.

The German fire had slacked, and they reached the shelter.

Now there were several men waiting for them, as well as Ebury. Veronica lay on her back, staring at the trees.

"We must get her to a doctor," Harry said.

"But the woman is dead, monsieur," said the bearded man.

"Dead?" Harry dropped beside her. "God damn it."

"Are you Harry?" the Frenchman asked.

"That's my name."

"Just before she died, she opened her eyes for a moment, and she said, 'I love you too, Harry'. I think she thought I was you, monsieur. She could not see clearly, you understand."

"I'm not sure she ever could," Harry said.

"Great God Almighty!" Lightman said. "I never expected to see you again." He came round his desk to shake Harry and Ebury by the hand, gazing at their ill-fitting and well-worn clothes. "Only you?"

"We brought Harbord out too, sir," Harry said. "But he was pretty badly wounded. He's gone straight to hospital."

"And you came out through . . . ?"

"Vichy France, Spain and Portugal. It took a little time."

"Three months." It was now high summer. "Well . . ." Lightman looked somewhat uncertain, unusually for him. "At least we'll now find out what really happened."

"We were betrayed, sir," Ebury said. "They knew we were coming. We walked straight into a trap."

Lightman sat down again. "That's very serious. Sadly, it's fairly obvious too. We shall have to work on that. You don't suppose that woman . . . ?"

"No, sir," Harry said.

Lightman raised his eyebrows.

"She helped us to escape, sir," Ebury said. "And died doing so."

"Good God!" He gazed at Harry for several seconds.

"She was quite a heroine," Harry said.

"So it seems," Lightman agreed. "Look, get yourself settled in, and then I'd like a full report. Everything."

"Yes, sir. And then?"

"Oh, back to work. And don't go away with the idea that the mission was a disaster. It was a resounding success."

"A success, sir?" Harry asked. "Something like six hundred men, dead or captured?"

"Remember what Lord Louis told you, Harry. Your job was to eliminate St Nazaire as a possible naval base, regardless of casualties. You did that. So things didn't go according to plan. But with you here to tell us what went wrong, why, we'll do better the next time. And there will be a next time. Very soon."

"Yes, sir."

"Forester will fix you up. And Harry, I'm damned sorry about Fraulein Sturmer."

"Yes, sir. So am I.

"With respect, sir," Ebury said. "In my report I intend to recommend Captain Curtis for the Victoria Cross."

"Indeed?"

"He saved Lieutenant Harbord's life, sir. Under enemy fire."

"Well, well, yes indeed, make your recommendation Captain Ebury, and we'll certainly see about it."

"I was merely doing my duty, sir," Harry said.

"You make out that report, Ebury," Lightman said. "And gentlemen, it's good to have you back."

Belinda had not been in the outer office when they had arrived. Now she was, somewhat out of breath.

"I just heard! Oh, Harry!"

She was in his arms, while Ebury patiently looked the other way.

"God," she said. "I'm weeping. To have you back . . . ?"

"Three," he said. "Out of six hundred."

"Shit," she commented. "What a mess. And . . . ?"

"She's dead."

"Oh. Does the boss know?"

"We just told him. Never batted an eyelid."

"That's our boy. Well . . ."

"We need all sorts of things. New uniforms, leave . . ."

"Of course. I'll sort everything out. Does your wife know you're back, Captain Ebury?"

"Not yet. I'd like to be in touch."

"Right away. I'll have her brought up to see you. Harry . . ."

"Have we been reported dead?"

"Missing, presumed dead."

He nodded. "I'd like to get up to Frenthorpe as quickly as possible."

"Tomorrow do you?"

"I don't suppose one more day is going to make all that much difference. I'll need someplace to spend the night."

"Would you like me to organise that?" She screwed up her nose.

He thought of Veronica. So beautiful, so desirable, and so much her own woman. Had she betrayed them? He didn't suppose they would ever know. If she had, it was a result of that deep chasm in her personality which had left her uncertain which side she was truly on.

She had said she loved him, with her last breath. But had even that been the truth? He would never know that either.

She had been the experience of a lifetime. But here in front of him was England, Home and Beauty.

"I'd like that very much," he said.